All Roads Lead to Whitechapel

All Roads Lead
to Whitechapel

A Baker Street Inquiry

Michelle Birkby

FELONY & MAYHEM PRESS • NEW YORK

All the characters and events portrayed in this work are fictitious.

ALL ROADS LEAD TO WHITECHAPEL:
A BAKER STREET INQUIRY

A Felony & Mayhem mystery

PRINTING HISTORY
First UK edition (Pan MacMillan, as *The House at Baker Street*): 2016
Felony & Mayhem edition (first US edition): 2019

Copyright © 2016 by Michelle Birkby

All rights reserved

 ® and BAKER STREET INQUIRY
are trademarks of the Conan Doyle Estate Ltd.
The Baker Street Inquiries are based on copyrighted works
by Sir Arthur Conan Doyle, used by permission of
the Conan Doyle Estate Ltd.® www.conandoyleestate.com

ISBN (trade cloth): 978-1-63194-224-2
ISBN (trade paper): 978-1-63194-220-4

Manufactured in the United States of America

Library of Congress Cataloging-in-Publication data
may be found on page 271

For Claire, in eternal gratitude.

The icon above says you're holding a copy of a book in the Felony & Mayhem "Historical" category, which ranges from the ancient world up through the 1940s. If you enjoy this book, you may well like other "Historical" titles from Felony & Mayhem Press.

For more about these books, and other Felony & Mayhem titles, or to place an order, please visit our website at:

www.FelonyAndMayhem.com

Other "Historical" titles from

FELONY&MAYHEM

CAST OF CHARACTERS

MRS MARTHA HUDSON

*housekeeper to
Sherlock Holmes
the Great Detective,
landlady of 221b Baker Street*

MARY WATSON

*friend to Martha Hudson,
married to Dr John Watson*

SHERLOCK HOLMES

the Great Detective

DR JOHN WATSON

Sherlock Holmes' friend and biographer

BILLY

pageboy at 221b Baker Street

WIGGINS

head of the Baker Street Irregulars

JAKE *and* MICKY

members of the Irregulars

IRENE NORTON
(PREVIOUSLY ADLER)

*the Woman, and ally to
Mrs Hudson and Mary Watson*

INSPECTOR LESTRADE

representative of the police

All Roads Lead to Whitechapel

Prologue

It started with champagne and promises on a sunny afternoon.

It was an adventure, a dare, to while away the hours, to prove ourselves just as good as them. It started in laughter and hope and joy. It is ending here in blood and pain and fire, in the darkness.

I am afraid, so very afraid, and I am tempted to run, to get help, to scream for rescue, but I won't. She is there, tied to a chair at the point of a gun, half-unconscious, bleeding, having suffered worse than me, but she won't call for help either. We made a pact—we would do this ourselves, without help from the men upstairs. It was a lightly taken oath, half in jest, but now the reality was deadly serious.

'Who's there?' the vile creature calls, and I draw back into the blackness even further. My place is in the shadows, off the page, silent behind the clever and the good. I am the watcher, the listener, the minor player in the game. To be here, now, in this situation, in danger, is not my role.

Yet my role has changed.

'Holmes? I know you're there!' he calls. His voice rings with triumph. It is the cue for my entrance.

'Mr Holmes has no idea who you are,' I tell him, and although my hand shakes, my voice is firm, and she stirs a little behind him.

Together. We started this together and we will end it together.

'Who the hell are you?' he demands, confused. His hair is wild, his clothes disordered, his face suffused with blood. I step forward, into the light.

'I am Sherlock Holmes' housekeeper. I am Mrs Hudson.'

CHAPTER 1

Farewells and Greetings

April 1889, London

If you have read John Watson's thrilling stories, and I am sure you have, you know me best as housekeeper and landlady to the Great Detective, Sherlock Holmes.

Such a short sentence to write, and yet, oh my, what a wealth of information is there. Such adventures, such stories, such people. And as for me—I did so much more than bustle in and out with the tea. Although to be fair, I did bustle, and there was an awful lot of tea consumed by everyone. And I feel you should know John did make a few mistakes in his stories. He claimed artistic licence, though I feel it was faulty memory. But what people don't know about me is that I had adventures of my own, with Mary Watson, and sometimes other friends and acquaintances, and the occasional enemy, of Mr Holmes. So now it's time I told a few stories of my own...

Believe it or not, I was a young woman once. For the first nineteen years of my life, I was Miss Martha Grey: sweet, innocent, and ever so slightly bored. Then, one particularly dull evening, I met Hector Hudson, and I wasn't bored any more. I loved him on sight. He was a soldier, so tall and handsome in his uniform, with dark blond hair, and a special smile just for me that made the lines around his grey-blue eyes wrinkle in a fascinating way. To my delight, he loved me on sight too. He proposed just a week later, and I said yes before he had even finished asking.

We were a love story come true, but unlike most love stories, it did not end with a happy marriage.

It ended with his death.

He was a soldier and we were at war. Six months after our marriage, he died alone, on a blood-soaked battlefield, in some place I had never heard of, leaving me only with his child growing inside me.

But he didn't leave me destitute, like so many other poor widows of the war; Hector provided me with the rent from several properties he had owned in London, which were now mine. Including, of course, 221b Baker Street.

But I didn't go to London then. I stayed in the country with my son. He grew strong and clever and adventurous. He would stride out in the morning and not return till tea, full of tales of what he had done and seen, his pockets stuffed with treasures that he laid on my lap with pride. I know I should have tried to keep him indoors, keep him at his lessons, but he would not be shut up. He would escape into the world, and I did not have the heart to stop him. He looked at me with his father's eyes, full of wonder and joy, and I knew he would grow up to be a great explorer, or writer, or something thrilling and exciting.

Except that he didn't grow up. One day he was tired and stayed indoors, quietly watching me do my work. Poor fool me, I was glad of his company. One week later, he died—his last, great adventure—leaving me behind, as his father had done on that godforsaken battlefield.

I don't want to talk about what my boy's death did to me. Not yet. Not now. I will just say that I could not stay there, where every object, every sound, just the light in the trees, reminded me of what I had lost. I moved to London then. I became a landlady and looked after my properties efficiently, all those rooms in all those houses. All those bright young men and lovely hopeful young women in my rooms became ill and old and bitter. London can do that to some people, when they are alone, and poor, and lose all hope. It's not kind to everyone. London can be cruel. I did not find friends. I did not find love. I did not find my place.

However, I did learn to balance account books and make agreements with tradesmen and haggle for the best prices and everything else that came with running a business. I learnt how to appraise a maid or a tenant on sight, and how to get rid of them too. I learnt how to offset loss with profit, and what was a good investment, and what bad. Whilst Parliament argued over whether women had the mental ability even to own their own clothes, I quietly administered an empire—and no one noticed.

I also discovered cooking. As Hector's wife I'd had nothing to do except tell the servants what to do for me. As the landlady of all of these properties, I had to be capable of doing any work required, at any time. Therefore, I learnt to do every job of every servant. Cleaning bored me, laundry I loathed, but cooking I loved. Taking the ingredients one by one, all looking so simple, and then combining them and cooking them and using all kinds of secrets to make them into something delicious, I felt to be a form of magic. With all these discoveries about myself I changed and grew and became not Martha Hudson, grieving widow, but Mrs Hudson, formidable housekeeper and successful landlady.

As I got older, I gradually sold all my properties and moved into what I was sure would be my final home: 221b Baker Street. It was a very elegant new building, rising several storeys above the busy street, with a smart black door edged in white woodwork and red brick. There was room for me, and a suite of rooms for a pair of gentlemen, and I settled down for my long and inevitable slide into old age.

The first few men who rented my rooms were nice and polite. They had reasonable hours and required only breakfast and the occasional cup of tea, and kept themselves to themselves. They were the perfect tenants. Other landladies envied me.

But I was so bored.

They didn't need me, they needed an automaton. I did not need them. We were perfect strangers living under one roof.

Then *he* came. On a rainy night in September, he rang my bell and asked if my rooms were still vacant.

He was so tall and thin that at first I thought he was quite elderly. Then he stepped into the light and I saw his face was young and lean, with restless dark eyes. He looked around then smiled and raised his hand, but oddly, as if he was remembering he was supposed to be polite. Those hands were covered in sticking plaster, and his jacket was strangely stained.

He was soaked to the skin, so I invited him in and said I would bring him tea and, in the meantime, he could pop upstairs and view the rooms.

I knew he'd like them. They were nice rooms, though I say so myself. Comfortable, but not shabby, well furnished, with plenty of space for my gentlemen to keep their books and suchlike, with two large bedrooms and all conveniently situated near the centre of London. The question was: would I like him?

When I brought in his tea, I found him standing in the middle of the carpet—the exact middle—looking around curiously, with a certain intensity. I felt sorry for him then. There he was on a rainy cold night, all alone, nowhere to go, wet through, searching for a home. He turned to me as I entered, and took the tea and drank it gratefully. I felt he too had looked at me and studied me and come to his conclusions.

'You keep a very clean house, Mrs Hudson,' he said. I liked his voice. It was low, but expressive and strong.

'I do, and a very private one,' I assured him. He struck me

as a man who treasured his privacy. 'I will supply your meals and do your washing and clean your rooms, of course, but I won't impose or interfere.'

He nodded.

'I may have many visitors, Mrs Hudson, in connection with my profession. Will that be an inconvenience?'

'Not at all,' I told him. Though I would regret that in years to come, running up and down those stairs to show in some very odd visitors, at all hours of the day and night. 'May I ask...?'

'A consulting detective. The *only* consulting detective,' he said, with a touch of pride.

'How interesting,' I said politely, as my heart stirred inside me. A detective! The things that could happen in those rooms, what I might see and hear, the kind of people who would visit— the lost, the lonely, the curious, even the dangerous...

Excitement, of a sort, even just second-hand—but still, excitement!

'I work with the police, but not for them, so discretion must be guaranteed,' he warned.

'I understand.'

'I have odd habits,' he admitted. He almost seemed to be warning me against allowing him into my home. 'I keep strange hours. I can be very messy. I do chemical experiments that always seem to smell,' he said ruefully. 'There may be noise...'

I raised a hand to stop him.

'None of that will be a problem,' I assured him. Oh, how I longed for noise and mess in my pristine home!

'Other landladies have found me difficult,' he warned. 'In fact, I have been thrown out of my rooms three times—the latest just two hours ago.'

'Why?'

He took a breath, determined to admit it all.

'I poisoned her cat. It was entirely accidental...'

I burst out laughing. I couldn't help it. His contrite face, his bizarre admission—it was all so ridiculous! He stared at me, and then smiled. I looked up at him, this man tramping the streets searching for a room. He seemed to have no family, no friends to turn to in his hour of need, nowhere to go, never quite fitting in anywhere, no place he belonged to, and my heart just went out to him. He was a lost soul, just like me.

'I don't have a cat,' I told him. 'Do as you will, sir, as long as you pay for any damages.' I was not a soft touch, after all. He nodded, serious again.

'The rent...' he started to say. His coat was patched, his bag worn. Consulting detectives were, I imagined, paid by results, and how many results had there been so far?

'There are two bedrooms. I would have no objections to your bringing a companion to share the rooms and the rent.'

'I have no companions,' he said, his face turning from me towards the windows. 'I have not that nature.'

'You can have the rooms half-rent for a month whilst you find one,' I told him. I could not let him go back alone into that dark and damp night. 'London is full of men looking for a refuge. Perhaps a soldier returned from the wars? They always need a place to stay and an understanding companion. Just be sure and tell them about your bad habits first.'

It was three weeks later that he brought him home. He'd followed my advice and found an ex-soldier, a doctor, with a pleasant smile, a hearty handshake and haunted eyes. He badly needed a place to stay, a task in life and someone to care for him. Although he thought he needed only one of those things.

In the first days they were there together the doctor fixed my kitchen door, the detective had sharp words with the butcher, who had been cheating me (I had suspected as much) and I made them the best meal of their lives.

They sat in their rooms and smoked and talked into the night, and I sat in the kitchen and listened to them through the air vent and there we all were. Sherlock Holmes, John Watson and Martha Hudson. Three lost souls who had found each other.

CHAPTER 2

How It All Began

Now that you know how I met Mr Holmes and Dr Watson, we can move on to my story. Well, the story of Mary and me. Mary Watson, the wife of Dr John Watson, and I sat quietly at the huge wooden table in the bright basement kitchen of 221b Baker Street.

The kitchen is my domain, my office, my refuge. Let me tell you all about it. This place is important. This place is my home. If you open the black-painted door of 221b Baker Street, you find yourself in a dark, panelled entrance hall. There is a table to the right, highly polished, and with a brass bowl on it. Facing you, on the left, are carpeted stairs up to the rest of the house. On the right is a short hallway, leading down four steps to my kitchen. Whenever I think of home, I think of that kitchen.

It had a black door, which was rarely closed. This door led directly into the kitchen, and on the other side of the room was a half-glassed door, leading out to a humble back yard. Beside the back door was my pride and joy, a large gas cooking range, which kept the kitchen hot even on the coldest days. There was a chair in front of this, comfy and worn, with a rag rug rolled up in the corner to be laid out in the evenings. To the left of this range was a smaller door leading to the scullery, pantry and various other offices of the house. Past that, against the wall, was a large pine dresser, stocked with shining copper pans and pink and white plates. They were not for Mr Holmes' use, of course. He got plain white china after he started using my plates for chemical experiments and shooting practice. Opposite them, across the linoleum printed to look like red tiles (oh, the joys of an easy-to-clean floor of linoleum!), was a row of cupboards, and a worktop with a cool marble slab where I made pastry. The kitchen swept all the way through to the window and door at the front of the house, where I could see everyone go past. In the centre of the room was a huge oak table, scrubbed white with use, covered in scars and burns. This kitchen was my home, and I spent the happiest times of my life there.

So now, can you see it, my kitchen? The place where I belong, and where I felt like I belonged. This is where it all began. John's stories begin upstairs, and mine, downstairs. On this day, I was not alone. Mary Watson had come to visit me, and was sitting at one end of that table. She had come into John's life in the adventure he called *The Sign of Four*. John loved her, Mr Holmes tolerated her and I was very fond of her. The personification of beauty of the time was a full-figured brunette, with dimples, but Mary didn't fit the fashion at all. She was slender, and tall, almost as tall as John. She had a firm chin, and a straight nose, and an intense blue gaze. She had masses of curly golden hair that firmly refused to stay in place, always falling out of its pins. She preferred, like Princess Alix, to dress in simple blouses and skirts, with barely a bustle, and usually wore a simple straw hat, often pushed impatiently to the back of her head. She had a mobile face that expressed every emotion she felt and every thought she had. She laughed easily, and she was clever. She loved

John to distraction. She had been subdued, quiet and correct, a good governess, when he met her. Now she was free, and she glowed with a bubble of happiness inside her.

I can still see her, so very clearly, after all these years, as if she still sat opposite me, smiling mischievously.

Beside her, I am small, middle-aged. I have brown hair, turning silver, and brown eyes, and am, to be fair, plumper than her. You cannot tell what I am thinking from my face. My complexion, once peaches and cream, has become a greyish-white in the dirt of London. My hair is always neatly done up in a bun, my clothes are demure and plain, I am the model of a tidy, calm housekeeper. I am not made to be noticed, and to be noticed is not my place. My hands are cook's hands—always covered in tiny scars and burns from the oven and the knives. I am proud of that, and I need nothing more.

There, can you see us? Sitting in my kitchen on this day, when it all began, sipping our cups of tea, eating slices of my home-made Dundee cake and eavesdropping on Sherlock Holmes' latest visitor through the air vent.

Ah yes, the air vent.

Now, you must understand, British builders don't really understand air vents. They put them in all sorts of odd places, from room to room, hidden away in corners, linked up to pipes that lead nowhere. Strictly speaking, an air vent should never have linked the kitchen and the first-floor drawing room, allowing the smell of cooking to drift into the house. But what with bad planning, and alterations and other quirks, one air vent in 221b, high on the wall of Mr Holmes' drawing room (which was also his consulting room, dining room, shooting gallery and chemical laboratory) led directly into the kitchen, between two cupboards, above the marble top where I made my pastries.

I had only realized this when, one evening, long before Mr Holmes moved in, I had heard singing as I rolled out a batch of scones. I dismissed the idea as the first signs of insanity until I understood I was listening to the young man in the rooms above me, singing rather vulgar music-hall songs to himself, and the sound was carrying through that vent.

I usually kept the vent closed, but since Mr Holmes had taken the rooms, I found myself opening it more and more, sitting at the kitchen table and listening. It was wrong. It was eavesdropping. It was dishonest. It was against all the rules of being a good housekeeper. I profess myself completely shocked at my own lack of discretion and privacy. I told myself so every time I opened the vent.

However, if you are completely honest, if you had the opportunity to open a vent and listen to Sherlock Holmes talk, would not you do so?

Of course you would, and that is why you read these stories.

That day Mr Holmes had a new visitor. I had shown her up myself as Billy, our pageboy, was running errands at the time, and had taken careful note of the new client. She was a shy young woman, small and pale, trembling with nerves. Her hazel, washed-out eyes kept glancing quickly behind her, as if she were afraid of being watched. I had shown her up to his room, and then hurried down to the kitchen to find that Mary had already opened the air vent. We settled down to listen. What could such a nervous little mouse want of the Great Detective?

Unfortunately, Mr Holmes was not in one of his kindly moods, and Dr Watson had gone out on an urgent call. Mr Holmes professed to despise women (not as much as he insisted he did, I am certain). He called them weak, over-emotional, hysterical and guilty of dragging a man's attention away from cool logic.

However, some women he did, against his disposition, like. Those women tended to be strong, intelligent and independent. Shrinking violets only annoyed him—and no violet ever shrank more than this poor woman. He asked her what was wrong and she whispered 'blackmail?' in just such a questioning manner. But she would not say who was blackmailing her, over what,

what the demands were or even her name. To every question she just offered an almost inaudible 'I cannot tell you'.

Mr Holmes always demanded complete openness from his clients and, in the mood he was in, he had no inclination to be kind. He sent her away with a cursory, 'If you will not speak, I cannot help you. Good day.'

I ran out into the hall to see her descending the stairs slowly, all meek and quivering.

'Would you like a cup of tea, dear?' I asked her. And with that, she burst into tears.

Mary and I got her seated in the kitchen with cake and a hot, sweet cup of tea. Eventually the sobbing subsided.

'I don't know why I came; I daren't tell him,' she said, in a voice barely above a whisper to us. 'I daren't. What if he approaches my husband? I cannot have him…he cannot know…' And she burst into tears once again.

'My dear,' I said gently, 'what exactly is it that you have done?'

'That's just it!' she cried, with that queer hiccupping cough people get when they've cried all they can cry. 'I've done nothing!'

'Then how can someone blackmail you?' I asked.

'He lies!' she cried, so loud I thought Mr Holmes might hear her. I had no intention of sending her back to him; he had been heartless at best and cruel at worst, and I was angry with him. He deserved to lose this client; perhaps then he'd be better behaved to the next weeping woman. I shushed her. 'He tells such lies, such disgusting lies!'

'If he lies, why would your husband believe this black-mailer?' Mary asked.

'My husband firmly believes there is no smoke without fire,' the woman said, clutching and re-clutching her gloves. 'He says a woman's reputation is a price above rubies, and is her most precious possession, and that nothing should stain it, not even rumours.'

Mary and I glanced at each other. So he was one of those husbands! I'd wager his own soul was far from spotless.

'Last year we heard the most disturbing tales about two women of our acquaintance. Nothing was actually proven, nothing spoken out loud, but there were whispers,' she continued. 'He said I wasn't allowed to see them any more. I argued—I know a woman should not argue with her husband, but I liked them. I could talk to them. I said there was no proof, but he said the rumours were proof enough. He said that a woman who behaved decently would not have a chance to have a reputation stained like that. He said even lies had a basis in truth, and...' Her voice trailed off.

'And they must have done something, or else how would the rumours start?' Mary finished for her. 'More than one woman has been destroyed by that spurious argument.' I could tell Mary was very angry, but she kept quiet as the woman continued to talk.

'He might believe me at first,' she told us. 'That they were all lies, and so on. But he would look at me, and wonder, and after a while, if the rumours spread...'

'He'd start to believe,' Mary finished. 'And even if he did not, other people would, enough for your reputation to be sullied in the world, and that would be the end for both of you. Our society is beyond cruel, especially to women.'

'He could not stand it. And that was what the letter said, the letter that first...that I...' the woman whispered. She could not even bring herself to say the words.

'Do you have the letter?' Mary asked, holding out her hand. The woman obediently drew from her reticule a folded sheet of paper, which she handed to Mary, who opened it, and read it aloud.

'*My dear Laura,*' Mary read and then paused, looking up at our visitor. 'Laura is your name?'

'Yes. Laura Shirley,' she said, very quietly. Well, we had got further than Mr Holmes! Mary continued to read the letter out loud.

'*My dear Laura, I am aware of the following stories about you.*

You have a choice. Either do as I ask, or I shall repeat the stories to everyone you know. Such pretty stories too. Let us begin.'

Mary stopped, read ahead and then said, 'There follows a stream of vileness that I will not repeat.' She tilted the paper this way and that, studying it carefully.

'He asks for nothing,' I pointed out.

'Not yet,' Mrs Shirley said softly. 'I have received three letters. The third said the next one would contain a request.'

'May I see that letter?' Mary asked.

'I burnt it. I burnt the other one, too. Please understand, my husband reads my letters. It is only good fortune that those letters arrived on days he was away on business.'

'Good fortune or good planning,' Mary remarked. 'Did you burn all the envelopes too?'

'Yes,' Laura said miserably. 'I could not bear to have those things in my house.'

Mary had stood up, and she held the letter up to the light streaming through the kitchen window.

'Thick paper, fairly decent quality,' she remarked. 'Watermark is a common brand. Handwriting is not particularly distinctive. It is basically that taught in any good school, all individuality gone. The ink is watered down. The pen is blunt and badly cut—see how it catches the paper? This isn't someone's personal paper, or he'd be aware of that particular fault with that particular pen on this paper. I say this was written in a gentleman's club—not one of the more exclusive ones, they have their own headed paper.' Mary turned to see me staring at her. She smiled. 'Well, I haven't listened to John's tales of Sherlock's methods without learning something, you know!'

Mary sat down at the table and placed her hand on Laura's arm.

'You must bring the next letter directly to us,' Mary said.

'Don't open it,' I said quickly. I didn't want this trembling little creature to read whatever foul request this man had made. Besides, there might be a clue in the way it was sealed. 'Just bring it here.'

'You're going to help me?' Laura said, looking from one to the other of us in amazement. 'You're really going to help me?'

Mary and I looked at each other. It seemed we had both made the decision independently, and had come to the same conclusion.

'Of course we're going to help you,' Mary said quickly. 'How could we not?'

Mrs Shirley left soon afterwards, much cheered. Well, she had stopped crying at least. She still drooped. I occupied myself clearing the tea things, as I listened to Mary escort her to the front door, reassuring her all the way, before she came back to the kitchen.

'Mary...' I said slowly. I was unsure we could do what we had promised. Mary did not need me to voice my concerns—she knew them.

'We can help,' Mary said firmly, as she put the washed cups away in the cupboard. 'We've learnt a lot ourselves, merely from sitting down here listening to John and Sherlock. We can do this.'

It always amazed me how she called him Sherlock, even to his face, whilst he always called her Mrs Watson.

'But, Mary...'

'And we're women. She trusts us, and she could not trust Sherlock,' Mary insisted. 'That's to our advantage in investigating too. No one suspects women. Most men think we're harmless, mindless little fools. No one will blink an eyelid if Laura Shirley acquires two new female friends whereas if Sherlock suddenly appeared in her life, everyone would be very suspicious, including that holier-than-thou husband of hers.'

'Yes, but Mary...'

'I won't leave her lost and alone. I won't!' she insisted, slamming the cupboard door, then looking guilty at the noise she had made.

'I agree!' I said quickly, trying to leap in. 'We're going to help her, I agree. I just wanted to say—we're not going to tell Mr Holmes, are we?'

'No, we damned well won't!' Mary cried. She glanced at the vent to make sure it was shut. Then in a lower voice, she said, 'No. He turned her away. He wasn't kind. She came to us and we helped. It's our case now.'

'Good,' I said, wiping down the table. 'I must admit, I do like the idea of doing something to help, instead of just sitting here, listening to those poor souls' problems and then Mr Holmes saving them, whilst I make tea. But, Mary, will you tell John?'

'John?' she asked, sitting down at the kitchen table. She obviously hadn't thought about John. She stared at the table a moment, then said, 'I will not tell John. If he asks, I shall say I'm helping a friend. And maybe when it's over I'll tell him. To be fair, there are some cases he and Sherlock have worked on that he refuses to tell me about. So, just helping a friend; no more than that. And,' she looked up at me, 'that's all it really is, isn't it?'

I nodded in agreement as I wrung out the cloth and draped it over the oven door to dry. This would be something we would do ourselves, with no interference or 'help' from the men upstairs. Our case, our turn to shine, our turn to feel we were achieving something worthwhile. On an impulse, I took two glasses from the cupboard and put them on the table. Then I went into the pantry and took a bottle out from the back.

'Mr Holmes is not the only one who can appreciate fine wine,' I said, putting it in front of Mary.

'This is more than wine, this is champagne! Proper champagne!' Mary said, awed and laughing at the same time.

'That is what one drinks when one is celebrating, is it not?' I asked, carefully extracting the cork.

'You are full of surprises,' Mary said. 'But can I point out it's only four o'clock in the afternoon?'

'I wish to drink a toast, and tea won't do,' I said firmly, as I carefully poured the champagne. I held my bubbling, fizzing, golden glass of champagne up to Mary.

'And the toast is: Mary Watson and Mrs Hudson—detectives,' I cried giddily. Mary laughed, stood up and raised her glass in return.

'Mrs Hudson and Mary Watson—detectives!'

Later, much later, once the Watsons had left for the day and I had sobered up somewhat—I had forgotten champagne made me quite so light-headed—I took Mr Holmes' tea up to him, with the evening post, which included a postcard sent from the Isle of Uffa. One arrived each year since 1887, with no message but 'all well', and signed Grice Paterson. I did hope he wouldn't have to go back there. It had not been comfortable, or safe for him. The sun was setting, one of those glorious deep red sunsets that make London rosy and glowing, as if the old city was new and clean and bright. Mr Holmes stood by the window, hands clasped behind his back. He watched not the sunset, but the comings and goings in the street below. I thought he was looking for Dr Watson, so I told him the doctor had gone home.

'I wasn't looking for Dr Watson,' he said. 'I thought she'd come back,' he murmured.

'Who?' I asked, as I laid the white cloth over the table and set out his tea things, in precisely the correct place, as he liked it.

'Mrs Hudson, the woman who just came to see me...'

'She left in tears,' I said, perhaps more sharply than I had intended. He must have caught the tenor of my voice, because he turned to face me in surprise.

'I only wanted her to tell the truth. I needed her to tell me everything. I expected her to return, duly chastened, and tell me what I asked. I had every intention of helping her, but I must have data!' he snapped, picking up his cup of tea. He was almost defensive. 'I was sure she'd come back. Why wouldn't she?'

'Perhaps she found someone else to help her,' I said quietly, picking up my tray.

Mr Holmes bridled. 'Who else can help her?' he demanded. 'Who else in London could there possibly be to help her?' He went back to the window, and his ceaseless watching.

'Who indeed?' I replied. 'Surely there is no one else suitable, in the whole of London.' And with that, I left him alone.

CHAPTER 3

A Circle of Four

For so long, the three of us had rubbed along together quite nicely. Sherlock Holmes, the detective, his reputation growing by the day, John Watson, the doctor, Mr Holmes' staunch companion and chronicler (and how good he turned out to be at that!) and Mrs Hudson, housekeeper, forever running in and out with cups of tea, and learning that these men would never keep ordinary hours, or have ordinary visitors. Not to mention the strange requests from Mr Holmes at all hours of the day and night. *Mrs Hudson, I need such and such a chemical. Mrs Hudson, do you know where I can get a tracking dog in Central London? Mrs Hudson, instead of putting breakfast on this plate, please put this roll of paper on it.*

It was the most exciting time I'd had since meeting Hector. Even if, every once in a while, when I watched them charge off hot on the chase, I wished I could go too. I swallowed that feeling.

It was not my place to hunt down the villains or track the clues or save the victim. It was my place to wait quietly at home, and look after my tenants when they returned. I was where I was meant to be. This was, I was certain, my place in life. And in this way, the three of us, I hope and think, were happy.

Then along came Mary Morstan, with her straight back and beautiful eyes and stubborn nature. Mary, who would have walked straight into hell with her head high rather than hurt any of us. Mary, who loved us all. Mary, who one day would tear our hearts into tiny pieces. But that is a story for another time, if I ever have the strength to tell it.

The morning of the day after Mary and I had drunk champagne and decided to become detectives, of a sort, I sat in my room and told myself I was a silly woman.

My bedroom was above Mr Holmes' sitting room, and I often lay there in bed at night, listening to him pace and up and down, muttering to himself, working out the complexities of a case that had baffled Scotland Yard. What made me think I could do such a thing?

I sat on the large iron-framed, neatly made bed and looked in the mirror. I saw a woman of slightly below the average height. She looked older than she actually was; even I forgot my own age sometimes. She had a plain, comfortable face, and a plump body, a sign that she enjoyed her own cakes too much. There was a mass of brown hair, turning grey now, tightly pulled into a bun on the back of her head. She wore a respectable black bombazine dress, with a long thin gold chain hanging around her neck, carrying a watch that was tucked into the waistband.

I sighed. In my mind I was still the slim, pretty, giggling girl who had caught Hector's eye. Then I would look in the mirror, and see an ageing, ordinary woman, not worthy of notice or attention, and wonder what had happened to me. Sometimes

I felt I was invisible, just one more number in the huge mass of London's respectable older women, always in black, always doing the right thing, always silent.

I glanced towards the wardrobe. In there were two dresses I had bought on an impulse. One was dark green, the colour of horse chestnut leaves in shadow. The other, even more daringly, was a deep russet red.

Hector would have loved the green dress. My eyes were brown, but they had flecks of green and blue which were always more noticeable if I wore those colours. Hector loved me in green. He said it made my eyes bewitching. But I was an almost-silver-haired widow now, nothing but a landlady, and we weren't supposed to wear green dresses and have bewitching eyes. As for red—that was beyond the pale!

I looked again in the mirror. Perhaps I would go along with Mary's idea, just for a little while. Just to occupy my mind. Just to chase out the sad thoughts I had sometimes. I went down to the kitchen. The bedroom was only where I slept. The kitchen was my domain, my kingdom, my refuge, my home. I loved that room, and I always felt at peace there.

Mary had already arrived—she often came to see me in the morning—and sat there, turning Mrs Shirley's letter over and over in her hands. Mary was the only person ever allowed to sit in my kitchen when I was not there, the only one permitted to make tea with my own teapot, the only one authorized to make the occasional small meal. Not cakes and pastries though; only I ever baked in my kitchen, and only I ever would.

'May I read it?' I asked.

'It is vile,' she warned. Yet she did not withhold the letter from me but held it out willingly.

'I understand,' I said, taking it from her.

It was indeed vile. It accused Laura of unnatural acts with any number of men, in most explicit and lascivious tones. I felt sullied just reading it. It was ridiculous to think of that quiet, small woman doing any of these things. I doubt she even knew half of them existed. And yet—it was a clever letter. It had a few small touches here and there that seemed true. The tone was not hysterical. This letter would be enough to raise a doubt in the mind of a man who truly believed an innocent woman's reputation remained untouched. Women—good women—had been ruined by milder whispers than these.

Mary sat at the table, turning her tea cup—the tea had long since gone cold—round and round in her hand, staring into the distance.

'Where to start? That is the question,' she said softly.

'With the letter, surely,' I said, sitting down opposite her. 'Mr Holmes always starts with the evidence.'

'I think we've got all we can from that letter,' Mary said ruefully. 'I've no doubt Mr Holmes would find some clue from the irregularity in the ink or the way the sunlight has fallen on the paper, but my skills don't stretch that far.'

We sat in silence for a moment, and then I said, 'With the victim—we start with the victim.'

Mary looked at me questioningly, expecting me to defend my hypothesis.

'This is not random,' I said slowly, thinking as I talked. This moment—this right here, what I was doing—was…exciting. After years of feeling like I was nothing more than a middle-aged lady doing nothing that required any intelligence, I was finally thinking. I was making deductions and connections and coming up with ideas and using my mind. It felt odd, it almost felt like my brain was rusty, and needed to be coaxed back into life—but I could feel it working, for the first time in years.

I loved it.

No wonder Mr Holmes was addicted to this. No wonder he turned to stimulants when there was nothing to think about.

'He has chosen his victim carefully,' I said to Mary, continuing my train of thought. 'A meek woman, no real friends, with a jealous husband. She is the perfect target.'

'Target for what?' Mary asked. 'He hasn't said what he wants yet.'

'That is not the point, presently,' I said urgently. 'The point is, he has not just picked a name at random out of the society pages. He has made a well-informed choice. And that means...'

'He knows her!' Mary cried, picking up on my thread of thought. I smiled. This was going satisfactorily. 'He's not just a passing acquaintance either.'

'Exactly—which means he is probably part of her social circle. We need to know who her acquaintances are.'

'It'd be someone she'd never suspect,' Mary said. 'Which means, she won't give us his name—if she gives us any.'

'Perhaps we should find a way to meet her friends?' I suggested. 'Pretend to be her new acquaintances, be introduced to her social circle?'

'I doubt Laura could lie to her husband,' Mary objected. 'I doubt she could even lie by omission. She'd blush and stammer. She'd never be able to calmly introduce us to her husband as her new friends that she just happened to make. And if this...man— and I use the word in its lightest possible sense,' she made a sound of disgust, 'does know them, he might be suspicious of a shy little mouse like Laura suddenly acquiring two new friends, even if her husband would not suspect a thing.'

She was right, of course. I'm not even sure I could have carried the lie off myself, anyway, let alone Laura with all her worries.

'Besides,' I said, 'he may not even be a friend. He may be someone Laura contracts business with. A dressmaker, a solicitor, a butcher. My grocer knows to a nicety how much my budget for weekly shopping is, and whether I have guests and whether or not I have the nerve to argue the bill, but I wouldn't invite him to afternoon tea.'

'I hadn't thought of that,' Mary admitted. 'You are right, of course. We need to find a way of watching Laura, seeing who she meets, and why, and we need to find a way of doing it without Laura, her husband, or anyone else knowing.'

'It would be good to keep the husband under surveillance

too,' I added. 'Perhaps it is one of his acquaintances. And he would have a far wider range of business contacts.'

Mary blew out her breath.

'That's an awful lot of spying for just the two of us,' she said.

'It can't be us. We don't have the skills,' I pointed out. 'Laura knows us, and would react if she saw us. And someone as devious as this blackmailer would be bound to spot us. We need someone he'd never notice.'

It didn't take the two of us long to come up with the answer. We'd practically talked ourselves into it. We looked at each other, grinned, and said together, 'The Irregulars!'

The Boys of Baker Street

If you have read John's stories, you will know about the Baker Street Irregulars—but if you haven't, then I will tell you their story.

Back then, during the last century, London's streets thronged with boys—and occasionally girls—running wild. They often had no home or family, or if they did, it was not somewhere they were welcome. They roamed the streets, living as best they could, running errands, carrying messages, doing any little task that needed doing and that they could earn a shilling for. Whenever Mr Holmes needed anything fetched from some shop or another, there was always a boy on the street who would run the errand. Sometimes they committed petty crimes—stole an apple, or a bun. And some were tempted into bigger crimes, into working for bigger criminals, destined to end up in jail—or at the end of a hangman's rope. And some just...disappeared.

One of the boys on the street was Wiggins. He was the wily, clever, cunning leader of the Irregulars.

Wiggins was a boy who could think and plan and see consequences. That made him unusual. He looked around him, at all the urchins running round the street, some surviving, some not, and decided they needed help. He banded them together, found a place for them to sleep, made sure they shared their food, found them work and kept them safe. He gave them a family, of sorts, and he watched over all of them. And at some point, they met Mr Holmes, and each could see the advantage of helping the other. They had worked for Mr Holmes often.

I did not even know they existed until one day I opened the front door of 221b Baker Street to find a group of filthy ragamuffins standing there. The one at the front, a young man all of twelve years with watchful eyes, said very politely, 'Wiggins and the Baker Street Irregulars, missus, here to see Mr 'Olmes. At 'is invitation,' he added quickly, and I looked round at the faces, some nervous, some hopeful, one or two angry. Something told me they expected to be kicked off the front doorstep, told to use the tradesman's entrance, told to just go away.

Well, I've let far worse people into his rooms, and certainly far ruder, so I stepped aside, and invited them in. They scampered up the stairs, led by Wiggins.

When they came down again, I was at the top of the kitchen stairs. I called to them, 'I have cake, if any should want some! And tea or milk. Enough for all of you.'

Their eyes lit up, poor half-starved things, but they looked towards their leader first. He, in turn, looked at me suspiciously.

'I shan't make you wash, and I shan't ask questions,' I promised. I vaguely remembered, from so long ago, what boys were like.

He nodded, and the boys (about ten of them, but as they dashed around and in and out it was difficult to count) rushed past me into the kitchen. He, the older boy, walked towards me, and said, 'That's very kind of you, Mrs 'Udson.'

'My pleasure,' I assured him. 'You know my name, and I know you are Wiggins, yes?'

'Yes, ma'am,' he said politely, touching his cap, and walked past me into the kitchen, as self-possessed as any city gent. I heard him tell the boys to eat properly, not like a bunch of savages. I followed him in and watched him pour milk for the younger ones, and make sure each and every boy got his share. He insisted on please and thank you, served himself last, settled disputes quickly and all the time he watched those boys.

I have known many worse men than Wiggins of the Baker Street Irregulars, but none better.

The boys wolfed down the cakes, all I had, and I was glad to see it.

'You're welcome here any time,' I said to them. 'I always make too much food, and it just goes to waste.'

Wiggins didn't trust charity. I could see it in his face. Charity meant the workhouse, and prayers and exhortations to remember your sins and then eat bad food, and never enough of it, and beatings, and separations.

'Mr Holmes doesn't eat his dinner half the time,' I told him. 'It pains me to see all my hard work over the stove going to waste.'

Wiggins nodded, but said nothing. He looked round at the others. He had his own stubborn pride, but would he deny his boys because of that?

Wiggins deserved the truth.

'I had a son once,' I said to him, in a low voice. I sat down beside him, at the head of the huge wooden kitchen table. I kept my voice low, so none of the other boys could hear me. This was between Wiggins and me. 'He died. So did my husband. To tell the truth, I would appreciate the company. Mr Holmes is out most of the time, and I am alone here.'

Then he smiled at me, and nodded his approval of my plan at the rest of the boys. From that moment on, the Irregulars would turn up at my door, two or three times a month, never more than two or three at a time. I would feed them, and talk to them, never asking questions, but listening to all they said. Sometimes I would treat scratches and cuts and bruises—even with Wiggins' protection, life on the streets was never easy. Every so often, Wiggins himself would appear, sometimes with a half-starved boy, sometimes alone. After a while, I came to realize that even though I thought I was looking after the boys, Wiggins believed he was looking after me. His visits weren't just to eat, but to make sure I was all right, not lonely, not scared, not in trouble. It touched me more than I can say.

And of course, one day he brought me Billy.

'How do you find the Irregulars?' Mary asked. 'John says they run all over London; they could be anywhere.'

'I leave a message in the newsagent's window on the corner,' I told her. 'That's how Mr Holmes contacts them. They check it every day, every hour sometimes.'

So I did. *BSI contact Mrs H. I have work for you.*

Wiggins came the next day, to the front door, as befitted a business transaction. Normally he slipped in through the kitchen door, as the boys did when they came for cake, but Wiggins was very conscious of the proprieties. He wasn't here as a boy, but as a worker. I invited him down to the kitchen, my own particular office.

'You all right?' he asked, coming down the stairs. He hesitated when he saw Mary sitting there. He wasn't used to seeing anyone else in the kitchen. I think he was worried that Mary was a do-gooder, come to take him away to some place to be prayed at and ordered about and locked away.

'This is my friend, Mary Watson,' I said quickly. 'Dr Watson's wife.'

I walked over to the hob and poured the tea as Mary and Wiggins took the measure of each other. She would have seen a boy of indeterminate age, somewhere between twelve and fifteen, thin but lean, with a suggestion of a hungry strength in the way he moved. He could be still, so very still, as if carved from stone, except for his eyes. His eyes watched and assessed and judged all the time. He was calm, though he never stopped thinking and his thoughts were not often pleasant. He was taller than most of his boys, with dirty skin, pale underneath all the grime. His dark blond hair was too long, and filthy, and his eyes were dark, very dark, and shadowed. He was dressed all in mismatched brown rags—a disguise to help him blend in on the streets. I knew he had better clothes as I had given them to him. All this Mary saw and understood as she looked at the boy standing before her.

'Mr Wiggins,' Mary said to him, nodding. He nodded back, all cool politeness.

'Just Wiggins, ma'am,' he told her. 'No other name?'

'Never needed one.'

'Wiggins, then,' she said, smiling at him. After a moment's hesitation, he smiled back. In that moment they had made their assessment and found each other perfectly satisfactory. Wiggins sat down at the table and I poured tea for all of us. 'Do you need help?' Wiggins said to me. 'The advert said you, not Mr 'Olmes.'

'I do. I'm not in trouble, but someone I know is. I said I'd help her, and for that I need you,' I told him, placing a very large slice of seed cake in front of him. It was his favourite. He looked at it suspiciously, recognizing it for what it was—a bribe. 'And I'd rather Mr Holmes did not know.'

Wiggins looked at us, from one to the other, warily.

'Not tell Mr 'Olmes?' He didn't like this. He had a great deal of loyalty for Mr Holmes, not to mention a healthy amount of respect. He knew it would be very difficult to keep a secret from his major employer.

'This is our case,' Mary said forcefully. 'Not his.'

'Your case? You setting yourselves up as 'tecs, same as Mr 'Olmes?' he said, with a mixture of incredulity and amusement.

'Yes we are,' I said calmly, sitting opposite him. 'Why ever not?'

His smile faded as he realized I was deadly serious. 'Your case,' he said, looking at the two of us.

'Our case,' Mary replied. 'Our client to protect. Our obligation to fulfil.'

He watched her earnest face for a moment, and saw how seriously she took this. He nodded, and ate an enormous bite of the seed cake.

'Fair enough,' he said. 'Mind, on one condition.'

'What condition?' I asked.

'If either of you get into trouble, or get hurt, I go straight to Mr 'Olmes,' he insisted.

'Agreed,' Mary said quickly. We were daring, but not fools.

'Right then, what's the job?' Wiggins asked, as businesslike as ever.

'To follow two people,' Mary told him, handing over a piece of paper. Wiggins, unusually for a street boy, could read and write. I do not know where he learnt these skills. I suspect the price for them was high. But they were skills he was determined to use and expand.

'Mrs Laura Shirley and her husband. This is their address, details of where he works, and so on. We need to know the names and descriptions of everyone who calls at their house, everyone they have any contact with, everyone they see or meet, no matter how insignificant.'

'Blimey, you don't half ask a lot!' Wiggins said, amused, peering down the list.

'Can you manage all that?' I asked, watching this boy.

'No more than I done for Mr 'Olmes a dozen times,' he told me with a touch of scorn as he folded the paper and put it into his pocket. 'Servants, too?' he asked. I hadn't thought of that.

'Not yet,' I mused. This was more complicated than I first thought. There must be so many people Laura Shirley had contact with, day in and day out, and those people had contacts, and then there were her husband's friends and colleagues...how would we track down all those connections?

'Unless you spot something significant in the servants' interaction,' I added.

'How will he know what is significant?' Mary asked.

'Wiggins will know,' I said confidently. 'Mr Holmes has great faith in his abilities.' This was true. I had often heard Mr Holmes say that Wiggins was destined to rule Scotland Yard one day—or set it by its heels and outwit it completely. Wiggins' back straightened unconsciously.

'Send Billy to me twice a day for reports,' Wiggins said. 'He'll know where to find us.'

Have I mentioned Billy? He was our pageboy. More on him later. He has quite a story of his own.

No one knew where the Irregulars slept, not even Mr Holmes. They guarded their lair fiercely, for who knew who would come for them in their sleep—the law, the beadles, the criminals. 'I'll come myself if anything happens.'

He nodded once at Mary and me, and turned to go.

'Remarkable boy,' Mary said, watching the door as Wiggins left.

'They all are, all the Irregulars,' I said, clearing up the tea things. I was suddenly angry that all that intelligence and kindness should go to waste. 'What kind of world is it where Wiggins and Billy and the like scrape a living on the streets whilst worse boys than them get an education and a home and parents?'

'A world where you take Billy in and Mr Holmes employs Wiggins and Wiggins cares for the lost boys,' Mary told me gently, handing me her tea cup. She patted me on the shoulder, and I sighed. She was right, of course. Others failed them. We would not. 'Now what happens?' Mary asked.

'Now we wait,' I sighed, and sat down. 'Mr Holmes hates this part.'

'I can't say I blame him.'

Mary left soon afterwards, to take care of her own home and husband. I made cakes all afternoon—it was the most restful occupation I knew. And all day, even until the nighttime, I heard Mr Holmes pace back and forth above me. I didn't know what he was working on, but his restlessness matched my own.

I have to admit the next two days were exciting. Dr Watson was spending a lot of time with Mr Holmes, so Mary was free to visit me. We sat round the kitchen table, the sun pouring through the window, tea always in front of us, and the two of us planning and deducing. The plight of Laura Shirley had touched us, but I must say it was the thrill of the chase that was driving us onwards. We came up with a dozen different scenarios to catch the black-mailer, each more ridiculous than the last. We pored over the letter, searching it for clues, making terribly far-fetched deductions from the colour of the ink or the smudge in the corner. We talked and planned and, most important and thrilling of all, we *thought*.

I did love my job as housekeeper, more than I had enjoyed being merely a landlady. Mary did love being married to John. Yet neither role offered much in the way of mental stimulation when the men were out, chasing about the streets of London. But now we had something to do, not just a way to while away the hours, like embroidery or baking, but a problem to solve and a puzzle to piece together. For the first time in years I felt my thoughts racing and my mind turning and my imagination creating and I felt alive: intensely, gloriously alive.

The kitchen vent stayed shut for two days. We could hear John and Mr Holmes moving about upstairs, the occasional slammed door, once in a while an excited shout. Mr Holmes would not eat the meals I brought him, and his light burnt all night, always the way when he had a case. Mysterious telegrams arrived for him (using various aliases of his) at all hours of the day and night. And yet, for once, I had no curiosity about his case. I was utterly absorbed in my own.

Reports from Wiggins and the Irregulars arrived twice a day, via Billy. We examined every word for something, someone out of place. Laura visited her dressmaker, her father's solicitor, paid her bill at the milliner's. Mr Shirley went to work and went home. He ate lunch in a local chop house with three other men of equal probity and averageness. The servants seemed ordinary; one of the maids had a follower, the boot boy was recognized as one who had run away from his previous post. Just tiny wrinkles in their perfect life, but enough to start a whole range of speculation in our minds.

Of course there came the moment when the door to Mr Holmes' rooms slammed open with extraordinary force, and Mr Holmes ran down the stairs shouting, 'Come, Watson, there's not a moment to lose!'

Mary and I happened to be in the hall as John ran past and out of the door, glancing apologetically at Mary.

'Go, go!' Mary shouted happily after her husband. 'Save the day, solve the riddle. Be sure to tell me every detail later!' She never begrudged John a moment with Mr Holmes, as long as he told her the entire story afterwards.

Mr Holmes called out as he passed us, 'The game, Mrs Watson, is afoot!'

Then they were gone. Mary closed the door behind them, turning to me, smiling sweetly, and said, 'And our game, Mrs Hudson, is also afoot!'

And we laughed for the sheer joy of it.

But we had been dreaming our hours away, imagining ourselves detectives but merely playing the game. The reality hit us that evening, hard.

John and Mr Holmes returned after sunset, well satisfied. Their case was solved, judging by Mr Holmes' suddenly prodigious appetite. Night fell, and it was bitterly cold, the last gasp of winter. Mary and I were in the kitchen when suddenly the area door banged open. There stood Billy, barely a shadow against the darkness, and he was supporting someone slumped against him. Someone, a boy—Wiggins! As Billy dragged him into the kitchen, I could see that Wiggins' arm hung loose, and blood, oh my God, the blood, dripped from his head, from his arm, from all over him. I grabbed him from Billy—who no longer had the strength to hold him after carrying him for miles through the streets like this—and propped Wiggins on a chair. His eyes did not open, his breathing was shallow and rasping, and his clothes were damp and stiff with blood.

'Mary,' I forced myself to say. My boy, what had they done to my boy? What had I done to him? 'Mary.' I sounded so calm. 'Get John. Now!'

The Friendship
of Billy and Wiggins

It was Wiggins who had brought Billy to me nearly a year ago. Wiggins turned up one cold, wet night with a bedraggled child in tow. This boy, who couldn't have been more than ten, slightly built, with dark brown hair, took off his hat when he saw me, and said 'please' and 'thank you' in a refined accent. I sat him at the table and gave him a huge helping of cold meat, cheese and a chunk of bread. I recognized the pallid tone to his skin, the hollows in his cheeks. It's the way the children look when they've been in the workhouse too long, and haven't had enough to eat. He ate the food quickly as Wiggins and I talked in the pantry.

'He's from an orphanage,' Wiggins told me, glancing over to Billy every now and again. 'Both 'is parents up and died of the typhoid, and there ain't no other family, so he got sent to a Church orphanage. Nasty places, those, specially for them that's used to a family and food and love. And he's posh and clever, and they don't like that sort of thing.'

'The other children bullied him?'

'Not them. The bastards—'scuse language, missus, but they are—the ones who run the place. They like their children small and quiet and obedient and knowing their place. They don't like children who know it ought to be different, and damned well say so.' Wiggins' voice, though low, shook with anger.

'So that's what he did,' I said softly, glancing over to the boy at the table. He'd finished the meal and was now looking around him, curious and bright. 'They treated him badly. Beat him, punished him.'

'They did,' Wiggins confirmed grimly. 'So I took 'im. That was right, weren't it?' he asked, a touch anxiously.

'That was right,' I assured him. I know I should have imposed authority, insisted Wiggins take him back to the orphanage, but I've seen those places. I wouldn't even send a dog I hated there. 'Will he stay with you?'

'He could,' Wiggins said, slowly. 'He could learn to be one of us, but he shouldn't. He could make something of himself.'

'You could make something of yourself, Wiggins.'

'Yeah, and I will, but not the kind of something he'll make of himself. He could be a doctor or a lawyer or suchlike. Me—I'm going to end up something a bit different, if you know what I mean,' Wiggins told me, his eyes for a moment full of a burning intensity. He was right. Given how Wiggins was growing up, on the street, no care, no guidance, precious little education and not always of the right sort, he could end up dangling at the end of a rope, or the richest man in London, but he could never be a well-respected member of society. He'd always be on the outside, looking in. Knowing that must have hurt, sometimes, but he never said anything.

I looked across at Billy, who had got up from the table and was walking around the kitchen.

'He notices things,' Wiggins said. 'Things I miss. And he works out what they mean.'

'Like a detective,' I said softly.

'Like a detective,' Wiggins agreed. 'Maybe Mr 'Olmes could teach 'im. Like an apprentice.'

'I'm not sure...' I didn't know if I could impose a boy on Mr Holmes—but Wiggins knew how to play me.

'Course, you'd be doing me a great favour, Mrs 'Udson. I can't keep an eye on him on the street, he'd be getting into all sort of mischief in no time flat, and I'd have to get him out of it. It would be a great relief to me to know he was safely here. In a proper home, learning a proper trade, where he belongs.'

'Wiggins,' I said warningly, knowing I was being manipulated.

'And 'cos I worry about you,' Wiggins interrupted.

'Me?' I asked, surprised and touched.

'Mr 'Olmes has all sorts in here, day and night. Thieves, murderers, politicians, brutes of all kinds. I don't like to think of you here all alone, having to show people of that sort up to his rooms. And Mr 'Olmes could do with a boy he could trust hanging round the place.'

'Could he,' I said dryly.

'Oh yes,' Wiggins replied earnestly. 'Very useful things, boys.'

He had talked me into it, though truth to tell I hadn't needed much persuading. A woman who'd lost her son, a boy who'd lost his mother—the entire thing was just like a story.

I took Billy on as page-boy. First I had a conversation with Mr Holmes and John. If Billy was going to do all the showing clients in and so on for Mr Holmes, they'd have to contribute to his wages.

Mr Holmes was reluctant at first. He didn't like change, and what ways he had, he was settled in, but John had sprung gallantly to my rescue, pointing out that at my age it wasn't good for me to keep running up and down the stairs at all hours, especially not with the kind of people who came to see Holmes. I'd had to show a drunken sailor in at 2 a.m. only that morning, for heaven's sake, and if this went on I'd have a heart attack and it would be Holmes' fault. What's more, I needed help to do all the errands to map shops and telegraph offices and cab stands—at which point Mr Holmes interrupted him, accused him of as pretty a piece of emotional manipulation as he had ever seen, and gave in.

Billy got a uniform with two rows of brass buttons and a home and an education.

Once Mr Holmes realized how clever he was, he did start to give the boy an apprenticeship, of a sort. Mr Holmes taught Billy something of what he knew. John, too, gave Billy lessons in all the knowledge Mr Holmes had forgotten (such as the solar system), though John's lessons always seemed to segue into thrilling stories that couldn't possibly have all been true. I do believe John honed his storytelling skills on Billy. I sent him to a succession of different tutors every Tuesday afternoon, and Billy played his part, too, reading voraciously. Within a few weeks Billy became an integral part of the household, and after a month even Mr Holmes called him 'useful'.

But Billy never forgot who had rescued him. Every hour that he had free—usually on Wednesday afternoons and Sundays— he ran onto the streets to spend with Wiggins. The two of them became close, as close as Mr Holmes and John. It touched me to see the care they took of one another, the concealing of their tight friendship with a joking manner, as boys do.

Now it was Billy guiding the injured Wiggins, with infinite care, to a kitchen chair. Wiggins was white and shaking. Thankfully John had come straight down as soon as Mary had called him, and gently knelt before him, examining the blood all over him.

'Where are you hurt?' he asked. Wiggins shook his head. He didn't have the strength to answer. I felt sick, watching him bleed, but Mary held me up.

'His head's bleeding,' Billy answered for him. 'A big cut, right here. Some other cuts and bruises, and his arm twisted under him when the man pushed him down the stairs. I think it might be broken.'

'Let me see,' John said, taking my scissors from the table and cutting Wiggins' shirt away. 'Tea, Mrs Hudson, strong and sweet and lots of it. Billy, hold him up, support him, he's going to be in a lot of pain and may pass out. Mary, boil some water, this wound needs cleaning.'

I'd never seen John in his role as the doctor before. It was a new side to him for me—this gentle, firm, knowledgeable, authoritative man. No wonder he was on call at all hours—it must have been comforting to have John Watson treat you. As soon as he touched Wiggins, the boy calmed, and let John take care of him. I wasn't surprised Mr Holmes deferred to John in all medical matters—he had a talent no mere learning could replicate.

'He's losing so much blood,' Mary whispered to him, as she placed the bowl of hot water and cloths on the table by John's side. She glanced up at me, and I saw she was stricken with guilt. How could we have put a boy, this boy, in so much danger?

'It's a scalp wound,' John said, taking one of the cloths and dabbing at the cut on Wiggins' head. It went across his forehead into his hair, a sharp straight line. He must have hit it on the edge of something. 'They always bleed heavily,' he continued. 'You'll have a scar, Wiggins, which will make you very popular with ladies. Tell them you got it duelling.' John winked, and Wiggins, thank God, laughed, just once, a queer, choking laugh.

John unpeeled the last scraps of Wiggins' shirt just as I put the tea on the table. I gasped—I could not help it; Wiggins' torso was covered in bruises. Wiggins saw the horror in my eyes, and in John and Mary's too. Even Billy winced.

'I fell down some steps. Stone ones,' Wiggins said hoarsely.

'Fell?' John said, disbelieving. 'Billy said you were pushed, and I'd say you were pushed with some force.'

'I fell,' Wiggins repeated stubbornly.

I could have told then, I would have. I would have told John all about the letters, and Mrs Shirley, there and then, and he would have told Mr Holmes, and it would all have been taken out of our hands. But then Wiggins glanced at me, he stared at me, and his message was clear. He was in on our secret now, had suffered worse for it than we had, and he didn't want it told. I gave in and sat down silently. If that was what Wiggins wished, that was how it would be. I owed him that.

I swear that is the only reason I kept silent.

'Some of these bruises are old,' John said, examining the mass of yellowing, purple and black patches on Wiggins' torso.

'Lots of fights on the street,' Wiggins told him, clenching his teeth. John's touch, no matter how gentle, must have hurt, but he would not react to it, not even a gasp of pain. It was I who gasped, and winced and wept.

'He always wins,' Billy said, half proudly, half anxiously. I saw his glance at Wiggins and wondered how many fights Billy had pulled Wiggins out of, how many bruises he had. Did he worry that, one day, Wiggins would not win? There was so much that went on in the lives around me that I only knew through glances, and glimpses, and half-overheard conversations. I did not have the authority to demand the truth, but I had the skill to watch and listen and understand what they would never say.

John, having bandaged up the cut on Wiggins' head and gently smoothed ointment across his bruises, turned his attention to the arm that hung swollen and misshapen at Wiggins' side.

'Well, it's sprained, rather than broken, but it'll hurt like the devil for a while,' John told him, as he bandaged it up. 'I know you're eager to be gone, but you need to rest, for a couple of days at least.'

Wiggins looked at him mutinously, but Mary laid a hand on his shoulder.

'Please, Wiggins,' she said softly. 'Give us a chance to make our amends to you.'

Wiggins went quiet, secretly grateful, I thought, and lay back against the chair. John stood up, snapped his bag shut, and turned to me.

'Mrs Hudson…' he started to say.

'Don't tell Mr Holmes,' I interrupted.

'Do you honestly think Holmes could miss one moment of a bleeding and battered Wiggins!' he cried, as close to angry as I'd seen him.

'John,' Mary said softly, and he turned to her. He could not help but look at her with love, and she gazed up at him. 'We can't tell you, or Sherlock, how Wiggins was hurt, but please, I ask you, trust us.'

'For heaven's sake, this house is full of secrets!' he snapped.

'They're not our secrets to tell. You have secrets you cannot tell me,' Mary said reasonably.

'Holmes' secrets,' he said gently, not wanting to argue.

'Exactly. Other people's secrets,' she whispered. He looked down at her, and she up at him, and they looked like Hector and I once did. When we were young, and in love, and we did not have to speak to have a conversation, we just looked at each other and knew what we thought. For a moment, as I watched John and Mary Watson, my heart ached for my dead husband and lost youth, and I had to look away.

'Don't look so worried,' John said softly, and I glanced round to see him looking at me. 'I can't tell Holmes anything, anyway. You haven't told me anything.'

'And you haven't deduced anything?' Mary teased gently.

'I'm not the detective, my love, merely the doctor.' He leaned down and kissed her on the cheek. Mary and Billy turned to Wiggins, preparing to move him to the other room beyond the pantry and prop him on the bed and tuck his sheets in and generally bother him under the guise of making him comfortable. But before John left, he turned to me and said gently, so that no one else heard, 'He was doing something for you?'

'Something simple,' I promised, clasping my hands, torn with guilt. 'I hadn't realized it would be so dangerous.'

'That's how it always starts,' John said grimly, 'something simple, then there's danger and guns and fights and people get hurt. What are you up to?'

I bit my lip. My life was a tangle of promises. Which ones would I keep? I dared not speak.

'Secrets,' John said softly, nodding. 'I'm surrounded by them, and if I'm honest,' he glanced towards Mary, fussing over Wiggins, 'I'm as guilty as all of us of keeping secrets. Only don't get hurt, will you?'

'Mary will be in no danger, I promise you,' I said equally softly.

He snorted. 'I'd like to see you stop Mary once she's set on her path, no matter how dangerous it is!' he said, just loudly enough for Mary to hear. He dropped his voice, took my arm and pulled me into the hallway. 'Look, if Mary got hurt, it would hurt me deeply too, and she knows that. Her safety is my responsibility, and hers too, and she is more than capable of taking care of both herself and me,' he added, in a whisper. 'I meant you, Mrs Hudson. Don't you get hurt. It would break both our hearts.'

'You and Mary...' I started to say.

'I didn't mean Mary and me! I meant Holmes and me!' he interrupted. I must have looked dubious, because he said, 'He does have a heart. He doesn't use it much, but it's there. And you've got your place in it.' He kissed me gently on the cheek, the kiss a son gives his mother. 'And a place in my heart, too. Don't you forget it.'

CHAPTER 6

Death at the Docks

I still remember the very first time I saw Mary Morstan. I answered the door one morning to find her standing there in a plain, neat but slightly faded light brown dress. She was taller than me, and slender. She held up her head, not proudly, but with a certain confidence. She was lovely, not conventionally pretty, but with a refined, expressive face, blue eyes, and coils of heavy gold hair. She carried a packet of papers tightly bound, and she had a determined set to her mouth. When I opened the door, she smiled at me, quite the sweetest smile I had ever seen.

'Good morning. I am looking for Mr Sherlock Holmes?' she queried, in a low, well-mannered voice. She had the faintest trace of a Scotch accent. My mother and my husband both being Scottish, I have a fondness for that proud and glorious country, and I instinctively smiled back at her. I opened the door wider, and directed her up the stairs.

She hesitated for a moment, and I saw the hand that gripped the packet tremble slightly, and then tighten. Her manner was poised, and yet there was something in the way she looked up the stairs, as if she were unsure of what she was doing, perhaps even slightly nervous.

'They will be kind,' I assured her spontaneously. I surprised myself. I never normally spoke a word beyond 'come in' and 'up the stairs' to Mr Holmes' clients, yet something about her touched me, and made me want to reach out to her.

She looked at me, her blue eyes wide, and then smiled.

'Thank you,' she said softly, and then, with what I was to learn was a characteristic gesture, she put her shoulders back. She took a deep breath, and ascended the staircase.

When she came back down again, I happened to be in the hall—out of idle curiosity, I assure you; I had nothing useful to be doing there. She saw me and stopped at the foot of the stairs.

'Thank you, Mrs...?'

'Hudson,' I said to her. She looked happier, almost glowing. 'It all went well then, Miss...'

'Morstan. A great pleasure to meet you.' She held out her hand to me; something that happened so rarely I almost didn't know what to do. I grasped it, and we shook hands, as men do when they decide to become instant friends. 'It all went very well. Thank you for your comforting words, they were a great boon. And you were right, they were indeed kind.'

I had wanted to dislike Mary for changing our perfect little household. Instead, she became my greatest friend and bound the four of us even tighter together. She changed all our lives, quite unwittingly. Mary Morstan—Watson these days—was now part of the family of 221b.

❀ ❀ ❀

Once John had left, Wiggins opened his mouth to say something, but Billy placed his finger to his own lips to shush him and walked towards the door.

It wasn't that we didn't trust John not to reveal what little he knew, or guessed, but Mr Holmes was so very good at deducing entire stories from tiny little details. When we were sure John was safely upstairs, I had Billy help Wiggins along to the small bedroom on the basement floor and get him into bed. I guessed Wiggins would rather not show weakness to Mary or me, nor would he wish to undress in front of us. Once we were certain Billy and Wiggins were out of earshot, Mary opened the vent.

We could hear that John was in the rooms above, cleaning his instruments. Mr Holmes must have asked what had happened, because John was telling him that Wiggins had got himself hurt in a fight, he had patched Wiggins up, and yes, Wiggins was going to be perfectly all right.

So far, so good. But then Mr Holmes asked where Mary was. John replied that his wife was in the kitchen, feeding cake to Wiggins, and was that coffee in the pot?

Mr Holmes hesitated, and then he said, in a low voice, 'I don't like to say this to you, but she's up to something. Mrs Watson, I mean. And maybe Mrs Hudson too.'

'Probably,' John said, very unconcernedly. 'After all, I usually am, why shouldn't she be? Where's the cream?' Mary smiled—some secret joke between husband and wife.

'She is keeping a secret, I am sure,' Mr Holmes said. This was followed by a rattle, which I believe was him passing John the cream. 'Are you not curious?'

'Very. But she will tell me what she has been doing eventually, just as eventually I will tell her what I've been doing all day with you.' It must have been a strain on John, balancing between his wife and his best friend, but it did not cause his voice to waver one iota. Mr Holmes was right; John had a spine of iron.

'Actually, I think I prefer tea,' John said lightly.

'John,' Mr Holmes started to say, and I held my breath. He called his friend 'John' so rarely I knew he was going to say something momentous, but John stopped him.

'Look at my hat, Holmes. It is dusted. My shoes are clean, my collar ironed, I am several pounds overweight. My wife still loves me,' he told him, laughing. 'Look, Holmes, I love my wife with all my heart and soul, and I am certain she loves me the same way.'

Opposite me, also leaning against the wall to better hear what came from the vent, Mary smiled.

'But,' John continued, 'I spend most of my free time running around solving cases with you—which I enjoy greatly, and which has given me a good deal of satisfaction, not to mention a wife. She has never once objected to my time with you—in fact, she encourages it. She sees it as my doing some good in the world, and I believe she feels she owes you a debt, for our marriage. If she, in her turn, wishes to spend her free time with Mrs Hudson doing something that interests them far more than sewing shirts and baking cakes, then I have no objection.'

'If you say so,' Holmes grudgingly replied. 'But is what they are doing safe? Wiggins seems quite badly hurt, judging by the amount of bandages you used.'

'Oh, I am sure they are safe,' John told him, suddenly sounding quite loud, as if he were right next to the vent. 'They made a promise.'

Then there was a loud bang—John had closed the vent.

Mary jumped back from the wall, startled.

'He closed the vent!' she cried, her cheeks flushing, either with anger or embarrassment. 'He made that remark about our promise, and then closed the vent. Do you think he did that deliberately?'

'That vent is high up on the wall, and very stiff to open and close,' I told her. 'So, yes, I think he did that deliberately.'

We stood there aghast for a moment. What a discovery! John

knew we listened—how long had he known? Had he known all along? I had only ever opened that air vent and listened when the kitchen had been silent. I had no idea he could hear me. Mr Holmes had certainly never hinted he could hear me.

But then we couldn't help it. We laughed. Like a pair of naughty schoolgirls caught eating sweets in bed, we laughed.

Once we had quietened down, I went to the room where Billy had settled Wiggins. He was just tucking his friend in, taking the greatest of care with him, keeping his arms free of the blankets. For once Wiggins looked like just a boy, small and hurt, needing help, though his eyes were as fierce as ever. I sat on the end of the bed, Mary standing behind me, and said, 'Tell us everything.'

He took a breath, calmer now, and cradled his sprained arm. I thought of leaving him, waiting for him to tell us later, but I knew he would not sleep until he had made his report. He was conscientious.

'I was following the gent—the husband. It was Billy and me, 'cos I'm teaching him a few tricks of the trade. The bloke was just having a normal day—went to the office, came out at one for lunch, went to the same chop house he always goes to. But then, instead of going back to work, he went for a walk down by the river. And not a posh part neither, he went down to the docks. Right into the dangerous bit. Right where he might get jumped or murdered by anyone, just for the hanky in his pocket, and no one would stop it neither, though it was broad daylight. And he knew it too. He looked...what was it you said, Billy?'

'Apprehensive,' Billy added. 'His face was pale and his hands were shaking. I do not think he wanted to be there.'

'No, he did not,' Wiggins continued. 'And neither did I, 'cos the docks is not a good place to be. Boys get snatched there.'

'Snatched for what? By whom?' Mary asked. He looked at her darkly, as if he regretted saying such a thing. I doubt he would have done, if he hadn't been so light-headed from loss of blood.

'I'd rather not say, missus,' he said.

'Oh…I see,' she said, glancing down at me. Wiggins occasionally opened up a whole new dark foul world to us, which we had no idea existed.

'Perhaps Mr Shirley was going to a shipping office,' I suggested.

'Ain't no shipping offices down there,' Wiggins pointed out. 'Leastways, not one a gent like him would use. 'Sides, he never went to no office. He kind of stopped, and looked round, to see if anyone was following him. He didn't see me, nor Billy either. We're too good at that game to be spotted by the likes of 'im! Then, all of a sudden, he darted down these stone steps, right by the water. He was in the open there, nowhere for us to hide, but I knew whatever was happening would happen down there, so I told Billy to wait up top and I went down the steps too, like I was just a river rat, looking for a bit of work, or a bit of rubbish, you know. There was a man down there, right by the river. Light shining up onto his face, sunlight reflected from the river I guess. Couldn't see him clearly. Mr Shirley went right up to him, and he kept saying something about not telling her, and begging he not tell her 'cos it'd break her.'

'Not tell her what?' I asked.

Wiggins shrugged. 'Dunno.'

'What did the man look like?' Mary asked, and Wiggins frowned.

'See, I bin thinking 'bout that, over and over again, but when I close my eyes I can't see his face, I just see the light from the river shining back at me, right in my eyes. I keep thinking, 'cos I saw his face, just before the light blinded me, I know I saw it, plain as I see you, but I just can't remember it!'

'It's the head wound,' Mary said soothingly. Wiggins was getting agitated. 'John says it plays havoc with the memory. Just don't think about it, and it'll come back to you.'

'What if it don't?' he cried, agonized by his failure.

'Then it don't…doesn't,' I told him. 'We'll find him another way. Did you see what he was wearing?'

Wiggins shook his head, but Billy said, 'Pea jacket, dark peaked cap, shabby trousers. But they didn't look right for him, he didn't even move right in them. He walked very odd, stiffly, as if he was trying to remember how to walk.'

'Faking it,' Wiggins said quietly. 'Faking the whole lot of it. Did you see his face?'

'No, the cap covered it,' Billy said quietly. 'Sorry.'

'No, you did well. Remembered the clothes, spotted the walk. Well done,' Wiggins said to Billy gruffly, and the boy shone with pride.

'I remember his voice,' Wiggins suddenly said. ''Cos of what he did next. He said to Mr Shirley, "I'm tired of you both. This game has reached an end." He had a posh, soft voice. It didn't fit with the rest of him, I know that. And then…then he just pushed Mr Shirley in the river. No warning, not even a threat. 'E just pushed 'im, like he didn't even care.'

'The river police fished Mr Shirley out,' Billy said quickly. 'I saw them. They just happened to be patrolling the docks in a boat, and I called out to them. He was unconscious, but alive. I'm sorry I didn't tell you before, I got distracted.'

'Understandable,' Mary said.

''E saw me,' Wiggins suddenly said, in a low, almost frightened voice. 'I don't remember much, but he must 'ave seen me. I think I ran up the stairs…'

'You did,' Billy said. 'But he came after you. He reached you at the top of the stairs, and he grabbed you and shook you and then threw you down. I'm so sorry I didn't reach you in time,' Billy told him, almost in tears. 'I ran so fast but I couldn't get there.'

'And what would have 'appened if you 'ad got there?' Wiggins demanded. 'He'd have thrown you down the steps too, and we'd've both lain there bleeding to death with no one giving a damn what happened to us.'

'We give a damn,' Mary said. 'We'd've found you.'

'Not down there you wouldn't have. You'd've looked, I'll grant you that, but you'd not have found us. No, Billy saved both our lives,' Wiggins reassured the traumatized Billy.

'And I brought him here,' Billy said. 'Apparently police and doctors ask too many questions,' he added, darting a glance towards Wiggins.

'Quite right too,' I said, standing up. 'And now, I ought to tell Mr Holmes.'

'No!' Wiggins and Billy cried in unison.

'But, Wiggins, you yourself said if anyone got hurt...' Mary objected.

'I said if you were hurt, you or Mrs 'Udson,' Wiggins said firmly. 'Not me, I'm not important.'

'You are very important,' I told him.

'Not in the way I mean,' Wiggins insisted. 'I know you sort of like me, and I like you and we talk and all that,' and he blushed fiercely. 'I meant, it's me that got hurt, and I'm used to it. But I got hurt by the bloke you've been looking for and that makes it my case now. I want it solved, I'm asking you to solve it for me, and I don't want Mr 'Olmes to do it. He's brilliant and all that, but I want you. You started it, you asked me to help, and I want you to finish it, and you owe me that. Understand?'

'A question of honour,' Mary said gently.

'That's it, missus,' Wiggins replied, staring back at her.

'Very well,' Mary agreed. 'I'm married to a soldier and I'm a soldier's daughter. I know what that means. No matter how foolish it may seem, we continue ourselves, without Mr Holmes' help. Agreed?'

I looked round at the bruised yet defiant boy, his staunch friend at his shoulder, my strong-willed friend standing beside me, and thought of all I could lose.

'Agreed,' I said.

Billy, determined as always (and, I think, racked with guilt over Wiggins' injury), tracked down Mr Shirley to an infirmary. He was alive, barely, still unconscious. It was severely doubted that he would live, let alone wake. Mrs Shirley had been by his bed since

the moment she had heard, and now she was making arrangements to have him moved to their home. She would not speak to
anyone about the incident or the letters. Billy, telling her he came
from Mary and me, stayed only long enough to tell her that if she
had secrets, so did her husband. The same man had hurt them
both and, Billy, wise beyond his years, told her the best revenge
was to love each other, no matter what. She nodded, and agreed.
I didn't feel we could do much more for Mrs Shirley. We had the
evidence from Wiggins, we had the evidence of what happened in
the docks, and a few days later, we would have far more evidence
from other victims.

Now it wasn't simply a case of Mrs Shirley and the letters. Now
it was a case of attempted murder, not just of Mr Shirley, but
Wiggins too. And who knew what else this man had done?
A man to write such despicable letters, to throw a defenceless
boy and a man to a probable death, must have a long history of
vileness.

Hours later, Mary and I sat in the kitchen, opposite each other,
both lost in our own thoughts—not pleasant ones, I fear. We
had the vent drawn back, though we were not really listening. I
was vaguely aware of John—who must have reopened the vent
at some point the previous night—complaining that Mr Holmes'
new tobacco made the rooms smell like a Turkish bazaar. (It
did. I have no idea what a Turkish bazaar actually smells like,
but I can imagine it smelled the same as the thick odour coming
through the air vent.) Mr Holmes retorted that the best way to
learn to distinguish between different tobacco types was to smoke
them all. The two were rubbing each other up the wrong way
today, and nothing in the house seemed right. A moment later,
John said he would see Holmes tomorrow and came downstairs.

'Tomorrow,' I said to Mary.

'Tomorrow,' she replied softly.

Once they had gone, I made some sandwiches and took them up to Mr Holmes. I recognized the signs—the increased tobacco smoking, the peevishness with company of any sort, the restlessness and silence. It was his time. He had a case to solve, something I knew nothing about, as I had been caught up in my own puzzle lately. Tonight he would solve it, he had that air about him.

He was sat on a great pile of cushions culled from the sofa and armchairs, in front of the blazing fire. The room was in darkness, lit by only the flames and the fast-fading twilight outside, lending the room a disturbing, almost sinister air. It is in atmospheres like this that ghost stories are told, and believed. Thick huge shadows flickered in the corners, lending the books and pictures a life of their own, heavy and mysterious in the half-light. All the precarious piles of manuscripts and notes and papers seemed to writhe and twist in the flickering firelight, as if they would be free. The room was full of smoke and fog, from the fire and from the street and from Mr Holmes' pipe, blurring the edges of the furniture, dimming my eyes, making the whole place seem almost hellish. It was more a cave than a room. In the dim, murky light, Mr Holmes sat perfectly still, his face saturnine, set in stone, a pagan statue of a god to be worshipped and feared and placated.

For a moment, in that room, I shivered, despite the heat— but my mother's sensible Scotch blood prevailed. I strode in, placed the sandwiches on the table, opened the windows wide to clear the smoke and stir the air, and poked the fire so it cast a kindlier light. Mr Holmes did not move during all these tasks. It was only when I was about to leave that he spoke.

'I'm not hungry, Mrs Hudson.'

'Not now, perhaps,' I told him. 'But you will be when you have solved your case at three o'clock in the morning, and I don't wish you to be ringing for me then.'

'At three o'clock?' he asked, curious, and turning to me. 'How do you know I will solve the case then?'

'It's always three in the morning, or thereabouts,' I said, with a touch of asperity. 'I am woken by a great shout, and the sound of you charging about your rooms, throwing things around, yelling out incomprehensible facts, and calling for Dr Watson or Billy.'

He grimaced. I do not think he liked to be known so well. Or perhaps it gave him a pleasure he was uncomfortable in acknowledging. Perhaps he did not actually know how often he set the household into an uproar in the early hours of the morning. However, when he was not in the throes of a case, or boredom, he was unfailingly polite to me, and so he said, 'I apologize. I shall endeavour to express triumph silently tonight.' He turned back to the fire, casting his face half in shadow again.

'No, don't,' I said impulsively, walking back into the room, towards him. 'I like to hear it. I like to hear you crow in victory, and know that another case is solved. The world seems such a dark and soulless place sometimes, especially at three o'clock in the morning. I lie awake in bed, and think of all I have seen and read, and it can be hard to believe that there really are good men and women, and if there are, that they can hold back the dark and the terror and the evil. Then I hear you, and I know that someone is out there, trying to bring light into someone's life. I hear you shout, and I know another problem has been solved, perhaps a life saved, or a danger averted, and I feel safe again. I feel there is hope again.'

I don't think I had ever spoken to him like that before. I had certainly never said so much. John had once told me that Holmes was the worst tenant in London, and I only put up with him because of the rent he paid. I put it up every time he destroyed another part of his rooms. He was paying—uncomplainingly—a very high rent by now. But it wasn't that. It was because I knew of the miracles he wrought, the pain he healed, the comfort he gave, under my roof.

Mr Holmes turned to look at me, curious and unsettled, as

if I were a cat that had sprouted a pair of wings and proposed to fly about the room.

'You have such faith in me, you and Watson,' he said quietly.

'Well-deserved faith,' I told him firmly, my hands clasped in front of my black bombazine dress, the very picture of a respectable housekeeper, oh-so-successfully concealing the raging emotions within.

'And if I should fail?' Mr Holmes asked, his voice even, his face unreadable in the firelight. 'I have failed before, Mrs Hudson. I will fail again.'

'But you tried,' I said, wanting so much to tell him what he, and what he did, meant to me, and yet shaking with nerves that what I was saying was inappropriate to speak to a tenant. Maybe this was not my place. My place was to incline my head silently and leave until called for. Yet now I had started, I could not stop. 'And you will keep trying. It matters that you try, when so many walk away.'

'It matters that I win,' he said, and a log fell in the fire and the flames shot up, and for that moment, that one moment, I saw his face so clearly. His eyes looked bleak, and I caught a glimpse of the desperate battle always raging in his mind. Sherlock Holmes against the world. Sherlock Holmes, one man, against all the evil and corruption and hate in London. Then the log settled and the fire died down and his face was in darkness again. I looked around. On the table I saw a small scrap of grey paper. I saw my name—Hudson—and a message about game and flypaper.

'Is this meant for me?' I asked.

'Not unless you sailed on the *Gloria Scott*,' Mr Holmes said dryly. 'It's a souvenir. That is where it all began, really. My first case.' He was silent for a moment.

'Wiggins will recover?' he asked, abruptly changing the subject, as he was prone to do.

'He will. I will look after him.'

'As he, apparently, looks after you, I hear,' Mr Holmes said. I glanced up at the vent. Sound could drift through it both ways...

'Good night, Mrs Hudson. Thank you for the sandwiches,' Mr Holmes said politely.

'Good night, Mr Holmes,' I replied, closing the door softly as I left.

Perhaps that would have been the moment to tell him about Laura Shirley, and all that had happened since then. He would have taken the case. I could have so easily lifted the burden from my shoulders and placed it on his, already so weighed down. But I could not. I remembered his bleak eyes, and I would not add one single grain to his problems. As he had his responsibilities, his promises, our faith to live up to, I also had. Mary and I had started this. Mary and I had taken on this burden. We would carry it until, one morning at 3 a.m., we finished it.

CHAPTER 7

The Adventure of the Whitechapel Lady

Seven months ago almost to the day, John had come down to my kitchen, sat down at the table, and told me he loved Mary Morstan but could never marry her. He sat right there, at the end by the stove where it was warmest, and drank tea and ate scones—or rather, sipped aimlessly at the tea, and crumbled the scones between his fingers. He talked of the fabulous Agra treasure, and a tale of mystery and betrayal in India and the Sign of Four and he talked most of all of brave, beautiful Mary Morstan at the centre of it all.

'She's clever,' John said, his eyes shining as he stared out of the window and thought of her. 'Even Holmes admires her intelligence. And she's kind; kind to everyone and so calm. Even in the most dangerous moments, faced by murderers and villains and death, she didn't shrink, though she must have been frightened. She just threw her shoulders back, as if she were a soldier like her father. And when she smiles...' He looked down at the tea cup in front of him.

'Your heart feels as if it has missed a beat,' I finished for him. He looked at me, suddenly seeing I understood. 'I remember mine used to feel like that when Hector—Mr Hudson—smiled at me. He didn't smile often, except when he was with me, and, each time, I felt something inside me give a queer little flutter. That was when I knew I loved him.'

John smiled, and blushed slightly. It was so touching, that blush, as if something of the schoolboy remained in the battered old soldier.

'I do,' he admitted. 'I do love her. I must love her, how can I not? If you knew her...'

'I will know her,' I said, picking up the cups, 'when she becomes Mrs John Watson.'

He didn't answer, and I turned to look at him. The blush had gone from his face and he stared ahead of him, bleakly.

'You are going to ask her to marry you?' I asked.

'She will be rich, when we solve the case,' John told me, and his eyes were so, so sad. 'She will finally have the fabulous Agra treasure that her father left her, and wealth beyond her dreams, and I am so poor. I barely scrape by on my army pension.'

'How do you know what her dreams are?' I said angrily. On the other hand, how did I know what her dreams were? Given the choice between treasure and the love of a man like John, I'd have chosen John, but what did I know of her? But still, I defended her. If he loved her, she must be worth his loving. 'Besides,' I told him, 'if it were the other way round, you rich and her poor, it would not matter.'

'A man is supposed to take care of a woman,' he said gently. 'He should support her, not the other way round. A poor man marrying a rich woman sounds—feels—contemptible, somehow.'

'She won't care!' I told him. 'If she loves you, the money won't matter.'

'I don't even know if she loves me,' he said, walking across the room to me. He looked so forlorn and lost.

'If she knows you, she loves you,' I said firmly. 'How can she not?'

I turned away, so he could not see my face. It was so unlike me to reveal how fond of him I was, how highly I regarded him. My emotions were mine alone, and I had not shared them since my Hector died. Besides, I could not bear to see the sadness in his eyes.

'She's so far above me, Mrs Hudson,' he said. 'And when I place the treasure in her hands, she will be unreachable.'

Of course, she was not unreachable.

Wiggins stayed on in the little room by the kitchen in 221b. He had wanted to leave, to recover with his gang around him, but Billy had given him a stern telling off about how hurt I would be if he left, and how rude that would be, so Wiggins stayed, temporarily.

Two days after he had arrived, he gave me my next step as I brought him soup. Billy was sitting on the bed, and the two of them were having an urgent whispered conversation. It was getting quite heated before they saw me and stopped talking.

I settled the tray on Wiggins' lap and exhorted him not to spill the soup, but to eat it all at once. John had said that Wiggins was healing quickly, and I knew that once the pain had gone, the boy would be away, back to the streets. Until he was, I was determined to feed him up as much as possible. The sight of his thin chest when John had undressed him had disturbed me.

As Wiggins ate his soup, I glanced round the room. I could see the pile of books, and the fresh flowers Mary had left. Wiggins occasionally glanced at the bright flowers as if he'd never seen anything so lovely in his life—which he probably hadn't. I don't know where Wiggins had learnt to read—I know it was a skill he had acquired before he met Mr Holmes—but he devoured any books he could find. I knew Billy spent every spare second in here with his friend, intensely chatting about whatever case Mr Holmes was working on, and cases he had worked on in the past. And, judging by the cigarette ash on the floor, Mr Holmes himself had visited a few times. Billy saw me glancing at the ash.

'Wiggins didn't tell Mr Holmes anything about the case,' Billy said anxiously. Wiggins glanced up at him, and I saw Billy nod at the ash and mouth 'She knows'.

'Not a thing,' Wiggins confirmed. 'I meant what I said.'

'No matter what anyone else says,' Billy murmured, and I saw Wiggins glance mutinously at him. I guessed the two of them had been discussing rather fervently, as boys (and men) do, the relative merits of keeping me safe or keeping promises. It looked like Wiggins had won. I glanced over at Billy and smiled at him, to reassure him. He nodded at me, this boy so near to becoming a man.

'There's something else, isn't there?' I said, looking at them. 'Something you're not sure whether to tell me about.'

'It may be nothing,' Billy said.

'Or everything!' Wiggins disagreed hotly.

'She'll end up going to Whitechapel! Do you want her in Whitechapel?' Billy shouted back.

'I'm not going to lie and, before you argue, not telling something is as bad as lying!'

I sat down on the bed, straightened the sheets, and said, 'Tell me.'

'There's a lady down in Whitechapel,' Wiggins said quietly.

'There's a lot of ladies down in Whitechapel,' I replied dryly. Even a musty old housekeeper like me knew a thing or two, especially one that regularly borrowed Mr Holmes' copy of *Illustrated Police News* and read the advertisements as well as the stories.

'No, this one's a proper lady,' Wiggins continued. 'And not like them other proper ladies what visits Whitechapel, always praying and wittering and moaning, like we don't have anything better to do than listen to them trying to save our souls, as if we had any souls to save in the first place.'

'Since the Ripper, ma'am,' Billy said shyly, as if he was embarrassed to even mention that name to me, 'lots of ladies—fine ladies—have taken to doing missionary work in Whitechapel. Setting up churches and trying to save the…the fallen women.'

'How do you know all this?' I asked, curious as to what Billy actually did with his time off.

'I read about it, ma'am,' he told me, which I knew was a half-truth. Wiggins had been known to run around Whitechapel, and Billy ran with him occasionally. Still, I knew better than to keep them apart, and knew Billy was probably quite safe with Wiggins. I didn't have the heart to split them up and keep Billy at home. I decided to swallow the lie.

'But this lady, the one I'm talking about,' Wiggins continued, 'she 'elps people. Proper 'elp, I mean. She has a sort of free clinic anyone can go to, and she gives out medicines and food and stuff and never mentions God or prayers or nothing. But she's sad, missus. Not like the others, all proud and happy and smug that they're doing God's work, whatever they think that is. This lady—the Whitechapel Lady we call 'er—she's always sad.'

'What else can you tell me about her?' I asked, watching him intently. This was a new side to Wiggins, and Billy too. This was an insight into the lives they lived away from Baker Street.

'She never leaves Whitechapel. Not never, not at night, not on Sundays, never. Sometimes I see her watching other people walk out of there, and she kind of stares after them, like she wishes she could leave too, but she never does. But it's hard to tell, 'cos her face is covered.'

'Covered?'

'The Whitechapel Lady wears a black veil, missus. So you can't see her face. And she won't tell no one her name, neither. It's like she's got no face, and no name.'

'Then how can you tell she's sad?' I asked.

'You know, the way you tell anyone's sad, even when they smile. Like you, sometimes. The way she stands, and the way she moves. Slow and 'eavy, like. And her voice—you can tell when someone's smiling, even if you can't see it, in their voice, can't you? Well, there's never a smile in her voice.' Wiggins leaned forward eagerly. I had no idea he was such a good observer of human nature. I had no idea he'd observed me that closely either.

'Have you ever talked to her? This Whitechapel Lady?'

'Once,' he said. 'I'd bin helping her one day hand out some stuff, some food to people who couldn't walk to the clinic. I do that sometimes, 'cos then I get a bit for the Irregulars too. Anyway, I could tell by the way she was spending that she had money, lots of it, and I asked her why she lived in Whitechapel all the time, why don't she just visit, like the other rich ladies, and she said, "Because of a cruel man. The cruellest man who ever lived."'

'We used to think she meant a lover or a husband,' Billy added. 'But when I watched Laura Shirley, she reminded me of the Whitechapel Lady. They moved the same way, sort of watchful and frightened. Always looking behind them and flinching away from strangers and jumping at any noise. And letters—the Whitechapel Lady always hates getting letters. I think that's what she meant. I think she's hiding from this cruel man in the one place he'd never think to look. I think the Whitechapel Lady was blackmailed too.'

It wasn't difficult to find the Whitechapel Lady. It seemed everyone knew of her, the kind woman with the veiled face, who never spoke of God or redemption. Billy guided Mary and me through the streets of Whitechapel. It was a foul place, crowded with sad-eyed souls, with vicious men and women and frightened ones too, scurrying back and forth, the only smiles accompanied by a drunken bellow of laughter. I can't blame them for that. I would have obliterated that world with alcohol too, if I were condemned there. Leading off all the streets were filthy narrow alleyways thronged with rats and rubbish. Even that rubbish had desperate people picking through it. The smell was choking and heavy, so I could scarcely breathe, with the only sweet scent coming from the old women who sold violets. Even in the daytime I saw women persuading and importuning men to come into an alleyway or a yard with them, or a room if they were lucky. Some of the women looked pretty and fresh, and talked and giggled. Most looked tired and raddled and wanting nothing more than for the act to be over so they could spend the money on drink, and forget. They must have had hopes and dreams once. Everyone does. But their dreams had choked and died on the noxious fumes of Whitechapel years ago.

Since the crimes of Jack the Ripper had brought the horrors of Whitechapel vividly to the attention of the rest of society, some work to alleviate the suffering had been done—but not nearly enough. It had become fashionable for society ladies to descend upon the place, dispensing food and clothes, but mostly handing out exhortations for the Whitechapel residents to give up their sinful ways and return to God. They handed out religious tracts about how much more glorious it was to die in poverty and hunger than live an unclean sinful life. These tracts made no mention about how painful dying of starvation was. These women were despised by the people they thought they were helping. I could see why. The people of Whitechapel starved. They choked. They bled. They suffered. They shivered. They died. What use was prayer to them? What use is a pure soul in a body that is falling apart? They did what they could do to live, and I would not condemn them for it.

Even now, it is the smell of Whitechapel I remember: a thick, choking, sour stench that lay in the back of my throat. It almost made me vomit. I craved cool water and fresh air. The only water I saw came out of the street pumps, and it was brown and brackish. The only air had come through docks and hospitals and graveyards and butchers and cobblers and dyers and was poisoned before it ever reached us. Even the sunshine was grimy. If I looked up, I could see a tiny patch of blue sky, way up above the houses, but the shadows of the street robbed the sunlight of any warmth. I shivered in my thick wool coat, but the people around me stood around in thin rags, never moving, as if they had never known what warm sun on the skin felt like. I was struck by their eyes. Dead eyes, all of them, as if their souls had died long ago, whilst their bodies continued the struggle to breathe.

We were not molested or called at in any way, which puzzled me, until Mary pointed out a tall, strong boy following us.

'He's one of Wiggins' lads,' Billy explained. 'He's here to protect you. You didn't think he'd let you come here unprotected, did you?'

Wiggins, always and forever my knight in grubby armour.

Billy took us to a sort of square, near the edge of Whitechapel. Three sides of the square were made up of houses that must have been prosperous at one time, but now were verminous and rotten. In the centre of the square was a pump, set in cobbles. On one side of the square was a large plain brown building. 'Clinic' was scrawled above the door in whitewash. Billy led us round the back of the building to a set of stairs that climbed to the second floor. Billy nodded to the tall boy, who left us.

'She won't open this door if there are strange men about,' Billy told us. 'Wait here, I'll check she'll see you first. She knows me; I've run errands for her before, to the finer parts of town, where Wiggins and the others boys would get thrown out.' Billy ran upstairs like someone who knew his way, and I wondered again about what his life away from my home was like, his life in these streets. This was not where he was born, but somehow he had a place here, just like he had a place in 221b.

He ran down again.

'She'll see you,' he said breathlessly. 'She wants to!'

He ran back upstairs and opened the thin, cracked door for us. We stepped through, uncertain what we would find. On the other side was a darkened room, with closed shutters. The only light came through the cracks in the shutters themselves. I could just see enough to make out there was only the bare minimum of furniture—a single bed, a chair, a crooked table. But it was clean—very clean. There was an overwhelming smell of lye and soap.

'The Whitechapel Lady,' Billy announced, with as much élan as if he had been in a Mayfair drawing room. 'May I present Mrs Hudson and Mrs Watson.'

He closed the door behind us, and then went to stand between us and the Lady.

'They'll help,' he told her. 'Tell them about him.'

The Lady sat in the darkest corner of the room, on a plain, straight-backed wooden chair. Her face was completely in darkness. I could only see her dress, also plain. It had once been fashionable, about ten years ago, but now it was shabby and patched, washed too many times.

'I won't tell you my real name,' she said, haltingly, as if she were not used to speaking. Her voice was low and gentle, but had a husky quality, as if she had a sore throat. There was an odd accent to it, an unfamiliar tone I could not place. 'They call me the Whitechapel Lady here. You can call me what you like. My real name was lost a long time ago.'

'We don't need your name,' Mary said, stepping forward into the room. 'We're sorry to bother you, but there is a man who has hurt people. We just want to…We just need to know…' Mary's voice faltered. She did not know how to ask what we needed.

'The man that destroyed you hasn't stopped. He's still destroying people,' I said, surprising myself as I spoke boldly and clearly. 'We need to know what you know about him. We will stop him.'

'Can you?' she asked softly, without even a trace of hope.

'We can try,' Mary said fiercely. 'Has anyone else tried?'

'I don't think anyone else really believes he exists,' she said, her voice so low I could barely hear her. In the street below people shouted and laughed and cursed and wheels rattled over cobbles and dogs barked but in this room, we were so still and quiet, the dust in the air barely stirred.

'He brought me to this,' the Lady said. 'From the happy, beloved woman who loved sunshine and laughter—to this.'

I saw her turn her head to look round the dingy dark room.

'If this is too difficult for you...' Mary said softly. The woman laughed then—not joyously, but one single bitter bark of laughter.

'Difficult?' the Whitechapel Lady cried. 'It is well-nigh impossible. But I will have someone know my story. I've kept silent so very long, I've been so afraid. And the truth is, there's been no one to tell. I'm still afraid, but I must say what has happened to me. It could save someone else. And you have such kind faces. I had forgotten what kindness looked like.' She took a deep breath and looked towards the window. There was so little light coming through the cracks, but perhaps through one she saw the tiniest patch of blue sky, and remembered sunshine on her face.

'The man who destroyed me was called Jack Ripon.'

'Ripon?' Mary asked quickly. The Whitechapel Lady nodded.

'I know. A name like that has such resonance in these streets, does it not?' she acknowledged. 'But this was long before Jack the Ripper. I do not believe it was his real name. I'm not sure he has one. He told his lie so well, how can he remember the truth?'

'What did he look like?' Mary asked.

'Just...ordinary,' the Lady replied. 'It was a long time ago, and what I remember—hair colour, accent, the way he dressed— would have changed since then. He was just one of my husband's friends—or at least, I thought he was. Just someone who went to the same parties we did. He was not someone I really noticed. I barely remembered his name. I think perhaps along with a name he put on a face he could change at will. Even after what he did, I believe I could walk past him and not know him. Think of that.

The most evil man in London, and no one can really see him.'
She stopped talking and clasped her hands together for a moment.

'He came to me soon after I married Richard,' the Lady
continued. 'I loved Richard, do you understand? I loved him
with all my heart, all my soul. But this man...this thing...this
foul toad had letters of mine. Letters from before I was married,
before I even met Richard.'

'Letters to another man?' Mary asked.

'To my first love,' she agreed. 'Such a silly, foolish little love
affair it was, too. He wrote such pretty letters though, and I was
never allowed to spend enough time alone with him to discover
what a shallow man he was, that all his love was a game of words,
and there was nothing in his heart. So I wrote pretty little letters
back. But then I met Richard, and I fell truly in love. There were
no more letters then.'

'The letters you wrote to the first man—were they indis-
creet?' Mary asked. Usually she always did the asking; I always
watched. My eyes had grown used to the dim light, and I watched
now as the Whitechapel Lady's hands tightened.

'No!' she cried. 'That was the point. I had written silly
little love letters to a man I should not have written to, but the
letters themselves were innocent. Richard had known about him,
known I had written to him, he didn't care!'

Her hands twisted and writhed in her lap—I don't think it
was because she lied, but in memory of pain.

'Then how could this Ripon blackmail you?' Mary asked.

'I'm not sure it was blackmail,' the Lady said softly.
'Blackmail is an attempt to gain money or power or something
else tangible, usable. I don't think he wanted anything. I think he
just likes to destroy. He sees something precious and shining and
bright and he smashes it. That is what he did to my life.'

I wanted to reach out to her. I wanted to touch her, and reassure her—but I could not. I did not have the nerve. I was not the
kind of person who comforted a stranger. But Mary impulsively
knelt before her and touched her knee. I saw the Whitechapel
Lady freeze, as if she had not been touched in a long time, and

she had forgotten how to react. Then one thin, deathly white hand stole over Mary's where it rested on her knee. She touched her, just for a moment, and then withdrew, so shyly, so softly. Mary moved away again.

'He forged letters,' the Lady continued, her voice cracking ever so slightly. 'Oh, they were very well done. He had letters in my style, in my handwriting, on my paper—but I had not written them. They spoke of acts that had taken place between me and that boy, my so-called first love. Foul, disgusting acts, worse than you can find on any Whitechapel street.'

'He threatened to show these letters to your fiancé?' Mary asked.

'No, my husband!' she cried, and she stirred in her chair, as if for a moment she would spring up, come back to life. 'He did not reveal the existence of these letters until after I was married. What was the point then?'

'Destruction,' I murmured. 'Destruction of your happiness.'

'Precisely,' she agreed, becoming still once again.

'But surely,' Mary asked, 'your husband, knowing you as he did, would not have believed in these forged letters?'

'Why not?' she said bitterly. 'The fakes were very good; even I was convinced for a moment. They were interweaved with letters I had really written and admitted to. Besides...'

In the filthy grey light, I could just see her hang her head in a gesture of shame. Poor thing, as if she had anything to be ashamed of now.

'My husband and I had...' She paused, and then gathered herself again. 'We had anticipated our marriage vows. We had lain together as man and wife before the vows were spoken. I know it was wrong, but...'

'Not wrong at all,' Mary said firmly. 'You were in love, and knew you belonged together even without the formality of a few words spoken over you. I freely admit, I did the same.'

Mary glanced round at me, as if anticipating my censure—but how could I condemn them? How could I even be shocked? John and she had loved each other from the moment they met, and there had never been any doubt, once she had agreed to marry him, that they belonged to each other, body and soul. The vows were almost an afterthought, just a formality to recognize their partnership. And I remembered my Hector. So tall, so handsome, and I so young and in love. Six weeks had been an eternity to wait for our wedding night—it had been Hector who had been firm, not I. And even then, we had not waited until night fell…oh, I understood passion far more than I understood the black and white rules of the society I lived in. The same rules this man was using to destroy women's lives.

'You understand,' the Whitechapel Lady said, looking at the glances Mary and I were exchanging. 'Then perhaps you can understand how my husband might, perhaps, think I had also committed that sin with my first love? I had not, I had not felt the same desire, but for him, it was so easy to believe. I think perhaps my husband never really understood why I loved him so much, he never understood he was air and water to me. And those letters, those vile letters, made it sound as if that man and I had done things so sordid, so filthy, a foul pairing blessed only by hell.'

'It's all very clever,' Mary mused, her eyes dark and troubled. 'If you wrote the innocent letters, why not the other ones? If you lay with your fiancé before marriage, why would you not have lain with others? He is creating lies based on truth—a very small amount of truth and a huge mass of lies, but it is enough to rouse suspicion.'

'Suspicion is what he thrives on,' the Whitechapel Lady said bitterly. 'It is meat and bread to him. You must understand, when he brought me the letters, and I saw I had no escape, I asked him what the price was. He refused to tell me. He just kept saying "we'll see". And in the meantime, at every soirée, every garden party, every visit to the opera, he would appear, whispering filth in my ear. Things he said he had done, what he said I would do, what he thought I could do. But worse than that, I would see Ripon whisper to my husband. It would drive me mad, seeing him whisper to my Richard, and never knowing what he said to him. I asked my husband what the man had told him, I cajoled him, I screamed at him, I begged him but he always said they talked of nothing. I could not believe him, and when I accused him of lying, we would argue. He was confused and I was afraid and we took out our frustrations on each other. Our marriage became a mass of bitter recrimination.'

The Whitechapel Lady moved slightly, and the light fell across her face. I could not see it. She wore a thick veil that blocked out everything underneath it. Her voice steady, cold even, she continued her story.

'That man never told me his price. Instead, at the height of our quarrels, he sent the letters to my husband. He had done well. He had prepared the ground. He had split us apart and destroyed all trust and confidence between us before my husband had even seen the letters. But once he saw them, my husband, my darling sweet husband who worshipped the ground I walked on, and wanted to believe I had touched no other man but him, shot himself. I found him in the study, the letters scattered before him, the gun still in his hand, all life gone.'

She stopped. She could not go on.

'I think we can guess the rest,' Mary said gently. 'You burnt the letters? And the verdict of the inquest was death by misadventure? The gun went off accidentally whilst he was cleaning it, was that the story?'

'That is it exactly,' the Lady said darkly. 'How well you understand the way we cover up our scandals.'

'John has attended some of these cases,' Mary said to me. 'It's amazing how many guns go off whilst being cleaned. The papers are full of these cases. Perfectly sane, intelligent men who suddenly decide, against all experience and knowledge, to clean a loaded gun.'

'Suicides?' I asked, thinking of all the inquest accounts I had read that had given just that story.

'Probably.'

'That was not the end,' the Lady continued. 'He was there, at the funeral. He stood beside me, in the pouring rain, as they lowered my husband's body into the ground. It must have looked as though he was supporting me in my grief. But instead, he kept whispering in my ear: "Why don't you just die too?"'

Billy, sat in the corner, swore quietly under his breath.

'He would just turn up,' the Lady continued. 'Everywhere I went. Whispering in my ear. I should have told someone what Ripon was doing to me, but who would believe me? Somehow, the sordid tales of my behaviour had become whispered about amongst my friends. I was blamed for my husband's death. One by one, my friends left me, and I was alone—except for him. At every corner, on every road, in every shop or street, there he was, whispering in my ear. *Die, die, no one wants you to live. Die, die, what use are you. Die, die, you deserve to.* Until finally, I decided to do it. I just wanted peace. I wanted to sleep—no, I wanted to die.'

The room had become utterly still now. You could not even hear us breathe. The only sound was the Whitechapel Lady's slow, measured words of despair.

'I took laudanum,' she told us. 'But I misjudged it. I was not an expert! I had taken enough to send me into a stupor—but not enough to kill me. Instead, unbeknownst to my conscious self, I rose from what was meant to be my deathbed and wandered the house in an unwitting daze. I went into the study where my husband died. A fire was lit there. I tripped—I think I tripped— and fell into the fire. In my inert state I could not pull away. I burnt for several moments before I was found.'

That was when the Whitechapel Lady leaned forward into the light, so we could see her. She raised her veil, and we saw her face clearly for the first time, the face she went to such lengths to keep hidden. Billy cried out. Mary caught her breath. I put my hand quickly up to my mouth, suddenly nauseous.

The Lady's entire face was covered in shining red scars, suppurating pustules, badly healed sores. I could even smell the rotting flesh underneath. No wonder that room smelled of lye, she must spend her life trying to wash away the stink of her own flesh. Her eyes, lidless, stared out at me, unable to look away.

Her lips had half burnt away to reveal the blackened teeth underneath. It was a face out of a nightmare, a fiend from hell to be fled from.

'I have not seen that man again,' she said, and now the strange accent was explained. She could not form her words properly with that destroyed mouth. 'I paid his price.'

Scandals and Secrets

We stumbled out. We had made our polite excuses and left and almost ran down those wooden steps to the square and struggled for breath. Even Whitechapel air smelled sweet at that moment. I glanced around me in despair; I wanted nothing so much as to leave, run away from that face, this place, her words. I needed to escape. It was an awful thing to do. She had expected kindness and met instead with revulsion. It was what she was used to, but that did not lessen my guilt.

I looked up, searching for a way out. Instead I saw a woman leaning against the wall, clearly a prostitute, strapping a knife to her thigh. She saw me looking and called out, 'Getting ready for Jack, dear, just in case.'

'Jack?' I said, gasping. For a moment I thought she meant the man the Whitechapel Lady had spoken of, the one that had whispered her husband to death, and her to a living horror.

'The Ripper!' she answered, as if I was stupid. Perhaps, then, I was. 'He may be gone now, missus. Nothing to say he won't be back tomorrow. They say he 'ad enough, but men like 'im, they never get enough blood.'

She left for her evening's work, and I turned to Mary. She still looked horrified.

'What have we got ourselves into?' she begged of me breathlessly. 'What have we promised?'

We left Whitechapel quickly, guided by Billy and tracked once again by a member of the Irregulars. Although I wasn't sure we needed a protector now. We had changed in that hour: we no longer seemed so innocent. Whitechapel fought and cheated and thieved and killed and sold itself all around us, but we were no longer shocked. No wonder the Whitechapel Lady lived here, and not in some rich, beautiful place. In that mass of angry, damaged humanity, she was practically invisible.

'She can't be the only one,' Mary said as we walked along. She had recovered quickly, quicker than I had. 'If what she says is true—and I see no reason that she should be wrong—he gets his satisfaction not from money, but from the destruction of lives. No, wait...' she said, stopping in the street all of a sudden. 'Not from the destruction of lives,' she went on slowly. 'If that were the case, he'd still be haunting the Lady. He gets his satisfaction from the total power he has over their lives.'

'He'll leave the Shirleys alone now then,' I said, gripping her arm and persuading her to walk on again. 'I think he can have no more power over them.'

'That kind of torture is too exquisite to have been refined overnight,' Mary continued, oblivious to the street surrounding her. I had to pull her around great hulking men, and blowsy, argumentative women. 'He's practised this on many other people, mark my words,' she said firmly, as Billy led us down an alleyway that came out into a more salubrious part of town. The streets here were wide, and clean, the company more respectable. Still, a part of me believed there was as much cruelty and anger here as in Whitechapel, but it was better hidden. We walked down the street, past a row of shops. Mary was still talking.

'But who else? Who else has he inflicted this on? It's not the sort of thing that gets into the papers. How else do we find these poor people?'

We stopped for a moment, so I could catch my breath. I was still upset, and had walked far too quickly to get out of Whitechapel. We had paused before a photography studio, the kind of place that displayed photographs of famous society women. We stood there for a moment, aimlessly staring at the pictures of these proud, lovely women, dripping with jewels and silks, so secure in their place in life. Given what we had just heard, how could we help but wonder which of these women was being hunted by him now? Mary suddenly gasped, and laughed a little bit. I swear it was very akin to the way Mr Holmes was when he made a sudden discovery.

'I know how to find his other victims!'

'How?' I asked. She gestured towards the display of the society ladies.

'We need to find women who have disappeared from society. The kind of woman who attended all the balls and galas and plays, who went to court and hunting and so on, and then who just disappeared.'

'I agree,' I told her. 'But we don't move in those circles, and we don't know anyone who does. How do we find these women?'

She frowned for a moment, but then inspiration struck.

'Doesn't Sherlock know someone? Didn't he mention a man he knew, a man who knew all the secrets of society? A man who sat in a window in St James', gathering gossip?'

'Sherlock?' I said, a tad giddily. It still seemed presumptious of her to call him Sherlock, but he didn't seem to mind. 'Oh, you mean Langdale Pike.'

'I know him,' Billy piped up. 'Mr Holmes has sent me to him often. He watches everyone. He writes a gossip column, but he keeps a lot more secrets than he tells. Mr Holmes says he thrives on secrets like a bee thrives on flowers.'

'Actually, he sounds less like someone who can help and more like our blackmailer,' I pointed out, unsettled by his description of Langdale Pike. I had never been quite comfortable with Mr Holmes seeing him—I didn't like the idea of him telling Mr Pike secrets of his clients, even if it was in return for even greater secrets.

'No, not him,' Billy asserted. 'He's the kind of man who likes to watch, not to get involved. Otherwise Mr Holmes wouldn't have anything to do with him.'

'I suppose not,' I said dubiously.

'If Sherlock trusts him, I do,' Mary said staunchly.

'I know where to find Langdale Pike,' Billy volunteered. 'I can take you.'

I was so tired. It had been such a day; I could take no more. I needed to be alone to think. And besides, I had seen something.

'You go, Mary,' I said. 'I must go home.' I looked in the window again. Yes, right there. I had seen it.

'Will you be all right alone?' Billy asked anxiously.

'Perfectly all right,' I assured him. I waited until he had stepped into the street to hail a hansom, and then said to Mary, 'I think I have seen him.'

'What?' Mary said, startled. I put my finger to my lips, and nodded towards the window. She saw what I saw too. 'You can't,' she objected.

'I damned well can, and will,' I asserted (yes, I even swore). 'I am tired of only listening and watching. I must do something. You do your part, and I will do mine.'

Mary looked at me, and she knew. She was my friend, and she knew when she could help, and when I must be left alone. She nodded reluctantly, and then she and Billy got in the cab he had hailed.

I turned back to the window, seemingly absorbed in the photographs, but really looking at the reflection in the glass of the street.

Behind me stood a man. He looked perfectly ordinary. In fact, I would not have noticed him at all, except for a distinct splash of whitewash on the back of one sleeve. He must have brushed up against a freshly painted wall somewhere. He had no other distinguishing feature. He would not stand out in a crowd. He melted into the background of this street—just as he had melted into the background of at least three street corners in Whitechapel and the square outside the Whitechapel Lady's clinic. I now recalled he had been on the omnibus to Whitechapel. This perfectly ordinary man had been following Billy, Mary and me all afternoon.

I went straight home, aware of the ordinary-looking man following me all the way. Perhaps I should have made an effort to shake him off, but I didn't have the first idea how to do that. Besides, he probably knew where I lived—or if not, it would do no harm to let him know I lived with the Great Detective, Sherlock Holmes.

And I had another goal in mind. I kept trying to catch sight of his face so I could recognize him again, but he looked too bland. His features slipped away from me like water. I would catch a glimpse of him, but be unable to describe him. I could only recognize him by the white splash of paint on his sleeve, and no doubt once he saw that distinguishing mark, he would destroy the jacket. Even his clothes were ordinary, just a simple working man's jacket and trousers, such as could be seen all over London. If he was Jack Ripon, or whatever name he used now, I would not be able to recognize him again.

I admit I was shaking by the time I let myself into the house. I had done nothing wrong in my life, nothing to be ashamed of, yet I was afraid. What could he do to torment me? What could he do to torment those I loved?

The house was empty. Wiggins had taken advantage of our absence to run back to his own streets, as I had known he probably would. This, after all, was not his home. At least he left warm and well-fed. Besides, the Irregulars needed him. I was just surprised he had stayed so long. It was only a few days, but he never normally stayed longer than a few hours. Mr Holmes and John had gone out chasing a lead, leaving a hastily scribbled note on the kitchen table: 'Back at 11. Probably.'

That was not the only news. On the mat was a letter from Mrs Shirley's solicitor. It explained that Mrs Shirley was taking Mr Shirley to Harrogate to take the waters, and hopefully recover. Therefore, although she thanked me for my services, they were no longer needed. In the solicitor's dry, legal language, I was freed from any obligation to Mrs Shirley.

I felt lost, bereft almost, returning to that empty house. The minutes of being followed had left me with a creeping fear, and I had badly wanted company—preferably that of Mr Holmes. He had a way of making me feel safe. I went up to his room and looked at the street through the net curtains. I saw the ordinary man—or Ordinary Man as I now thought of him—stare up at the house, right at the window where I stood. I knew he could not see me through the curtain, yet I shuddered. Then he walked away.

Who had sent him? Was it connected to Mr Holmes? Or was it my case? Was he the tormentor—or was he sent by the tormentor? Why follow me at all? Why not just try to stop me? So many questions were filling my mind.

I stood there for a long time in Mr Holmes' rooms, by the window. I stood and watched the people of London go by. I saw other women in black like me, and young men hurrying through the street, and sandwich sellers flirting with maids and errand boys dawdling. Opposite 221b I could see a man, tall and blond, in his mid-thirties, very correctly and properly dressed, carrying a stick, though he obviously did not need one. He was very upright and respectable, with his blond moustache and dark suit. He was staring up at Mr Holmes' window, stroking his moustache with one hand, and stepping off the kerb to cross, and then back on again. I recognized the signs—he was what John called a ditherer. Possible clients of Mr Holmes who could not make up their mind to come in—they needed help, but were too embarrassed or too proud to ask, so they dithered on the pavement. Mr Holmes had been known to fling open the window and shout at them to come in, for God's sake! Twice this man made to cross the road, twice he checked the address on a piece of paper in his hand. Whoever he was, he was the pattern of a perfect gentleman—the kind of man who, if he was in trouble, would go to the police and expect them to solve all his problems. His problem must be deeply embarrassing to drive him to a private detective. He made up his mind—he walked away.

So he had a secret. He would not be the only one in this street. How many of them out there had a secret? According to Mr Holmes, they all did. How many of them were in pain, in fear, in need? How many of those calm faces hid a heart in turmoil, a soul in want? Far more than I previously suspected. Mr Holmes was out helping one right now. And I—I could help too. Maybe I could save a few souls in need myself, I just had to be brave enough. As dusk fell, I swore that Mary and I would carry this burden on.

Besides, I may have been frightened and confused, but I also felt alive for the first time in years. I was finally living my life, not just participating in someone else's. For the first time in a very long time, I was achieving something that was my own. I was thinking and deducing for myself, and it made my heart beat and my blood race. I felt like a racehorse that has spent its life in the paddock, and now, suddenly, has come onto the course and raced past the starting tape. I would not, could not, stop now.

So, when Mary and Billy returned, I was sitting at the kitchen table making notes of all that had been done so far.

Billy dashed straight out to find either Mr Holmes or Wiggins, whichever one he came across first, whilst Mary took off her fashionable lilac hat and walked across the kitchen.

She was as comfortable in that room as I was, and as she talked, she walked round the table.

'What was happening when I left you?' Mary asked. 'You didn't seem quite yourself.'

'Nothing,' I said. 'Well, no, not nothing, but I'll tell you later. I want to hear about Langdale Pike first.'

'But—'

'Later, Mary,' I insisted. I didn't want to talk about the Ordinary Man yet. I still wasn't quite sure that I had not imagined the whole thing. I didn't want to make a fuss about him and then look like a foolish woman if I was wrong.

'Well,' Mary said dubiously, but eager to tell her story. 'Very well. Mr Langdale Pike is a very strange man. He is very thin, very precise in all his movements and dress. He has dark hair—which I suspect is dyed, and very dark skin. Do you know, I almost think he wears make-up? His face was unnaturally smooth. He is dressed in the height of fashion, but more flamboyantly than is general. For example, his frock coat is green, not black. He spends all day—all afternoon, I should say, for he sleeps all morning—in the window of his club in St James' Square, where, of course, I could not go. However, he does spend one afternoon a week walking in Hyde Park. I believe he likes to spot lovers sneaking off into the bushes, and Hyde Park is where Billy found him today. Billy, knowing him already through Mr Holmes, very properly introduced him, and Mr Pike scrutinized me very sharply. He has the very darkest eyes, very piercing—I was almost afraid, for it seemed he could see through me to my very darkest secrets—then I remembered my secrets were not so great, and I merely stared back at him. He seemed to like that, for he dismissed Billy, and gestured me towards a bench.

'"A very worthy partner for Dr Watson," he said to me, as we sat—and do write that down for I want to tell John that one day when he is being difficult. "And how is Mr Holmes?" he inquired.

'"Well and busy and he has no idea I am here with you," I told him. I thought it best not to lie. I'll lay ten to one he can sniff out a lie like Sherlock can sniff out cigar smoke.

'"How secretive," he said, watching me very closely. '"Not at all," I replied. "I am merely working on my own recognisances."

'"Ah. How charming. How may I be of help?"

'He lit a cigarette then, a violet one from a gold case very clearly marked with initials that were not his own, and using a lighter with a rather florid inscription from a lover. I am unsure of which gender. And as he did that, he took the opportunity to look quickly around the park, and in that moment he took in everyone, the strolling soldiers, the nursemaids, the riders in Rotten Row, the boats on the lake. "Excuse me a moment," he said, and I saw his attention had been caught by a woman in a carriage, trying to hide her face with a parasol. He took out a small gold note case and scribbled something whilst watching a carriage go by. "Now," he continued, as he put the note case away, "tell me what I can do for you, and I will decide how you can help me in return."

"'I need information," I said. "I need to know the names of any ladies who have disappeared from society with no apparent reason—possibly after their husbands committed suicide. Or rather, accidentally shot themselves whilst cleaning their guns, or whatever other lie was used to cover up their fates."

'I saw no point in being coy. It might while away an afternoon, playing games of allusion and hints, but it wasn't going to get me what we needed to know.

"'You're very direct," he said, and I think he was surprised. I don't suppose he's used to people being that straightforward with him.

"'I see no point in dissimulation," I told him.

"'Quite," he agreed. He has an odd voice, smooth and silky. You could listen to it for hours, and tell it everything just for the pleasure of hearing him soothe you. And he chooses his conversation so carefully—he uses exactly the right words with exactly the right intonation. He never strikes a false note.

"'You wish to know a lot of secrets," he said. "What can you offer me in return?"

"'I don't have much money..." I began to say.

"'I don't want money," he said sharply, and I think I almost insulted him. "I deal in stories, my dear. Tell me a story. A true story."

'I could not think what to tell him for a moment. Then I realized I had the perfect story for him.

'"I know a tale," I told him. "It concerns a woman who also disappeared from society. I don't know her real name, but you may. My story may solve another mystery…"

'"How intriguing," he said, and I had his complete attention. I remembered what Billy said—that Langdale Pike doesn't pass on nearly half the stories he has been told. He just likes to know everything. He wants to know the secrets of everyone's soul, but he's content to keep most of them locked away.

'So I told him the secret story of the Whitechapel Lady.

'It was a good story, and I think I told it well. I held him spellbound. But when I spoke the final words, he sat back, and he was shocked. He knew of her, of course, of the suicide and the accident with the fire, which was very memorable, but he had no idea about the blackmailer. He had no idea she had been driven so far and had lost so much thanks to this one man. And all just for his satisfaction.

'"This cannot go on," he said, and he was very determined. "I will not have the brightest lights of society dimmed for this man's pleasure."

'He told me the name of the Whitechapel Lady and who she had once been. She was once so high in society! You would recognize her name from court circulars. And then, without any more demands or questions, he gave me a list of women who have disappeared, and asked me to make sure no one else suffered like the Whitechapel Lady. I think, perhaps, he had been rather fond of her.'

Mary sat down then, and handed me the list. It was long, of about thirty women.

'These are the women he could think of who have retired from society for no reason, or gone abroad suddenly or just disappeared.'

'Dead?' I asked.

Mary blinked. 'I didn't think of that. Yes, I suppose some of them must have died. Do you mean…?'

'Suicide. I mean they killed themselves. At least I think that's what I mean.'

'At least seven separated from their husbands despite seeming to be blissfully married up to that point.' Mary pointed their names out. 'Five of them, well…'

'Their husbands had inexplicable accidents?' I asked. Mary nodded.

'Next, we go to the library,' I said firmly. 'We shall research each and every one of these names. In *Debrett's Peerage*, in old newspapers, every reference source we can find. There must be a link between them: a family friend, a lawyer, a servant. Someone!'

'Mr Pike did give me one possible name,' Mary said. 'A man with a very bad reputation with women. He is apparently irresistible. He tricks them and uses them and then abandons them, and yet still they love him. I suppose they think they can save him. I swear, I have problems understanding my own sex sometimes. He did say he is not the kind of man to indulge in this kind of nasty abuse. Violence is not quite his style; he is, at heart, a coward. Still, he is the kind of man who easily gains power over women, and then abuses it.'

'"A most convincing rogue",' I quoted. 'How many of these women is he linked to?'

'So far, Mr Pike knew of five.'

'That's not many, in a list of thirty.'

'There may be more. Besides, it's a start,' Mary said, rising.

'Then we'll research him too. What's his name?'

'Sir George Burnwell.'

'To the library!' may not have the same dramatic ring as 'the game's afoot!' but it was far more useful. Mr Holmes employed a Mr Mercer for the endless slogging work, trawling for information from papers and journals and registries and records. (Not a fact John knew yet. At this time, Mr Holmes liked to maintain his infallible image with John, especially after his remarks in writing about Mr Holmes' lack of knowledge of the solar system.)

But Mary and I had to do it ourselves, with the occasional help of Billy. Mary haunted the periodical section of the library, Billy took advantage of Mr Holmes' absence—he was away a lot at the time, there must have been a very complex investigation going on—to plunder his cuttings books, and I went through the piles of newspapers that had built up in the attic. Mr Holmes hated to have anything that might one day be useful thrown away—and his definition of 'possibly useful' was very wide-ranging.

By the end of a week, we had two names—or rather, confirmation of one name and a new one. I had found several divorce notices, as well as advertisements for sale of goods 'to be applied for via the solicitor'—a sure sign the seller had left the country quickly. Mary had found several names that simply disappeared from the society pages for no good reason, notes of at least two court cases quickly abandoned and several wills changed at the very last moment.

The same person had kept popping up in all the gossip columns, court cases, divorce notices, even court circulars. The same man was named in connection with all these women, sometimes as little as being mentioned as being at the same ball as them, but it was there.

Sir George Burnwell.

The other man was the reporter who covered these stories. Of course, most of the reports were anonymous, just snippets in a gossip column. However, whenever the story was meatier, often it was the same man who wrote the story. He seemed to take a subtle pleasure in the downfall of these women, and the further they fell, the better. He also seemed to hint that he knew far more than he was telling. It was a tenuous link, but a link nonetheless. His name was Patrick West. I did not have the first idea how to investigate a reporter, but Billy did. He was anxious to use some of the skills he was learning from Mr Holmes, so I set him on to the task of discovering all he could about Mr Patrick West—discreetly, of course.

Before I went out, I popped up to Mr Holmes' rooms to check the street. I did that a lot lately, only if he was out, though.

I just looked down the street, one way and the other. As usual, there was nothing sinister, nothing odd, just busy Baker Street, same as always. But the ditherer was back, the tall blond man standing on the opposite side of the street, still staring at our windows (and incidentally getting in the way of everyone on the pavement). Billy came in at that moment.

'There's a ditherer,' I said to him. 'Maybe we should make up his mind for him and just invite him in.'

Billy peered out of the window, and then leaned in closer, staring hard at the man.

'I know him!' he said, making sure the lace curtain covered us. 'I saw him when we were following Mr Shirley—he's a friend of the Shirleys.'

'Get him in here,' I demanded. Billy ran down the stairs, but by the time he got there, the man had gone, marching briskly down the street.

'Sorry,' Billy said, coming back in as I walked down the stairs. 'He's fast!'

'You definitely saw him with the Shirleys?' I asked. Billy nodded.

'It's not a coincidence he's here, is it?' Billy wondered.

'I doubt it,' I told him. 'Someone directed him; he had the address written down. He may be a victim too. If you see him again, grab him.'

Two hours later, I had left Baker Street to meet Mary. I stood on a street corner in the drizzle, ostensibly staring at dress patterns in a haberdashery shop window but really checking my reflection to see if the Ordinary Man was behind me. Not that I had much confidence in recognizing him without the distinctive splash of paint on his jacket. I had not seen him since that day, and I was beginning to tell myself I had imagined the whole affair. Perhaps he, too, was a Baker Street resident who just happened to have business in Whitechapel that day. Perhaps I had been over-sensitive, my nerves heightened by the Whitechapel Lady's story. And yet…and yet…no. When I thought about it, calmly and sensibly, I knew he had been following me. Was it for some reason of his own, or did Burnwell have his victims watched? Or was it not linked to our investigation at all—was I being followed merely because of my connection to Mr Holmes, in which case, should I warn him? Questions, questions, questions, but at least I was getting close to answers now.

Mary came round the corner, wearing a dress of primrose yellow, carrying a jaunty umbrella and smiling to herself. She looked bright and lovely and sunny, as if she didn't have a care in the world. That impression was misleading. All those stories of despair she had uncovered had hit her hard. She had dreamed of them, she told me. She had dreamed of all those women, all those families, so happy, so lively, and then that man had appeared and whispered in an ear and it all came crashing down. The dreams had not made Mary fearful or cautious though. Instead she had announced we would catch him, and stop him, and there was a steely look in her eye when she promised me this. Kind as Mary was, she would nevertheless make an implacable enemy.

She joined me, crying, 'Proof! That's what we need,' as we walked off down the street together. A tall, lovely woman in yellow, and a shorter, plainer one in black. We must have looked like mother and daughter, instead of the closest of friends. 'What are you looking at?' she asked, as I glanced over my shoulder.

'Sometimes I think we're being followed,' I said. 'Maybe it's my imagination.'

'Maybe not,' Mary replied, looking around the street. 'You notice things more than I do. You observe, as Sherlock says. Followed by whom?'

'I don't know. Just an ordinary man,' I told her. 'I thought I saw him in Whitechapel, and then in Baker Street.'

'Are you sure?' Mary demanded.

'No, I'm not sure,' I told her. 'I'm not used to this, Mary, how can I tell if someone's following me? I honestly don't think I could pick his face out of a crowd if it wasn't for the stain on his jacket. But it's probably just my imagination. I was a bit shaken by Whitechapel, and anyway he's not here now. It doesn't matter. So how do we get this proof?' I asked, as Mary blithely ignored a man trying to make eyes at her, and steered me round a puddle.

'Well, the man we're hunting must keep all kinds of letters and souvenirs and so on. I doubt he trusts a bank, or a solicitor.'

'Why not?' I asked, as we turned the corner into a quieter street, lined with trees.

'All it takes is one nosy bank clerk or solicitor's clerk or burglar, and he'd be undone. Besides, he likes power. I'd lay good odds he likes to gloat over those letters of an evening. How can he do that if they're at the bank? No, I reckon Sir George keeps them at home.'

'"Good odds,"' I quoted, amused. 'Has John been taking you to the races again?'

'I won five pounds last week,' she said complacently. 'John, on the other hand, lost ten shillings.'

'Mary,' I said, pulling her to a stop. 'Are we sure about this? Sir George is very rich and very powerful.'

'Doesn't mean he's not a blackmailer,' Mary insisted. She had that stubborn set to her chin again.

'But he's very well known. The Whitechapel Lady said her blackmailer was an ordinary man, a man with an alias...'

'Then Sir George hired an agent! It's not hard to do, find an ordinary-looking man, and tell him to go and whisper certain phrases in a lady's ear. I should imagine he's very well paid...or he too has a secret that Sir George holds over him!' Mary said quickly. A heavily moustached man tutted at our blocking the path, and Mary pulled me out of the way, so we could stand against a bookshop window. The earlier grey drizzle had cleared, and now the damp street sparkled in the sunlight. Even this usually quiet road was full of people, sober-faced men in dark suits, laughing girls in colourful dresses, errand boys dashing between the crowds, flower girls offering their bright violets. It was such a lovely, perfect London street in the spring sunshine.

'I have seen his name everywhere,' Mary urged. 'His name appears over and over in the divorce court records. I've even seen it in records of the criminal court. Never the accused, but always there in the background, always just where a good man would not be, always with a faint patina of villainy on him. I have found his name over and over again. I do believe it is him: Sir George Burnwell is our man.'

She was intense in her belief, and she was persuading me. But I needed more than a feeling.

'Proof, then,' I said. 'Which we are agreed is in his home, which we have no way of being invited into.'

'Then we break in,' Mary said, a touch breathlessly. She smiled, a dazzling, daring smile, as if it meant nothing to her to suggest committing a crime. Yet the hand that rested on my arm trembled slightly.

'How on earth do we break in?' I asked. Mary had wild, wonderful ideas, but she sometimes forgot the practicalities of putting them into action. 'If we smash a window, or break open a door, he'll know someone's been there and then he'll redouble his efforts, punish his victims and find us!'

'Pick the locks?' Mary suggested.

'A skill neither you nor I possess,' I said, looking down at my hands, lined and small, draped in very proper black gloves, grasping my very proper reticule; respectable hands of a respectable woman. Yet as I thought about breaking into Sir George's home, my hands did not tremble. How very cold-blooded I was becoming.

'It's time we had some assistance,' I said.

'Not Mr Holmes,' Mary insisted. 'He would...'

I held up a hand to stop her. An idea was forming in my mind—a most delicious idea.

'Not Mr Holmes,' I agreed. I raised my head a little. The remaining clouds had drifted away and the sunshine felt so lovely on my face. I decided to remove my gloves, feel the sun on my skin for a change.

'The Irregulars?' Mary asked.

'I'm not encouraging those children to break the law,' I said firmly, as I folded my gloves into my reticule. I stretched out my fingers. 'I know they do break the law, but I'm not going to give them a reason to. No, I know someone far better. Or at least, I know someone who could suggest an appropriate person. Someone who will definitely not tell Mr Holmes.'

Oh, what an idea I'd had. What a perfect, thrilling, amusing idea. I almost giggled with the perfection of it.

'Who?' Mary demanded. 'Why are you smiling like that? Tell me who!'

'I did see in the papers that she has just returned, for a brief visit, from her year's sojourn in America,' I said, grinning. It was fun teasing Mary like this.

'Who? Tell me now, or I'll burst!' Mary demanded.

'Well,' I said. 'Mr Holmes always calls her "the Woman".'

The Woman and the Strange Request

After Irene Adler had escaped him, and taken her new husband to America, Sherlock Holmes had stormed round his rooms for hours, alternately raging and laughing. She had changed him. Before her, he had never really respected women as intellectual equals. We were necessary, he supposed, to the continuation of the human race, and to perform certain tasks, but our minds were small and narrow. Even Mary, whom, when he met her, he called intelligent and organized, was still castigated as 'just a woman'. And now, not only was he beaten—a rare occasion in itself—but by a woman!

From then on, he never underestimated women again. Sometimes I would catch him staring at Mary or me with a puzzled expression as if he no longer knew what to think of us. Occasionally, John would bring up the subject of Miss Adler, mostly to amuse himself. I, of course, was usually listening, in the kitchen. John had never underestimated any woman, and he found it very funny that Mr Holmes had been beaten by one. Mr Holmes would shout about her perfidy, or admire her mind, or show John a new cutting about some incident that he swore bore her hallmark. And he always ended these tirades with 'And married to a country solicitor. What a waste!'

Once John said, in a rather too carefully careless way, 'Would you have preferred her to marry you?'

'Don't be ridiculous,' Mr Holmes had said. 'Emotion is an indulgence of the intellectually inferior. I will never marry. Especially not that woman. We'd be planning to murder each other within a month. And the worst thing is…' I heard him tune his violin, 'we are both more than capable of getting away with it.'

And yet he never said her name. She was always 'the Woman'. It was as if her name were difficult to utter. She confused and puzzled him, she infuriated him, and yet it seemed to me he took a certain pride in being beaten by her.

And now she was back.

I thought perhaps she would return to the house she had known before, that unassuming villa called Briony Lodge in Serpentine Avenue with the convenient secret cupboards tucked in mantelpieces. I knew exactly where it was, and I disguised myself as a perfectly respectable housekeeper as I made my way there. Not much of a disguise, I admit. My heart still ached for the green dress in my wardrobe though I was becoming less respectable by the day. Mary was with me, in a plain grey merino dress, with her hair smoothed back, so she looked just like the governess she used to be. We caught the omnibus to St John's Wood and found Serpentine Avenue easily. We walked arm in arm sedately down the street, just a pair of old friends enjoying the sunshine. An inquiry of a policeman, charmed by Mary's sparkling yet demure eyes, confirmed our suspicion that *she* was back, her house was indeed still in that street and, what's more, she usually came home in about an hour or so.

We walked up and down, just talking, not about the case, but about Mr Holmes and John, and the latest fashion, and what we had seen at the music hall and flowers and the seaside and everything except blackmail and murder. We had always talked well, not always agreeing but always content to discuss. Some of the happiest hours of my life were spent in Mary's company.

It was a wonderful day, and a wonderful place just to walk and talk. The street was busy, full of knife-grinders and fruit-sellers and grocery boys, but not crowded. The houses here were clean and white and freshly painted, and the newly swept street almost shone. There was a large public garden on one side of it, and the scent of the breeze in the trees wafted over us. It was more than a world away from Whitechapel, just a few miles down the road.

As evening began to fall, Mary squeezed my arm.

'Is that her?' she whispered, looking towards the corner of the street.

A woman had just turned the corner and was walking towards us. She was dressed in a trim grey suit, with narrow edgings of purple velvet. She was shorter than I expected, with dark hair and eyes, and a milky white skin. Her figure was well suited to the hourglass fashion currently prevalent and she walked with a certain sway that was not quite modest. She carried no parasol, and she turned her face up towards the sun, not caring if her skin tanned, apparently. She held her head high, and watched everyone—not out of concern or worry, but for interest, for she smiled at the lovers and laughed as the barrel organ started to play and nodded in a friendly way to the policeman. To be honest, she was not, by all the rules we had been taught, beautiful, but she was attractive and charming and fascinating.

Halfway down the street sat a war veteran, crouched on the pavement. He was old and worn, with one leg missing, the empty trouser leg neatly folded and pinned. His battered crutch lay beside him. He still wore his uniform, though it was barely more than rags and patches now. He tipped his hat to all who passed by, and nodded to anyone who left money in front of him, but he did not speak. He seemed to look beyond the street, beyond London, to far-off lands and long-lost friends and scenes we could only see in books.

Everyone who had passed him had given him a coin or two. Everyone knew someone who had been lost in the wars. Mary had brought him two hot pies. She had a special affinity for injured veterans—after all, her husband was one, and if he had not met Sherlock, who knows if he might have ended up begging for his meals.

The woman in grey paused before the veteran, then knelt down before him, heedless of the dirt on her skirt. She talked to him in a low voice, and gently touched one of his faded medal ribbons, as if she knew what it meant, and what it had cost. He smiled at her, a soft, sad smile, and she emptied her purse into his lap.

As she stood, I glanced at Mary. She too had seen the woman's gentle care of the veteran, and she watched intently. She had been captivated.

The woman walked past us, and then stopped. She turned back, and looked at us with a puzzled expression.

'Mrs Hudson?' Irene Adler asked. 'What on earth are you doing here?'

She invited us into her parlour. The room was fresh and clean, with simple but comfortable furnishings, and a few beautiful, jewel-like paintings. After the heavy, dark, velvet-cloaked, ornament-choked rooms of my usual acquaintances, this room felt deliciously cool and relaxing.

Miss Adler unpinned her hat, and placed it on a side table, motioning us towards the sofa.

'Did Mr Holmes send you?' she asked curiously.

'No,' I replied. 'He has no idea we are here and I would be grateful if you did not tell him.'

She smiled, and studied me with her dark brown eyes.

'How intriguing,' she said lightly. 'So why are you here? Is Mr Holmes well? Not in any kind of trouble?' There was a momentary expression of unease on her face. Taunt him, tease him, defeat him, escape him she might, but Miss Adler had a liking for Mr Holmes.

'He is perfectly well, as well and safe as he ever is,' I reassured her, aware that Mary sat next to me staring with unabashed wide-eyed curiosity at Miss Adler. 'He is busy, very busy. I...we... are here for our own reason, Miss Adler,' I stammered, suddenly nervous. I had just realized how impertinent it would look to ask Irene Adler if she knew a willing burglar to help us rob a house.

'Mrs Norton, now,' she reminded me gently, as a sweet-faced little maid entered with the tea. Irene held the door open for her, and glanced up at me. 'Yes, I am still married,' she said, and that was when I realized I had been assuming she was not. 'I love my husband, and he loves me. He is currently in America, but when we are together, we are still a honeymoon couple. Given both my past and my nature, no one is more surprised at this turn of events than I, but I am happy.'

Irene thanked the little maid and dismissed her, and sat on the sofa opposite Mary and me.

'My husband is also understanding enough to indulge my sudden craving to visit London alone. I mean to revisit some memories, transact some business, see some old friends. Milk, Mrs Hudson?'

There was always something about the way she spoke—as if her words said one thing, but everything else about her was saying something else. Not that she lied to us, or dissimulated— though often she did!—but what she told us was never the whole story. Still, even then, I knew better than to ask her outright why she had returned to London. Besides, another question had just struck me.

'Forgive me,' I said. 'But as I recall, we've never actually met before. I know who you are, from Mr Holmes, and from the newspapers—but how do you know who I am?'

She poured the golden tea into the thinnest of china cups.

'I researched my adversary well, Mrs Hudson,' she said. 'I knew Mr Holmes was a formidable foe, and if I was to defeat him, in the matter of the King of Bohemia's ridiculous photograph, and I did defeat him thoroughly, I had to know him. Not just his strengths and weaknesses, but the people around him. Have you heard that a man can be judged by his friends? Therefore I had to know about the few friends he had, his family...'

'His housekeeper,' I finished for her bluntly. I hadn't meant to. Something about Irene Adler—Norton—brought out the brutally honest in me. It always would. She liked that.

'More than just a housekeeper, so much more,' Irene said, her dark eyes meeting mine, a wealth of knowledge in them. I smiled, almost blushing. I could not help it. It felt so warm, to be thought of as more than just Mr Holmes' housekeeper.

'You I'm afraid I don't know,' Irene said, turning to Mary and holding out a cup of tea. Mary, who had been watching the exchanges between Irene and me with a delighted fascination, suddenly realized she had been silent until now.

'Oh, how rude of me!' Mary said, taking the tea. 'I'm Mary Watson. John's wife. Dr John Watson, I mean. Well, of course, you know who I mean.' Mary was babbling, but she stopped herself by drinking her tea.

'Really?' Irene looked at her steadily, examining her top to toe. Mary met her inquiring glance frankly, staring back over the rim of the tea cup with her fierce blue eyes. She put the cup down, and smiled. Very few people could resist Mary's smile. Irene smiled back. 'I approve,' she said. 'A perfect match.'

'I think so,' Mary said. 'I am very excited to meet you, Miss Adler—I mean Mrs Norton. John has told me all about you—well, all he knows.'

'And is his opinion of me good or bad?' Irene asked dryly, handing me my tea. I noticed it was made exactly how I like it, though I had not got round to telling her if I wanted milk or sugar.

'All good,' Mary told her. 'He appreciates the way you fooled Sherlock. And approves, too. He thinks Sherlock being beaten by a woman did him the world of good.'

'You call him Sherlock? Does he call you Mary?' Irene asked, intrigued.

'No, I'm always "Mrs Watson" but I persist in calling him Sherlock. He's practically a brother-in-law to me, after all.' Mary took a sip of tea, and then said thoughtfully, 'John says that does him good, too. He says at this rate Sherlock might begin to think of women as at least half as good as men by the end of the century.' She glanced up at Mrs Norton, laughing. 'Between the two of us—I mean the three of us—we could reform him!'

'I doubt that,' Irene replied, though she laughed. 'But ladies—excuse me, you were not in the neighbourhood for a gossip, or idle curiosity. You want something. How can I help?'

Mary and I exchanged glances. This was it, the vital moment. The moment where we reached out, and knew not what the answer would be. We had enlisted the help of Billy and Wiggins, but we knew them, we knew what they would say. Now we were going to ask this woman neither of us had ever met for help, and what's more, we were going to ask her to help us with something utterly illegal. We didn't know what would happen next. She might be insulted. She might be angry. She might tell the police. Doubtful, but possible. She might tell Mr Holmes, which was more possible, and then he and John would—in the gentlest possible way—either tell us to stop, or worse, push us to one side and take over the investigation themselves. Mary and I would become bystanders again. This moment was quite a risk.

Ah well, as my Hector often observed, risks are there to be taken. I put down my tea cup, faced Irene, and said, very directly, 'We want you to introduce us to someone trustworthy who could pick locks and break into safes and generally burgle a house so no one knows we have been there.'

I said it quickly, all in one breath. Beside me, I heard Mary give a tiny cry of surprise at my audacity, which she quickly silenced. Irene stared at me, her tea cup in her hand, eyes wide.

Give me my due, I'd achieved something Mr Holmes never had. I'd surprised Irene Adler.

She put the tea cup down very slowly and said, 'What makes you think I know such people?'

'Because you managed to retrieve the photograph of you and the King of Bohemia, even though it was safely locked away,' I said swiftly. 'Because you knew enough about the habits of burglars not to keep it in a safe. Because from all I've read about you, I suspect there are many other pictures and souvenirs you had to get back before you married and I don't think you could have got them all yourself. You must know someone with the necessary skills.' I stopped. My mouth had gone dry and I could not have said more if my life depended on it. Irene's face froze. I felt my hands twist against each other in my lap, and I grasped them tight to control them. If she was going to feel insulted, that last statement should just about do it. I braced myself for the inevitable flood of anger.

She took a deep breath and then said, 'Why?'

'Why?' I asked.

'Why do you need to find such a person?'

Well, that was not what I expected.

We told her. We told her of the crying woman and the man in the river and the attack on Wiggins. We told her of the Whitechapel Lady, and all those other women who had disappeared from their ruined lives. We told her of the destroyed families, and the suicides and the whispering, the constant, corrosive whispering. We told her of the foul, faceless spider of a man who squatted in the centre of it all, pulling strings and playing tricks and feeding off the pain, growing fat on terror and loss and heartbreak.

'I see,' Irene said when we were done. 'What a horrible story. I never knew all this was happening. I should have understood, I have seen some terrible things, but I never put all the pieces together. Blackmail is such a foul crime.'

'He's not even blackmailing for money,' Mary said. 'He just likes to destroy.'

The day had grown dark outside, and Irene rose to light the lamps. She took a spill from a jar on the mantelpiece, and lit it on the fire. She held the flame up to the gas lamp, briefly throwing her face into a bizarre, flickering shadow.

'You think you know who this man is?' she asked, as she lit the lamp.

'Sir George Burnwell,' I told her.

She blew out the burning spill and turned to me in surprise. 'Are you sure?' she asked. 'I am aware of him. The man is a heartless manipulative bully who hates women even as he seduces them, but to go as far as this…It really does not seem to be in his nature.'

'The evidence points that way,' Mary said. 'For now. It's only circumstantial. We need something solid.'

'I see,' Irene said. She threw the spill into the fire, and walked up and down the room a few times, deep in thought. Then she turned to us, straightened her back, and said, 'The person you are looking for, the trustworthy and skilled house-breaker, is me.'

'You?' I asked, surprised—but not actually that surprised.

'I am quite good at it, I assure you,' she said gently, but very seriously. 'Actually, very good at it. Let me not underestimate my own talents. I had the best of all teachers.'

'But…' Mary started to say. Irene sat down on the sofa opposite us again.

'As you say,' Irene confirmed, 'there have been objects— photographs, letters, locks of hair—that I have needed to retrieve. I could trust only myself, therefore I alone took back those objects from those who kept them. If anyone else had seen them, I would have been open to blackmail myself. I have some interesting, highly scandalous information. Even the information I lodge with my solicitor must be sealed. I have had some narrow escapes in my time,' she said, in a quiet voice. She shuddered, as if an old and bitter memory washed over her. Then she turned back to us, and smiled brightly.

'I accept,' she said. 'Whatever you need, I will do.' Her smile became mischievous. 'I'm in the mood for an adventure.'

'Um…thank you, Miss…I mean Mrs Norton,' I said, stammering in my surprise. Mary laughed, utterly delighted with the outcome.

'Irene, please,' she said. 'If we're to be criminals together, let us use our first names. I am Irene.'

'And you know I'm Mary,' Mary said cheerfully. They both turned to me.

Criminals. We would be criminals. We would rob and steal and who knew what else?

I looked up to see Mary and Irene looking at me, waiting. My first name? No one had used my first name since Hector died. I had not even told Mary my name. For a moment, I wasn't sure I could remember it.

'Martha,' I said to them. 'My first name is Martha.'

Martha, Mary and Irene. Criminals together. So be it. It was for the best of causes.

We planned late into the night, accompanied by a lovely supper, only stopping at ten, when Mary mentioned her husband might possibly be wondering where she was. I knew Mr Holmes would not care where I was. If I was not there to serve his supper, he would merely go out to eat at his favourite Italian restaurant. Everything was settled for two nights hence, when the moon would be new, and cast less light. Mary and I walked up to the main street to hail a cab. Mary ran ahead, seeing one in the distance. I, trailing behind, happened to turn as we left Irene's street.

It was empty now, apart from one last, solitary straggler. He lounged against a postbox, not even bothering to hide the fact that he was watching us. He could have been there all day. He must have been there ever since it was dark. He could have watched us through the well-lit window of Irene's house. I did not recognize his face—the street was too dark, his face too plain. I looked at the arm of his jacket. There was no paint, but I could just see, under the gaslight, a paler patch where it had been cleaned vigorously. He tipped his hat to me and strolled away.

I had led the Ordinary Man right to Irene Adler's door.

A Good Night's Work

John glowed the day he came to tell me he had won his Mary. I wept—I told him it was for joy, but it was loss. John had been the tie that bound us all, and now he was slipping away. I know that Mr Holmes felt it keenly, but he never said a word. He merely sat and brooded in the dark. His adventures for a while became more frenetic and more dangerous, and I sat in the kitchen and listened.

The afternoon before his wedding, John came to visit. I was touched he chose to spend this time with me, and I would not stop talking, for fear if I fell silent, the afternoon would end. But dusk will always fall, and soon it did.

'I have bought a medical practice,' John told me, as I rose to light the gas lamps. 'Not so very far away.'

'But not here,' I said, before I could stop myself.

'Close,' he said, and reached to light the highest gas lamp for me, the one I had to stand on a chair to reach. 'A short cab ride away. You and Holmes will always be welcome there.'

'Good luck getting Mr Holmes to leave 221b for anything other than a case,' I said, more brightly than I felt, putting the matches away in the kitchen drawer.

'Mary is talking to him now,' John told me. 'There is a room set aside for him in the new house, and she is consulting him on how he would like it to be decorated.'

For a moment my heart fell away, and I had to grasp the kitchen dresser for support. If Mr Holmes left too...

'Not that he will use it,' John said quickly. 'He is too fond of 221b.'

'He'll miss you,' I said softly, my back still to John.

'Billy is bright,' John said lightly. 'He soaks in everything Holmes teaches him, and Holmes has noticed. He'll enjoy making an apprentice of the boy.'

I said nothing.

'I will visit,' John promised. 'Not a week will go by that I will not be here. I will still keep a bed here, if I may. Billy will be here too. And Mr Holmes...'

'Is used to me,' I finished for him, straightening the plates on the dresser, still refusing to turn to look at John, in case he saw the tears in my eyes.

'Is fond of you, in his own brusque way,' John said gently. 'Highly insulting way sometimes. He's the same with me. Calls me all sorts of things, usually around the theme of "idiot", day and night, but I know I am his closest friend. Only friend, I think.' John came over to me, and placing his hands on my shoulders, turned me to face him. 'We will neither of us abandon you, mother to us that you are,' he said, and kissed me on the forehead.

I wept again, as he wrapped his arms around me, but this time I wept with relief.

'Now,' he said to me. 'I want you to meet my Mary. Yes, I know you've met her before, but I want you to meet her properly, as my wife, well, my wife after tomorrow. You will love her.'

And I did.

This had been seven months earlier, and I felt a little ashamed of how weak and foolish I had been. Of course Mary would not take John away from me. It was, in fact, quite the opposite—he had brought Mary to me. Given we were now working on our case, I felt Mary and I were as much partners in work and friendship as Mr Holmes and Dr Watson.

In work as long as we could solve this case, that is. The morning after meeting Irene, I sat down to sort through what we had learnt and see what I could deduce from the few facts and many suppositions. Mr Holmes was out, John and Mary were, for once, in their own home, and I had sent Billy to instruct the Irregulars to discreetly watch Sir George's house. Therefore, I was left all alone in 221b.

You mustn't feel sorry for me, that I was alone so much. I was of that nature that thrives on solitude. Much as I loved Mary and Billy and the others, sometimes I felt as if I could only breathe when I was alone. In solitude I found a peace and freedom I could never find in company. Even my husband and my child had known to give me time alone just to become myself again. Only when I was alone could I think. I have to admit, some of the most content moments of my life were spent alone, in the kitchen of 221b, the sun streaming through the window, with absolutely no demands on my time.

But then again, being alone by choice is so very different from being alone in an always empty house.

That day I was trying to get my thoughts in some sort of order. This case had started as blackmail and libel, evolved into attempted murder and had now become something so dark and disturbing I did not have a name for it.

What did we know? We knew this man held secrets. How did he gather them? He must have had help—disgruntled servants, foolish relatives, corrupt officials. But he himself hid in the background.

Just like me.

I doubted that it was him who had whispered in the Whitechapel Lady's ear. I should imagine he went to great lengths to keep his distance from his victims. He watched. He did not act—unless he had to. He set in motion a chain of events and stepped in only at an opportune, final moment. Only at the moment of greatest satisfaction, when his work had finally come to fruition. He must be a man of supreme control over himself— able to twitch and pull and loosen and tighten the strings of his puppets without ever giving himself away or going too far. At least not until the time was exactly right.

I sat back in my chair and sighed. This speculation was all very well, but as Mr Holmes would say, I needed data!

. This man liked power. Well, who did not? But for this man, it was not the power to create or protect. No, he liked the power to control, to destroy. Not quickly, as a murderer would, but slowly, painfully, infinitesimally taking apart a life, bit by bit, whisper by whisper, blow by blow.

I wondered if he had ever killed. I was certain he could. He had almost killed both Mr Shirley and Wiggins. I was certain now that man was him, not some sort of lackey. That moment of Mr Shirley's capitulation would have been a crowning moment. I was certain he would not have delegated that. Besides, Wiggins seemed to hint that he had taken some joy in the act of almost killing both him and Mr Shirley. No, I felt it in my bones, that man had been him.

Although murder seemed to run contrary to the cold crea-ture of control whom I envisaged. Perhaps that control was beginning to slip. Perhaps the urges and desires that had led him to this life were beginning to break free of his grip. In that case, who next? Would he slip into some sort of madness? Would he control himself, or just kill and kill again?

Perhaps he had killed before, and then forced himself to stop. Perhaps he had found the destruction of body less satisfying than the slow, merciless destruction of mind and spirit.

Why women? I said to myself, as I sipped a rare cup of coffee. The pungent odour swirled through the kitchen, lending an unaccustomed sharpness to the air. All his plans, his hate, his ire was directed towards women. Men had suffered, but only as an adjunct to the destruction of a woman. A man's suicide, his ruin, his rejection would be a way to hurt her more. So why only women?

Was it because we were the supposed weaker sex? Or because we were deemed the fairer sex? Had a woman rejected him? Although his actions seemed an egregiously over-the-top reaction to rejection.

Was it not just one woman? Had he been unsuccessful with all women? Could he only find satisfaction—of a sort—in hurting and hating women? Was it merely because women were more easily destroyed by secrets and lies than men?

My suspects:

Sir George Burnwell. A rake (to use my mother's term), a bully (to use Irene's term). A man who used and abused women, and yet was very attractive to them. According to Langdale Pike, he was very good at tempting women, and wheedling secrets out of them. Would he go so far as to blackmail them to destruction?

The Ordinary Man. He followed us, all the way from Whitechapel. At the moment he was just a face in the background. I wouldn't recognize him if it wasn't for the stain on his jacket. Although I think I was beginning to recognize an occasional feature, from time to time. I was observing, and noticing, and remembering. Why didn't he get rid of the jacket? Could he not afford to, or did he not realize that the mark was enough to distinguish him?

The reporter Patrick West. A gatherer of secrets, certainly; it was his job. He seemed to take pleasure in telling those secrets to the world, hinting at far worse. But all we knew of him was a name.

Someone else entirely? An utterly unknown quantity? Some link we had not found? Someone who was down on women, yet kept hidden? Had I already met this man, this monster? Perhaps I had passed him on the street, nodded good morning to him, even spoken to him.

A sudden thought struck me. Another possibility. Someone who had certainly hated women, had hurt them. He had made every woman in London afraid. His victims had once been respectable women who had fallen. He had sent letters, like my suspect. He had taunted and threatened and boasted. Perhaps he had learnt to enjoy the fear far more than the act. Perhaps he had moved from physical hate to emotional hate.

Slowly, hardly believing I was writing this, I wrote down the name of my final suspect.

The room felt suddenly cold. I almost glanced over my shoulder, convinced someone stood there.

Then, taking a sharp breath and shaking myself, I firmly crossed out the name. It was a silly idea! What a ridiculous, pointless thought! What a far-fetched thought!

What a terrifying thought.

I told myself I was being a fool, and yet that crossed-out name haunted me all day.

Jack the Ripper.

It wasn't that I believed it was really him—really Jack. But in my mind, our blackmailer was becoming a bogeyman as big as Jack, as terrifying. And after all, that case had never been solved.

Mary arrived in the early afternoon to find me scrubbing down my kitchen table. My daily help had cleaned the rest of the house that day, but I always cleaned the table and my pots and pans myself. I needed to be sure they were perfect. My notes were now neatly tidied away in the dresser drawer. Before we could even draw breath to greet each other, Billy burst in.

'He's coming! The ditherer, he's crossing the road!'

'It's a man who keeps coming to see Mr Holmes,' I said, in response to Mary's puzzled look. 'But he never quite makes it through the door. What's important is that Billy saw him with Mr Shirley—they seemed to be friends.'

Mary's eyes widened.

'Is Sherlock here?' she asked. I shook my head. 'Good, it's still our case. Billy, when he gets here, don't tell him Sherlock is out, just show him up to his rooms.'

The bell rang, and Billy ran for it, buttoning up his uniform.

'Do you have scones?' Mary asked. 'If we give him hot tea and scones he's less likely to up and leave.'

'I do, and the kettle is hot,' I told her. I could hear Billy guide him up the stairs to Mr Holmes' rooms, and say that someone would see him presently. 'Mary, are you actually going to question him?'

'If I can,' Mary said breathlessly, arranging a cloth on a tray. 'I hope I can. It's worth a try.'

She swept up the stairs, shoulders back. I followed her, carrying the tea tray piled high with fragrant tea and my best scones. Mary walked into Mr Holmes' rooms with barely a hesitation.

'Mr Holmes is presently absent,' she said, in her most charming voice. 'But we expect him back at any moment. In the meantime, may I offer you tea, Mr...?'

'Ballant,' he said unhappily. In the rooms he seemed even taller, towering over Mary. He had strong shoulders stretching the expensive material of his grey suit, and the sun glinted off his fair hair. He was a very handsome man, with a very fine moustache, and he seemed to be quite aware of the fact. He kept stroking his moustache with his right hand.

'Will Mr Holmes be long?' he asked, still standing. 'I have a letter I need him to see. It is of utmost importance.'

'Barely any time at all,' Mary told him in her most honeyed voice. She gestured towards the sofa as I poured the tea. 'Please, sit, have some tea. I am Mrs Watson, by the way.'

It would have been impolite to refuse, and I felt this was a man who lived his life by the strictest of proprieties. He sat down, and told me how he liked his tea. I handed it to him, with a scone.

'Mrs Watson?' he asked, as he sipped the tea. 'Dr Watson's wife?'

'Indeed,' Mary said. 'In fact, since my marriage I too have worked with Mr Holmes. In a strictly information-gathering capacity, of course.'

'Of course,' he said, biting into the scone. My scones are divine, if I say so myself, and he relaxed slightly as he savoured the taste.

'In fact,' Mary said, 'I often take notes of cases before Mr Holmes sees his clients, to save time, in strictest confidence.'

'Do you?' he said, surprised. He glanced up at me. Taking the hint, I left the room—but went no further than the corridor outside the open door, where I found Billy also shamelessly eavesdropping.

'Mr Holmes likes me to draw all the facts from the clients, and then arrange them in a logical order to present to him,' Mary told him, managing to sound both meek and competent at the same time. This was not a man who liked his women strong. 'Perhaps I could take a few details from you?'

I heard him shift in his chair.

'It is not a subject suitable for a woman,' he objected.

'Alas, very few of Mr Holmes' cases are,' she said gently. 'Do not think of me as a woman. Think of me as a recording device.'

'I have heard Mr Holmes can be difficult,' he admitted. I wonder where he had heard that from?

'He can,' Mary agreed. 'That is why I help him, to smooth the path. Please, Mr Ballant, you must have come so far, it would be a pity to leave now. You may leave the facts with me, and I can pass the case to Mr Holmes.'

I heard the man stand and start to stride around. He was so tall, he could not stride far in that rather small room, and I could hear every word he spoke.

'You must understand, I work for the government,' he told Mary. 'It is a highly trusted position, and there is a great degree of confidential work that passes across my desk. You understand, therefore, that I am reluctant to involve the police.'

'Mr Holmes has dealt with the highest echelons of government most discreetly,' Mary murmured. She was laying it on thick!

'Yes, I suppose he has,' Mr Ballant continued. 'The point is, my position makes me open to…well, to…'

'Blackmail?' Mary finished. She was getting impatient. I heard him take a deep breath.

'Yes, blackmail. And the worst of it is, I haven't even done anything! The blackguard makes all kinds of insinuations based on the flimsiest of evidence! Disgusting insinuations!'

'May I see the letter?' Mary asked. 'I will give it to Mr Holmes sealed.'

I heard the rustle of paper as something was handed over.

'I take it this man has not asked for anything as yet,' Mary queried, sounding considerably less meek and far more competent than earlier.

'No. But when he does—my God, the things I could tell him! It could bring the government down!'

'Then you shall not tell him,' Mary said, and she stood. 'You are not the only person to have received these letters, and Mr Holmes is already working on the case.'

'Who else?' he demanded. 'No, of course, I suppose you can't tell me. But can I ask—was it Shirley?'

'It was,' Mary confirmed. Well, it had been Mrs Shirley, and Mr Ballant meant Mr Shirley, but this was at least confirmation that Mr Shirley had been a victim too.

I heard Mr Ballant thank Mary and give her his address, allowing me just enough time to nip round the corner and out of sight before he left. Billy appeared to show him down the stairs and out of the door. As soon as the door was closed, Mary came out onto the landing, clutching a letter.

'Another victim,' I said to her.

'Yes,' she said, musing. She ripped open the letter and read it through.

'Well?' I asked. She glanced at Billy, watching us from the stairs, and frowned. He left, unwillingly creeping into the kitchen.

'Mr Ballant is accused of unnatural acts,' she told me. 'With Mr Shirley.'

'I see,' I said. I was not shocked, and neither was she—a soldier's wife and a doctor's wife already knew far more than most women. But it carried a taint a man could not scrub off. It would need more than a whisper, but the libel itself had been enough to bring down some very powerful men, and ruin a few more careers very quietly.

'So the only two men in the case share a secret,' I said.

'Strange, isn't it?' Mary replied.

'What?'

'Most of the victims are women. Just two are men—Mr Shirley and Mr Ballant.'

'You think that makes him a suspicious character?'

'You know what Sherlock says,' Mary said. 'Suspect everyone.'

So I did. I set the Irregulars to follow Mr Ballant. They sent Jake, a thin, though tall, boy, who had a reputation for never being seen by his quarry. He was the best. And so, he was very annoyed when he lost Mr Ballant.

'Lost him?' I asked, incredulous. Jake was still getting his reward of crumpets and lemonade, but he picked at the crumpet reluctantly, as if he felt he didn't deserve it. 'Did he see you?'

'Could 'ave sworn he didn't,' Jake said disconsolately, sitting at my kitchen table. 'Followed 'im all the way down Oxford Street, and on the omnibus, 'im striding along bold as brass, never trying to lose me, and then, he just disappears.'

'Do you think he did it deliberately?' I asked. Jake nodded, eager to absolve himself.

'Yeah, I think he did, laid me a pretty trail and then just when I was too confident, he slipped away. And I tell you what—you don't just know how to do that. Someone's trained him.'

Trained him? Who would know how to do that? I could see why Adam Ballant might be suspicious of someone following him, but he would have to be very good to have seen Jake. It had taken some skill to evade him.

'Where did you lose his trail?' I asked.

'Whitechapel,' Jake answered, his mouth full of crumpet.

Billy had not been idle as we worked. He had tasks of his own. Billy had done his research diligently. He had read many of Patrick West's articles. He had researched the women Mr West had written of. He had drawn up complicated diagrams showing the connections between Mr West and possible victims. Then, after a few days, he had actually stationed himself outside Mr West's pleasant home in Kensal Rise—to observe only, he assured us. Now Billy sat at my kitchen table, sipping tea, and refusing cake. That wasn't a good sign.

'I waited there a whole day,' Billy said to Mary and me. 'I know no one saw me, but no one came out. In the end, I got talking to the policeman who walks that street.'

'And?' Mary pressed.

Billy took a deep breath, and continued.

'Patrick West is eighty-four, cannot walk without a stick and is completely blind,' Billy said dejectedly. 'He has a few apprentices who gather his information, and take down his dictation—and they're all young women. It's a complete dead end.'

Mary smiled, and turned away so Billy couldn't see.

'So, not our man, then,' I said softly. 'Sorry, Billy.' The poor boy had worked so hard on this, so proud to have a suspect of his own.

'I should have checked!' Billy cried out. 'I did all that work and it was all useless!'

'Not useless,' I reassured him. 'Not completely. At least it's another name crossed off the list.'

'It could have been crossed off days ago if I'd just checked the man could actually walk,' Billy said miserably. 'And wasn't blind. He could never have been that man at the docks.' He got down from the table and left the kitchen, no doubt off to find Wiggins.

'Oh dear,' Mary said, still smiling, when he had gone. 'I ought not to have laughed, really.'

'No,' I told her. Then I burst out laughing too.

Sir George Burnwell's house was a flashy, newly built, rather tasteless red-brick construction by the brink of the river in Twickenham.

'Badly placed,' Mary remarked. 'I'll wager the basements get flooded monthly.'

The Irregulars had been watching the house for a week. I'd told them I wanted to know who came and went, and by the way, just out of interest, what were the security arrangements? Wiggins had snorted, demanded to know if I took him for a babe in arms and offered to burgle the place for me. But when I told him we were looking for papers, he allowed that we were more likely to know what to look for, and agreed to just carry on following the comings and goings of the household.

I hadn't told him we were coming tonight, I just told him the task was done, and to stop watching. He'd have insisted on sending one of the Irregulars with us, and I was trying so hard not to pull those children into further crime.

It turned out Sir George hardly spent a moment of the day at his house, but he returned every night, no matter how late he was, no matter what amorous adventures he was currently pursuing. Micky, the smallest and shrewdest of Wiggins' boys, who was specially detailed to watch Sir George, was shocked by how many ladies the man was trying to seduce. And he wasn't trying to seduce rich ladies who knew how to handle an affair, or maidservants, who expected it, but the middle-class, respectable women who would fall deeply in love, and not survive his rejection and the loss of their reputation.

Sir George, however, seemed to prefer to sleep at home. No doubt he had certain comforts installed there. His servants were given Saturday night and Sunday morning off, with strict instructions not to come to the house during this time. They were even given money to sleep elsewhere. That left Sir George free to bring his most secret liaisons to his home, with no servants to spy and gossip.

However, the Irregulars had discovered that, on this particular Saturday, Sir George was attending a house party in the Cotswolds and therefore his house was completely empty.

'He won't leave the party,' Irene told us. 'I know what he's like. He's already seduced the mother and the eldest daughter. Rumour has it he has set his sights on the youngest daughter now. He'll be preparing the way this weekend. He won't leave until she is utterly charmed by him.'

'It'll destroy the whole family,' I murmured.

'He claims they seduced him,' Irene said darkly. 'That's his trick, to make it seem like they are the guilty party and he is an innocent man being taken advantage of.'

'Burglary isn't enough,' Mary said vehemently. 'Let's burn his house down.'

'Oh, we'll find a way of injuring him, never fear,' Irene told her, laughing gently. 'Perhaps, though, in a more subtle way. Even if he is not your criminal, he is certainly guilty of a great many crimes.'

We all three stood in the dark, in a lane by the river, close to Sir George's house in Twickenham. The river lapped up against the bank, creating a peaceful, soothing atmosphere, completely at odds with what we were planning to do. I don't know about the others, but I felt sick with nerves. But no, I did not once think we should go back.

Larch and chestnut trees arched above us, rustling gently in the wind. Animals darted, unseen, in the undergrowth, and occasionally, an owl hooted. There was only a thin sliver of moon, and the entire world was cast in grey and black shadow. On a night like this, in a place like this, it was all too easy to believe in the old gods, in Pan himself, whispering behind us, blowing gently on our cheeks. We were only a few miles away from Baker Street, yet it felt like a different world entirely.

Before us stood a high red-brick wall, with a small wooden door set into it. Wiggins had found the perfect entrance. The door had no key hole, and Irene oiled the hinges from a small bottle and simply pushed it open. We were lucky—it should have been bolted on the inside, but the servants were careless and the bolts were rusted open. Beyond the door lay a smooth lawn, almost black now in the night; beyond that, the three-storey square red-brick home lay silent and dark.

Though we knew there was no one in the house to see us, we still crept round the edge of the lawn, shrinking into the shadows of the trees and bushes.

Irene had met us here, in Twickenham, dressed like a man, in battered brown trousers and a loose jacket, a cap pulled down over her face. Mary had wanted to dress like a man too, but she had not been trained as an actress as Irene had, and doubted she could carry it off. Irene walked and carried herself like a man; Mary would have been all too obviously a woman in trousers. Besides, the only male clothes she had access to were John's and she would have been swamped in them. So instead, she wore her bottle-green walking habit, which had shorter skirts than her usual dresses, and no petticoats to get caught. Irene had warned us not to wear black, as it did not fade into shadows like grey and brown and green did, so I wore an old dress, black once, which had turned grey and lost all lustre.

You have never seen such an odd collection of house-breakers.

We went up to the large French windows on the ground floor that opened out onto the lawn. Irene studied the lock, as Mary kept watch. I kept out of the way.

'Can you do it?' Mary whispered.

'A very simple lock,' Irene said. 'You'd think he'd have better security arrangements.'

'Can you see it, in this light?' I asked.

'Just about. It's easier to pick locks by feel than sight anyway,' she told me as she pulled a thin wire and what looked like a nail file (which I'd read about in some ladies' magazine, but not seen for myself) out of her pocket and began to manipulate the lock.

'He probably keeps anything incriminating locked away in his study. That'll have better locks—and a safe too,' Mary said. I looked along the line of the house. There was just enough light to see, and I have always had good vision.

'Look,' Mary said, pointing upwards to the first floor, the second window along from where we stood. I looked up. The white moonlight shone directly onto the windows, casting sharp shadows and highlighting flaws that would not have been noticeable by day. I scrutinized the window Mary had pointed to. All the other windows had white painted frames, but the paint was old and blistered and was heavily worn where the sashes were pushed up and down. The paint on this window was pristine.

'Sealed, I bet,' Mary whispered.

'That must be his study,' I agreed.

The lock clicked open, and Irene led us into the dining room.

The curtains were half drawn inside the room, and we walked slowly, trying not to bump into anything. We could not see much, but what we could see was opulent and substantial. The table was large, mahogany, with chairs set around it. At one end of the room was a dumb waiter—Sir George clearly didn't want his meals interrupted by servants. Curtains shielded all kinds of alcoves around the edges of the room, and couches were scattered here and there. There was a trace of a thick perfume and the room felt airless, which I could imagine would cause a tightly laced woman to faint after a while. It looked like something out of one of the Gothic novels I secretly read on stormy winter evenings.

'A seducer's paradise,' Irene remarked.

'Wouldn't work on me,' I remarked, with more than a touch of asperity. Well, it wouldn't, not now. But when I had been young and impressionable...Irene smiled at me, as if secretly reading my thoughts.

'Nor me, but neither of us is a romantic fifteen-year-old,' she replied.

'Fifteen?' Mary exclaimed, pushing back the curtains over the alcoves, either trying to find the door or being unashamedly nosy.

'His favourite age,' Irene replied grimly.

'I still say we burn his house down,' Mary said, darkly angry, as she found the door and opened it. We had not been whispering; we knew no one could hear us. The house had that waiting, echoing feeling that buildings do when they are empty. Behind me, I could hear Mary and Irene chatting with each other.

'Does your husband know you have such a pyromania?' Irene asked.

Mary giggled. 'Oh yes!' she replied happily.

I knew the joking was just to cover nerves. I imagined they were like me, inwardly quaking, jumping at every single noise, nervous to touch anything, in case we left a trace, no matter how invisible. The hallway was opulent too, full of rich colours and glittering fittings, with doors leading off all over the place. The house felt not just lifeless, but joyless—as if the acts of pleasure that took place here were just a matter of a mechanical act rather than a matter of love.

The stairs rose above us, and we climbed up them to the first floor, counting along to what we thought would be the room with the sealed window. There was a heavy mahogany door to the room with a large lock, but when Irene turned the door knob, it swung open.

'He's an idiot,' Irene remarked.

'Or very clever,' Mary mused thoughtfully. She was frowning as Irene went into the darkened room, and motioned for us to wait outside. She peered round, and then waved us in. We were silent now. It was beginning to feel serious.

There was a candle and matches on the desk. Irene placed the candle on the floor by the desk and lit it. Shielded by the wall, it cast a dim light, whilst not being visible from outside. We looked around.

The study was, like everything else in the house, stupefyingly dull. There was a thick green carpet, with thick green velvet curtains looped at the window. A large, heavy mahogany desk (the man must have destroyed an entire mahogany forest furnishing this house) was by the window, with a row of locked drawers and a green leather blotter—but no blotting or writing paper. One wall was lined with books, and the other walls were hung with hunting prints on panelling. In the centre was a large table with ornate legs, the top covered in scattered maps and timetables. Obviously he had been planning his country weekend carefully. Sir George Burnwell might be an accomplished seducer, but judging by his study, he was a deeply boring man.

That was when I started to think we were wrong.

In the far corner, by the window, sat a massive bronze-green safe. Irene and Mary stood in front of it, assessing it. It was three feet by three feet, and stood on four legs designed to look like lions' feet, which were clamped to the floor. There was no manu-facturer's name, but I could see where the plaque had been before it was removed. Of course, if someone knew who made the safe, they could also find the original plans. The door of the safe not only had two large bronze key holes, but a combination lock too. It looked impenetrable.

'Can you…' Mary asked.

'I doubt it,' Irene said, staring at the safe, but not touching it. Mary reached out to it, but I grasped her arm and stopped her.

'Look,' I said, pointing. A thin wire led from the back of the safe and into the wall. It looked like a telegraph wire.

'Electric wire,' Irene told me. 'Either it will give anyone who touches the safe an electric shock, or it will send a signal to someone. I'm sorry, Martha, I have no idea how to crack this safe.'

It all felt like such an anticlimax, but I admit, there was a hint of relief in my sigh.

'We'd better leave then, whilst we can,' I said. I bent down to blow out the candle, but noticed Mary standing in front of the safe, smiling slightly.

'Mary?' I asked.

'An easily opened back door,' she murmured. 'An unlocked study door—and then an impregnable safe? That doesn't make sense.'

'No, it doesn't,' Irene agreed.

'It feels like…it feels like we were led here,' Mary continued, still staring at the safe, still smiling that strange smile. 'As if everything was designed to pull us towards this safe, which we cannot open, and so there we stop.'

'Mary?' I asked.

'Clever man,' she murmured. 'Leading us here, and then sending us away.'

'Mary, can you explain?' Irene demanded. Mary turned round to face us, grinning widely.

'Do you know what I would do if I had something very precious to keep safe? Pictures, jewels, papers, that sort of thing? Something that must never be found?' she asked. 'I'd buy the biggest safe I could find. I'd put it where everyone can see it. I'd make it easy to get to. And then…I'd make it impossible to crack. I'd make it the kind of safe that someone would spend hours trying to get into, and then fail, or just give up and walk away. The kind of safe that looks like it'd keep all the secrets, so no one would look anywhere else. And then I'd put all my secret papers in a shabby old cardboard box in plain sight.'

Oh my. What a clever plan. Why would you search anywhere else except that challenging safe? And even if you did crack it open and find no secrets, you'd assume there was an even more formidable safe somewhere—you'd never think to look elsewhere. Hiding in plain sight!

Mary's deduction was worthy of Sherlock Holmes himself.

'Mary, you are a devious woman, and I hope John Watson appreciates that,' Irene said, laughing.

'He does, he likes it,' Mary told her. 'Now, let's search the rest of the room for some sort of shabby old box.'

'It might not be here,' I objected. It seemed like such a clever plan for a man like Sir George.

'No, it's here,' Mary asserted. 'The rest of his house is for seduction. Anyone could stumble across it.'

'I agree,' Irene added. 'This is his room alone, the one he can be sure no one would want to enter—or is allowed to. I bet even the servants don't come in when he's not here to keep an eye on them.'

'John doesn't allow the servants into his study either,' Mary said. 'Men don't, as a rule. I'm certain the papers are here.'

We all looked around the room. There were a few boxes scattered on the floor and the bookshelves—gun boxes, I guessed. They were wooden and polished and locked. Mary checked the bookcases, pulling the books out to make sure nothing was behind them. Most seemed never to have been opened. Irene went through the drawers in the desk.

'I found his bank book,' Irene said. 'He's not rich, certainly not rich enough to keep up a home like this.'

'Then how does he pay for it? And his lifestyle?' Mary asked.

'Credit, for now, probably,' Irene said. 'But sooner or later he's going to need to pay the bills.'

So the man needed money. Then I noticed, behind the candle, between the bookshelf and the desk, an old travelling case. It was battered brown leather, about two feet square. The monogram on top had nearly worn away. It looked as if it had been thrown there after a journey and never put away. It looked unimportant.

I moved the candle to one side, knelt down, and pulled the case out onto the floor. I pulled off the dusty lid and peered inside.

On top was a tray full of glass bottles. Whatever was in the bottles had long dried away to a sticky residue. The tray fitted tightly, and I had to pull at it hard to remove it. Underneath that should have been more fixtures and fittings—but they had gone. It was full of letters. Dozens of them. All kinds of letters, from plain white ones covered with sharp black ink to scented violet letters with palest purple feminine writing. From the case rose a mixture of perfumes—rose, jasmine, and more musky scents I could not identify. It was an entire case of love letters—and down one side of it was a heavy black ledger.

'This is it!' I hissed. Mary and Irene came over to join me. I pulled out the ledger and they pulled out handfuls of letters.

The ledger consisted of a record of his conquests. Each page was given over to one woman, with her name at the top, a place and a time, and a note of the technique he had used to charm her into bed. There were a few little odd facts here and there—the placement of a mole, a liking for Turkish delight. One or two of the names had amounts of money written next to them, but not as much as I would have expected from a blackmailer—the odd hundred, here and there. I was surprised by how many names I recognized, but these were names from the papers and court circulars, not from my case. There was no mention of the Whitechapel Lady or Laura Shirley.

I felt uneasy. The idea of keeping the ledger here was clever, I admit, but the actual book showed little sign of intelligence. Oh, Sir George was devious and cunning as a snake, but he seemed to have little of the insight into human nature that would create the trick with the safe. No, someone had told him that, someone cleverer than he. There was someone there, in the background— far in the background, watching him, guiding him...oh.

Oh.

Not him. He was a seducer, and blackmailer and abuser of women, but he was the weapon, not the perpetrator. Perhaps he was being used to destroy these women, prise secrets from them, then hand those secrets over to whoever controlled him. Maybe he didn't even know he was being controlled. Perhaps he had taken the suggestion of the safe and easily picked door locks as a damned clever idea, never realizing that meant whoever had suggested it now knew they could sneak in any time they pleased and read these letters and the ledger.

Not him. Sir George Burnwell could be crossed off my list. I sat back on my heels, and in my head, I swore a little. I swore a lot.

'These are very foolish letters,' Mary said, reading through them, not noticing my sudden distraction.

'Love letters generally are,' Irene said dryly. 'Why do we insist on immortalizing our feelings so? Engraved jewellery, letters...'

'Photographs,' Mary interjected.

'Photographs,' Irene agreed, amused. 'I've been as foolish as any of these women, I know.'

'Good grief, what language!' Mary gasped, peering at an ivory-white letter covered in florid handwriting. 'I'm surprised the page doesn't blush. And this one—no, wait, that's a solicitor's letter. And that's a boot-maker's bill. It's all mixed in together.'

'No sense of order at all. Not what I expected from our black-mailer,' Irene said, puzzled. 'Surely he'd be more organized?'

I looked up. I could see she was beginning to come to the same conclusion I had.

'Have you noticed,' Mary said, 'none of these letters make any mention of blackmail? Though several refer to lending Sir George money.'

'Lending?' I asked, standing up again and peering over Irene's shoulder at her letter. It was on pink paper, very thick, and quoted Byron. Judging by the handwriting, this girl was barely out of the schoolroom.

'To pay his tailor's bill, his hotel bill, various debts of honour,' Mary explained, flipping through several letters. 'But looking at what they've written, they are giving him the money through a twisted sense of love, not blackmail.'

Mary was beginning to realize it too.

'I've looked through this ledger,' I said, holding it up. 'Of the names I recognize, all are still alive and prospering.'

'He's not our man, is he?' Mary said to me, understanding. Irene shook her head.

'No, he isn't,' I agreed. 'He is foul and disgusting and should be stopped, but he is not the one destroying these women's lives. We were wrong. Someone else is behind this.'

We all three stood in Sir George Burnwell's study looking at each other. We felt oddly deflated, disappointed and scared now. Not only were we wrong, we were no closer to discovering the truth than before. 'His tailor charges a prodigious amount of money,' Irene replied inconsequentially, staring at a letter. 'Far more than I imagine his clothes are actually worth.'

'So does his solicitor,' Mary added lightly. I knew what they were trying to do, they were trying to cheer me up, but I felt only a great weight upon me.

'According to this, he has been named as co-respondent in five divorce cases!' Mary added.

'Only five?' Irene replied dryly. 'There's evidence for at least eleven in my hands right here…oh, that's what we'll do!' she cried, suddenly excited. 'We'll take the lot with us! The letters, the ledger, everything!'

'Why?' I asked warily.

'Why?' Irene demanded. 'Do you know what damage Sir George could do if he published these letters? Do you know what these letters represent?'

'Some of these women have stolen items for him,' Mary said, waving a letter at me. 'He's corrupting them, and this is his proof!'

'Proof of his guilt!' Irene added. 'We know someone who could use that!'

'And besides, it means the secrets don't fall into *his* hands. You know, the man we're trying to catch,' Mary told me. 'Because I think even if Sir George is not our man, I bet he has some connection to him, he sells his secrets to him.'

'Not wrong, then,' I said, looking up at her. She was right. They were both right. 'Not the man, but a step away from the man. Another link in the chain.'

'Another move in the game,' Irene murmured. 'Now it's your move, Martha.'

Oh, I knew what to do. Take the letters from Sir George, keep them safe from our blackmailer, give them to Mr Holmes, and achieve several objectives at once. I pushed the ledger down the front of my dress.

'Mr Holmes will never let him get away with this. One day, somehow, he'll find a way to deal with Sir George,' I said.

'Damned right!' Mary cried. She looked round at our surprised faces. 'Sorry, it's something John says.' Laughing again, with a purpose again, and justice on our side again, we began picking up the letters and stuffing them into every pocket we could find, down our dresses, even in our garters. We couldn't take the case, it was too large and awkward, but we were taking as much out of it as we could possibly carry.

All Roads Lead to Whitechapel

The case was half empty when we heard the front door slam, and the sound of laughter from downstairs. Feminine laughter, and then a man's voice, well-bred, amused.

Sir George Burnwell had returned.

The Great Escape

We froze, crouched on the floor, in the dimmest of moonlight, gathered around the case of love letters. Irene quickly leaned forward and blew out the candle, and we stayed as still as we could, barely breathing. We listened as Sir George and his lady (who did not quite laugh like a young society miss—he must have been very firmly rebuffed and returned to an easier alternative) climbed up the stairs to the first floor, down the corridor, up to the door of the study. There he seemed to pause for a second and we held our breath, but the pair walked past it, down the corridor into a room further down.

We three breathed again, and stood up slowly. My knee cracked as I stood, and it sounded unnaturally loud in the tense silence, but no one came. We could dimly hear the sound of laughter and glasses being knocked together and chairs creaking. Irene raised her fingers to her lips (as if either of us would speak!)

and pointed towards the door. We could see it outlined in the yellow light from the gas lamp in the corridor, just enough to guide us to it. We walked across the room as silently as we could, uncomfortably aware of papers rustling in various pockets and garments. Irene reached for the door, just as we heard Sir George say:

'Just a moment, dear, it's in my study. I'll fetch it.' His footsteps started down the corridor. In a flash Irene turned the key in the lock and pulled it out, letting the keyhole guard drop. Barely a moment later, the handle rattled as Sir George pulled at the door.

We backed away to the other side of the room, staring at the door in horror. What if the lock was faulty? What if he broke it down?

'He'll know we're here if it's locked,' Mary whispered, as Sir George swore and shook the door.

Irene shook her head and showed Mary the key. If it wasn't in the lock, hopefully he wouldn't know it was locked from the inside.

'Left the key upstairs,' Sir George called to his lady friend. 'I won't be a moment.' We heard him pause before the door a moment, puzzled. Perhaps if he had been less drunk he might have noticed that something was wrong. Then we listened to him walk away and climb the stairs to the second floor.

We heard the lady drifting up and down the corridor, singing softly to herself. We couldn't get past her. We certainly couldn't run for it. Not with all the letters overflowing from our pockets. There was no time, even if I had been as young and fit as Irene and Mary.

'Now what?' Mary whispered. Irene looked round, and then began pulling at the window, trying to push it open. But this was the window we had seen from outside, the one that had looked sealed, and it didn't move.

'Help me!' she hissed.

'We can't jump from here,' Mary advised her, though she went to the window and started helping Irene to raise it. 'There's a stone terrace down there; we'd break our legs.'

'We're not going to jump,' Irene said through gritted teeth. The window was beginning to loosen. I stood by the door, listening, ready to warn them as soon as I heard Sir George returning. I could still hear him blundering upstairs.

'Then what?' Mary demanded.

'I'm going to use a trick Mr Holmes taught me,' Irene replied, grinning wickedly in the moonlight. 'Martha, bring the case of letters over here—and pass me those matches.'

I did as she said, as Sir George, upstairs, finally stood still. I could imagine him up there, realizing the key wasn't there, remembering where he left it, working out that someone was in here.

Do you know, I was not afraid? Discovery, shame, imprisonment, possibly even death stared me in the face, but I was not afraid. Instead I was quietly, so silently, intensely alive, and I liked it.

Upstairs, Sir George cried 'Damn it!' and rushed for the stairs. He had worked it out.

At that moment, Mary gave one enormous shove, and the window flew open.

I heard Sir George thunder down the stairs. Irene was trying to light the matches, but they would not strike. She had to discard two, three matches as faulty.

Sir George fell against the door. He shouted at his companion to get back into the other room.

Irene tried again. This time the flame caught, and held.

Sir George shouted through the door, 'I know you're there. There's no way out!'

Irene dropped the match into the case of letters. For a moment, nothing happened, then a tiny flame flickered in the middle. Irene blew on it to fan it.

'Who sent you?' Sir George bellowed, as he smashed his shoulder against the door. The wooden frame shuddered, but held. 'I warn you, I'm armed.'

The flame was still so small, but growing.

'To hell with warnings!' Sir George shouted. 'I'll shoot

you where you stand!' He slammed against the door again. It still held, but I could see the frame splintering. One more thrust against the door, and he'd be in.

The letters were fully alight now. I heard Sir George line up to shove against the door one more time. The frame was worn. This was the moment on which it all turned.

'Fire!'

Irene had thrown the flaming case of remaining letters out onto the lawn. The lady, who had left the corridor and was waiting in the other room, had seen it from her window and she screamed with all her might.

'Fire, fire!' she yelled, at the top of her voice.

Sir George swore again and ran down the corridor to find a window. Holmes had taught Irene that when someone screams fire, they grab what is most precious to them. She had guessed that for Sir George, it was his letters. He would assume we had them and were out on the lawn burning them. The woman continued screaming, and we heard Sir George curse loudly as he worked out what was burning outside. He ran further down the corridor; we hoped he was on his way down to the garden.

'Now!' Irene said, and we ran for the door. Irene turned the key quickly, and flung open the door. 'Front door!' she ordered, and we headed down the corridor, towards the front stairs.

'Halt!' Sir George called. He had seen us and I remembered he had warned he would shoot us where we stood. The warning was not in vain. Something ricocheted off the wall, and smashed a mirror as I ran past it—he was shooting at us! We hurtled down the stairs, running faster than I'd ever done in my life.

'Halt, you scoundrels!' Sir George called, and fired again. He was twenty yards behind, but that was close enough to hit us. The shot passed through my skirt and grazed Irene's leg, but she ran on regardless. She pulled open the front door, and held it open for Mary and me as we ran through. Then, giving a cheeky tip of her hat to Sir George, thus making sure the only shape he remembered was a male one, she ran through the opening, slammed the door behind us, and joined us as we ran down the drive. Sir George standing by the front door called after us, 'Who sent you? Who sent you here?'

We ran, and kept running, down little alleyways and tree-darkened lanes until we reached the main street. It was well lit, and the shops were still open, so we could blend into the crowd. I was out of breath, and convinced everyone was looking at us, but Irene made us slow down, breathe gently, and walk along as if nothing had happened. In this way, occasionally glancing in shop windows, and buying apples from a street vendor, we finally reached the railway station.

I saw a glimpse of the three of us reflected in the train window as it pulled into the station. For a moment, I barely recognized us. I saw one middle-aged woman, one pretty young woman, and one slender young man. We all looked very respectable and well behaved. There was no hint we'd burgled a well-known seducer, stolen half his secret papers (still stuffed in our clothes), started a fire, been shot at—and got away with it all.

We managed to get a carriage to ourselves and settled down for the train ride back into London. Once we were sure we were alone and on our way, and unhurt—apart from Irene's bullet graze, which she dismissed with 'I've had worse'—we looked at each other and then burst out laughing. We were laughing in relief, and joy and disbelief and just because we could, and it felt so good.

I handed the ledger to Irene and we gathered all the letters together.

'What will you do with them?' Mary asked.

'Such a lot of secrets here,' Irene mused, glancing through the ledger. 'So many lives he could have ruined.' She snapped the ledger shut. 'I shall post them all to Mr Holmes, unless you want to deal with these yourselves?'

I agreed with her. We had enough to do with our own case. I did not want to involve myself in Sir George's convoluted and filthy affairs. 'He'll know what to do with it all. He'll use it to destroy Sir George, when the time is right,' I assured her. 'And discreetly too, which is more than could be said for the police.'

'Why post it?' Mary asked. 'Why do we not just give it to him at 221b? Oh, yes, I see, you don't want him to know it came from us.'

'No, I don't,' I agreed, leaning back in my seat. I was exhausted now, but it was a good kind of exhaustion. It was not the kind of restless tiredness that I usually experienced, which kept me irritably awake all night and worn out all day. The kind of tiredness that came from a day spent doing nothing worthwhile. No, this time I felt I could sleep the sleep of the just.

'Won't Dr Watson wonder where you are?' Irene asked Mary.

'He and Sherlock are caught up in a case,' Mary explained. 'They're out all hours, and locked away when they are at home. They won't notice either Martha or me not being at home for a while.'

'Convenient,' Irene said wryly.

'Very,' Mary replied with a smile.

We sat in silence for a while, letting the night drift by us. Out there everything was calm and peaceful, dim countryside giving way to warmly lit suburban villas. Irene read the ledger, frowning every once in a while. Mary dozed in her seat, curled up like a cat. I stared out of the window. Every so often I would catch my reflection, and I could see how different I looked: younger, happier, more at peace. Being a criminal suited me, it seemed.

'Well, that settles it,' Irene said, closing the ledger. 'Sir George Burnwell is definitely not our man.'

'How can you be certain?' Mary said sleepily, half opening her eyes. Irene looked at her, very directly.

'Because I have read this book from cover to cover and one name does not appear.'

'Whose?' Mary asked.

'Mine,' Irene replied.

Well, she had certainly succeeded in surprising us. Mary's eyes opened wide, and I sat up in my seat. Irene smiled, a touch bitterly.

'That is why I'm back in England,' she explained. 'My husband received a packet of papers, with the promise of more to follow. The papers detailed certain incidents in my past which I was under the impression no one but myself and the parties involved knew about.'

Irene stared through the window, not seeing us, not the land around us, but perhaps, seeing her husband, the man she loved, the man she had given up her whole life for.

'He was horrified,' Irene continued, in the same steady voice. 'Not at what I had done, but that anyone could behave in such an ungentlemanly manner as to send these papers to him. I told him I would come back to England, alone, and make it stop. He agreed.' Irene smiled to herself, a soft, sweet smile I hadn't seen on her before. 'He really is quite perfect.'

'So that's why you were so eager to help us,' I realized.

Irene turned her attention back to me.

'One reason,' she said. 'I think I would have helped anyway, after what you told me about what this man had done. It just so happened that your cause and mine coincided.'

'But it's not Sir George,' I said. 'You didn't have an affair with him?'

'No, I would not!' Irene said, snorting in disgust. 'But if this is not merely a record of his seductions, but a record of victims of this blackmailer, I would be in the book.'

'And you are not,' I said quietly. 'Sir George is a scoundrel, a cad, and many other things I don't even have words for. But he is not the man we hunt.'

'No,' she agreed. 'Tomorrow you must start again, from the beginning. But first...'

'First?'

She smiled, but not like before. It was an odd, tight smile.

'First I have an impossibility to eliminate.'

CHAPTER

12

The Impossibility of Miss Adler

Many people have asked me what exactly the relationship was between Sherlock Holmes and Irene Adler, to which I always replied that it was none of my business. (And none of yours, either, I was tempted to add!)

In truth, I had no idea what their relationship was. It seemed to be a fluid, amorphous thing, never pinned down, never defined, never really understood by either of them. I know they respected each other deeply. I know that, to a certain extent, they relied on each other to behave a certain way. He was the hero, she was the dubious lady, but both had honour—at least, that was what they expected from each other. But beyond that, I do not know. Sometimes I believed they hated each other. When he railed against women in general and *her* in particular, when she stormed out of 221b shouting 'blasted man!', I thought they would never talk again. Perhaps they saw each other as adversaries, occasionally as colleagues. Perhaps there was an odd sort of friendship there. Every once in a while, I thought I could discern a trace of love, but I always was a romantic.

Oh yes, their relationship did not begin and end with *A Scandal in Bohemia*. There was so much more that John never revealed, perhaps because he understood it as little as I, perhaps out of a sense of respect for both of them.

Did I see love there? Mr Holmes and Irene?

She could love, I know that. She loved so deeply and so completely, but then Godfrey Norton was, by all accounts, an easy man to love. Perhaps she could love in a different way, a less comfortable, more stirring way. Could she love someone as remote and controlled and cold as Mr Sherlock Holmes?

And he. That man. He always denied his ability to love, and yet he did, against his will, against his nature, against his very knowledge. John told me once that he caught an occasional glimpse of a great heart behind the great brain. Perhaps some of that was given to Irene—but if so, he never told me. Perhaps he never told himself.

So no, I cannot tell you what their relationship was. What I can tell you is that though it changed from day to day, hour to hour, with each new discovery of a hidden part of the other and themselves, it was, as the old sonnet says, 'an ever fix'd mark'. All through their lives, Sherlock Holmes and Irene Adler danced round each other, coming close, drifting away, never losing sight of the other.

Given all that it was hardly surprising that Mr Holmes was the impossibility Irene had to eliminate. He could have discovered the secrets in that packet of papers sent to her husband. He might, in one of his harsh, cold moods, have felt it was his duty to warn Irene's husband exactly who she was. The packet had been sent from London, after all. I knew better than to suspect Mr Holmes, of course, but she did not. Not then, anyway. So I did not stop her when she arrived to see him the morning after our burglary. Besides, I wanted to see what would happen when they met face to face.

She stood in my kitchen in a rich red gown, hat tipped coquettishly over one eye, somehow looking less vulnerable than she had in her men's clothes the night before. She looked round the room—and noticed the vent. She knew what it was the moment she saw it. I suspect she had listened through a few vents in her time.

'Very useful,' she remarked.

'Don't tell Mr Holmes,' I said quickly.

'I have no intention of telling him!' she said indignantly. 'However, please do me a favour and keep it closed for the next half hour? I will tell you everything, I promise. I just...'

'I understand,' I said. Irene wanted to be able to pick and choose what the 'everything' she told me was. She nodded, and headed towards the stairs—then paused. She stood there, at the foot of the seventeen steps leading to Mr Holmes' rooms, her hand on the newel post, just staring up at his door.

'You look very beautiful,' I reassured her. She turned to look at me, and there was uncertainty in her face. Beauty was not what she needed right now. 'And very assertive,' I added. Those were the magic words. She took a breath and headed up to his room.

I kept to my word and did not open the vent, though it was a hard-won battle, I can tell you. This is what Irene told me when she came downstairs again.

'I let myself into his rooms, quite as if I had every right to be there. He was standing by the window, alone, peering down into the street, his hands behind his back. I wonder now, did he see me arrive? He did not seem startled or disturbed by my entrance. He turned to look at me, his hands still clasped, and nodded once.

"'Miss Adler,'" he said.

"'Mrs Norton,'" I corrected. He did not seem shaken, as you assured me he would be, not even in the slightest. Nor did he seem pleased or angry or show any other emotion. He was the stone image of cool politeness.

'Except his hand. His left hand. He had unclasped his hands to gesture me to sit, and then he kept tightening his left hand, over and over again. I do not think he knows he does it. It is as if any emotion he does feel is clasped in that left hand, and he keeps tightening his grip, lest it should escape.

"'Welcome back to London. You are well, Mrs Norton?'" he asked, calmly, a polite inquiry, nothing more, as I sat down at his table. If he was surprised to see me there, he concealed it very well. But then he would, wouldn't he? God forbid Sherlock Holmes should show an emotion! He continued to stand by the window, clear daylight illuminating every plane of his face. I wonder if he is aware how handsome he is? He has a stern, unforgiving profile, his face is all angles and sharpness, but perhaps he knows that when he smiles, it is enough to set a girl's heart beating like a drum. Yet he did not smile, and I am not a girl.

"'I am well,'" I told him. I could damned well play this politeness game too! "'Though I have reason to believe someone wishes me ill.'"

'He stopped tightening his left hand then.

"'A packet was sent to my husband, Mr Godfrey Norton.'"

"'The solicitor,'" he said, his voice dripping with scorn.

"'The solicitor,'" I agreed amiably. "'The packet contained many details of my former life. Details I had kept from him. Sordid details.'"

'I own, Martha, I blushed. Not at the thought of what the packet contained, but because I had kept the facts from my husband. Facts Mr Holmes knew, facts I would carelessly tell him, but facts the man whose ring I wore did not know. Mr Holmes' expression did not change. He merely watched me.

"'Including some details I thought only you and I knew," I finished, sharper than I had intended.

'His face did not flicker. "You think I sent these papers to your husband?"

'I looked at him then, and he looked back at me, so very steadily. The silence in the room hung so thickly that the sound of the hansom cab driver calling outside seemed to ring through us.

"'No, I don't think it," I said, and I believe my voice was barely above a whisper. Mr Holmes' gaze is a fearsome thing to withstand, and yet I like the honesty of it. It is sometimes a relief to find someone before whom you cannot hide. I have played a part all my life yet all I am to Sherlock Holmes is Irene Adler.

"'But I must eliminate all possibilities," I added. He smiled at that, a quick, involuntary twitch of his mouth. "Given the secrets contained in these papers, you are a possible suspect. A faint one, but a possibility nonetheless."

"'I could assure you I am innocent, but then so would a guilty man," he said, without a trace of anger.

"'Quite. But now I have spoken to you I am…I mean…I do not believe you capable of such spiteful behaviour," I said, and I had stammered! I actually stammered. I don't know why. He merely inclined his head in thanks to me.

"'Perhaps you would be better chasing the motive," he said, quite as if I were a fellow detective asking for advice. "'I believe whoever sent this packet wishes to destroy my marriage," I told him, "persuade my husband to abandon me and leave me alone and unprotected."

"'Miss Adler, you may be alone, but you are more than capable of protecting yourself."

'He would insist on using my maiden name!

"'You know that; whoever sent the packet does not. Another reason I now do not believe you sent the papers."

"'No, I did not," he said, standing by the window, watching me, and only me. Not a single noise in the street outside drew his attention. No, he would not send those papers. He has honour, that man. A strange, unconventional kind of honour, I admit, but honour all the same.

"'No, you did not," I agreed. I started to fiddle with my gloves. I always do fiddle when I'm thinking. "It seemed like a dirty blackmailer's trick, but no one has tried to blackmail me lately. Thank you for your help." I moved to stand, but he spoke quietly.

"'Did it have the desired effect?'"

'I sat back down in my chair and looked at him, so clear and defined in the light from the window, so utterly unreadable.

"'My husband," I said, choosing my words deliberately, "read the entire packet of papers. He then asked me if I had ever been cruel, and I said not to anyone who was not rich, healthy and proud. He asked me if that portion of my life was over. I said it was. He then handed the packet over to me, and asked me if I cared for some coffee. He has not spoken about it since."

"'Then the blackmailer did not succeed?'"

"'No, Mr Holmes. It is true that I am here alone, but I am here investigating these letters, with both his knowledge and blessing. Business affairs keep him in the States, but if I call, he will come. He will be calm, he will be magnanimous, he will be reasonable and he will love me with all his heart and soul. He will never throw my past in my face, and he will never walk away from me unless I behave dishonourably. That is the man I married."

"'Yes," he said quietly. "That is the man you married. I was there."

'We were both silent for a moment. I cannot tell you what we thought—he, because I do not know, myself because I only watched him. Then, all businesslike again, he spoke. "Do you wish me to track down whoever sent you this package? Is that your commission for me?'"

"'No, I can manage that for myself," I said, rising.

"'Alone?'"

"'I have help. The very best help."

'For a moment he looked puzzled. Then he glanced down

at the floor, as if he would peer right through it into your kitchen and see you down here. Then he looked back up at me.

"'Sometimes I forget I do not live here alone," he said ruefully.

"'Well, you shouldn't," I admonished him, as I headed towards the door. "Mrs Hudson and Mrs Watson are very intelligent and stimulating company." Oh, I do enjoy teasing that man, and leaving him all bemused like that!

'I had just opened the door when he called out, "Irene!"

'He had such a note of urgency in his voice, I turned back, and forgot to tell him to call me Mrs Norton.

"'You may not know what you are getting into..." he started to say.

"'I know perfectly well..."

"'You may but Mrs Hudson and Mrs Watson may not!" he snapped. Do you know, my dear, I think he cares for you? Both of you, in his odd way. But emotions are something he has no room for in his attic of a mind, so he throws them away. Or so he thinks, until one day, something will happen to shove those self-same emotions right in front of him.

"'I will not offer my help, or intrude," he said, more calmly. "I understand why you must do whatever you are doing alone. I applaud it. But Miss Adler," and he came across to where I stood, still in the doorway, half in and half out of his rooms. "Sometimes, the puzzle is just a game, and it is studied and played and solved and you walk away. But sometimes, the puzzle becomes something much darker, more dangerous, deadly even. No one walks away untouched. I am here, if you need me."

'He meant it. He would keep us safe, all of us, if we asked. Do not be afraid to ask, will you? For as I left, he walked back into his rooms, his left hand clutched so tight the knuckles were white, and he murmured, as much to himself as to me, "Be careful. For God's sake, all of you, be careful."'

Irene stopped and looked at me across the kitchen table. It was not the story I had been expecting. I expected badinage, or flirting, or even anger. I had not expected cool conversation and emotions tightly hidden in a clasping hand. I had not expected him to know we were helping Irene, or his concern for the three of us. I was touched, and a little sad, for both Mr Holmes and Irene.

Irene rose.

'I said I would solve this myself, but you and Mary are far further along than I had reached. I have to admit, you seem to be better at this particular game than I am,' she told me seriously. 'You have the mind to solve this, Martha. And the skills, too— you and Mary.'

She glanced round my clean, tidy kitchen, her eyes calculating and thoughtful. She was planning her next move, but I could not read it in her face.

'I act, but you two think,' Irene said, reaching out and slightly moving a tea cup on the table. 'That's what this case needs—thought. Therefore,' she concluded, leaving the cup alone and looking at me, very directly, 'I will leave this case with you.'

'To us?' I questioned. 'Irene…'

'I will draw back, until you tell me to act,' she said to me, overriding my objection. 'Martha, I have lost all the contacts and influence I had when I lived here before. I also know that you know more than you are telling me.'

I looked up at her. She was right, but how had she known? I had kept other women's secrets from her. I had kept my own deductions from her. I kept the fact that for a brief second, just the briefest of moments, I had suspected her. She had so many skills, so many talents that an opera singer from New Jersey had no business having.

'I need you more than you need me, right now,' she said to me gently, and I felt a wave of guilt for my suspicions. 'Mary and you are most kind, and interesting company, but I am extraneous to this investigation.'

'No,' I said, trying to tell her I wanted her to stay.

'Yes,' she said. 'I made a mistake. I made an emotional judgement, and it was wrong, and very misguided.'

She did not glance up, but I did, towards Mr Holmes, silent in his rooms.

'I was a fool,' she admitted. 'This case, all of it, has shaken me more than I can admit. I think I would be best served by passing the case over to you. I am too emotionally involved. I have full confidence you will give me a satisfactory answer. I shall leave this in your capable hands. However,' she said, standing and pulling on her gloves, 'if you require any more nefarious help, you know where to find me. I am completely at your disposal.' She smiled mischievously. 'I expect to hear from you very soon.'

I cleaned furiously that whole afternoon. I always found cleaning very conducive to thinking. I turned the case over and over in my mind whilst polishing banisters and blacking grates and sweeping carpets. And always, all afternoon and into the early evening, just at the edge of my hearing, I heard Mr Holmes pacing up and down.

It was dark and the gas lamps were being lit when Mary came running into 221b and straight into the kitchen. She looked white as a sheet, and stood in the doorway, panting for breath.

'Oh Martha!' she gasped. 'Oh, Martha…'

She held out the evening paper.

The headline, big and bold across the front, read: 'New Ripper Outrage' and underneath that, 'Notable Whitechapel Resident Murdered'.

I read the article carefully, and then again to be certain, and then side by side with Mary to make sure we understood.

The story was florid and sensationalist, but the facts were these.

A woman—a respectable woman—in Whitechapel had been murdered. It could not have been suicide, nor an accident. She had been stabbed several times, with a large knife. She had been slit from sternum to belly. Her entrails had been removed and scattered around the room. Her tongue had been cut out and torn to pieces. The room swam in her blood. This was not a prostitute. This was not even one of the thousands of homeless, nameless women. This woman had a home, and a name everyone knew. Not her real name, but a name given to her. The ripped woman was known to one and all as the Whitechapel Lady.

The Game Changes

Murder. It was murder now. Mr Holmes was right: the puzzle had become something far darker. The game had changed.

Perhaps we should have called in Mr Holmes then. We did not even discuss it this time. We were under an obligation we were honour-bound to fulfil ourselves. An obligation to the dead.

I think Mary would have been incensed if I had even mentioned handing the case over to Mr Holmes. She was never quite as much in awe of him as I was. Besides, Mary liked to do things her own way. She never quite obeyed the rules all good wives should have obeyed.

Mary Watson suddenly appeared in my kitchen two days after her wedding to John. We had become friends, but our friendship was still new, and we were still discovering the character of each other.

I was standing at the counter, ostensibly kneading bread, but actually listening to the conversation coming through the open vent. Mr Holmes was telling John about his latest case. I was so caught up in listening that I stopped kneading and stood there, hands half covered in dough, head turned towards the vent, utterly unaware that Mary was standing in the doorway, watching. It was only when she gave a discreet little cough that I turned around to see her there.

I was horrified to be caught eavesdropping. My stomach dropped, I felt the colour fade from my face. She would tell; I knew she would. She would tell Mr Holmes and John that I listened to them, that I was a gossip, or worse, a lonely old woman. How could she not? I was eavesdropping on the most private of conversations! They would despise me. They would shut me out!

'You can hear everything that goes on in Mr Holmes' room through that vent?' she whispered. I swallowed, and nodded.

'Mary...' I started to say, but she interrupted.

'How wonderful! I always wondered what John and Sherlock talked of.'

I'm afraid I gaped, rather like a fish. Of all the things I expected to hear, that was not one of them.

'Do you mind if I join you?'

'Of course, be my guest,' I said. She came and stood beside me, and started to pat the dough I had kneaded into a tin. She smiled at me, the loveliest, most confiding smile I had seen in a long while.

'This is going to be fun,' she said.

All Roads Lead to Whitechapel

The very next morning after the newspaper reports of the Whitechapel Lady's death, Mary arrived at my door as soon as dawn broke, tense with anger and sorrow, her dress pulled tight across her taut shoulders. We caught a cab to Whitechapel together. All the way there Mary sat bolt upright, staring ahead of us, silently willing the driver to go faster. He would not take us into Whitechapel itself, but dropped us off on the Whitechapel Road. We didn't invite one of the Irregulars. I didn't want them to see what we would see.

'Which way?' Mary asked, looking around.

'This way,' I told her, taking her arm and leading her down Leman Street towards the tiny square at the end.

I hardly noticed Whitechapel this time. Not the stench, not the dirt, not the poverty. The tiny streets and narrow alleys were already bustling with life, but there were no cheerful calls, no shouts, no arguments, not this time. Everyone watched each other, warily, suspiciously. It was utterly quiet in Whitechapel, almost safe, apart from the whisper 'Ripper'. No one bothered us. They were too afraid for themselves to think about us.

We came into the square to see a man walking down the steps from the Whitechapel Lady's home, a man who obviously did not belong in Whitechapel. He stepped fastidiously over the dirt, his boots shining brightly, his trousers pressed and brushed and achingly clean. He was of middle height, slightly plump—I doubted he had ever gone hungry in his life. He had dark hair, smoothed down with pomade on either side of a pudgy, unhealthy-looking face. His small nose was wrinkled against the smell we were now immune to and his golden pince-nez pinched the bridge of it. He would have been unnoticeable in Baker Street or Oxford Street, but in Whitechapel he stuck out a mile, as the residents would have said.

Mary picked up her skirts and ran to him.

'Are you the police?' she demanded.

'No, they left. Who are you?' he said, quailing slightly before her anger.

'Friends of the murdered woman,' I said calmly, as I walked towards him. He looked us up and down, saw the quality of clothes, and the way we carried ourselves, and the bloom of health on our cheeks, and knew we were not Whitechapel friends. He sniffed.

'I see,' he said, a touch reluctantly. 'Well, I am…was…her solicitor. Richard Halifax, at your service,' he added mechanically, holding out a card to Mary. She only glared at him. I reached past her and took it. 'I can tell you now she left all her money to the clinic, and left behind no papers, so your search is pointless.'

'We're not here for papers!' Mary snapped. 'We're here to pay our respects.' She pushed past him and ran up the stairs and into the room. Mr Halifax looked deeply disconcerted. He held on tight to the shaky wooden banister as he descended the last few steps.

'My friend is very upset,' I explained. I too was upset, but I seemed to hide it better than Mary. That was a new discovery for me, that I could remain so cool and calm whilst inside my emotions churned. 'Have you had many people come to look for her papers?'

'One or two, Mrs…?'

'Smith,' I lied blithely. 'I hope you sent them away?'

'Quite away, with a flea in their ear to boot!' he told me. Then he looked at me, and decided, like so many people have, to confide in me. 'Truth to tell, there's nothing left. Nothing to be found. She had destroyed everything that spoke of her former life, and what caused her to leave it. And the few papers that she was obliged to leave with me, I shall, by the terms of her will, burn unseen.' He looked up the stairs at the Whitechapel Lady's last home, and then around at the shabby cobbled, dirty square. 'I knew her, before. A fine lady, a great lady I should say. That she should end so horribly, in this place…' He shuddered, then replaced his grey bowler hat on his head. 'For her sake, for her memory, I shall follow her instructions exactly. Nothing shall be left. Good day to you, Mrs Smith.'

I watched him exit the square onto St George Street, where a carriage stood waiting. His face was pinched and unhappy. Then, once he was gone, I heard Mary come out of the room and stand at the top of the stairs.

'Is that vile man gone?' she called.

'Quite gone. He was only doing his duty, Mary.'

'It doesn't matter. Martha, come and see, do come.'

She held her hand to me, beckoning me up. I hesitated. I did not want to see that room full of blood. I pictured the lurid illustration in the *Police News*, but full of colour, full of browns and reds and blacks, dried blood. I didn't want to see that.

'Martha, you should see,' Mary said softly, still holding out her hand. She was right, I should. I walked up the stairs and looked at Mary.

Her face was wet with tears. She took my hand and led me into the room where the murder had taken place.

The room was full of flowers. They lay over an inch deep on the floor. They were piled up in the corner. They were scattered thickly on the bed and table. Not a drop of blood was to be seen. Instead the room was full of yellow and bright pink and delicate blue and the softest, most exquisite petals.

'They're not expensive flowers,' Mary said from behind me, her voice breaking. 'They're the kind you buy from girls on the corner, or that you scavenge from Covent Garden. Some of them are wild flowers. I cannot think where they found those.'

'Who…how…?' I asked breathlessly. I stroked the petals of a daisy, so beautiful and pure in the morning light.

'There aren't many notes,' Mary told me, as she walked into the room. The flowers caught on her skirt, and tumbled on the floor. 'I don't think many of the people who left the flowers can read or write. Or perhaps they felt that nothing needed to be said. But there are one or two. They speak of her kindness, and her gentleness. They call her a saviour. And they are sorry that they could not protect her. All the flowers, Martha, all of them, they're from people who live here. All of Whitechapel has given her flowers. Whitechapel loved her.'

I hope the Whitechapel Lady knew. I hope that somewhere in her sad and lonely life she knew she had a place, and was honoured and treasured and loved. I was so afraid she had not known. I looked around. They must have searched long and hard for these flowers. Some must have gone without a meal, or two, to pay for a bunch of peonies. Here and there I saw a bright yellow dandelion that must have pushed its way up through the cracks in the pavement. The sweet, soft, pure scent of them pushed away the stench of the blood. These flowers were a far better monument than any massive stone sarcophagus could have been. I knelt on the floor, took off my glove, and ran my fingers over the flowers, silently adding my sorrow for her loss. My shame that we could not save her, my anger that someone could have done this to her, my promise that he would pay.

I pushed aside the flowers, and then I saw the blood. Everywhere beneath the delicate petals was stained in dark, harsh blood. It had even splashed onto the walls. This room had seen something horrific. I looked up at Mary. She stood by the window, staring intently about the room, her face pale and set and hard as a statue.

'I know,' she said. 'I saw the blood too. It's horrible.'

'It's insane,' I replied, standing up. 'This isn't right.'

Mary looked at me, her eyes burning in anger. She had misunderstood.

'No, I meant…this doesn't fit!' I explained quickly. 'I presume we both believe that the man who drove her to this place is the same man who killed her? The same man we are hunting.'

Mary nodded mutely.

'Then this does not fit,' I repeated. 'From what we have learnt, this has always been a man who prized control. He got his pleasure from controlling others and himself. He enjoyed being powerful in the background. He enjoyed being unsuspected, unseen. This,' I knelt down and pushed aside the flowers again to reveal the ugly stain. It still felt slightly sticky to the touch, 'is an utter lack of control. He doesn't do this. He kills by proxy.'

'He kills, though,' Mary said, in a low, grating voice.

'Not like this,' I insisted. 'I'm not saying he has never had blood on his hands. He probably did, I think perhaps he would want that experience, that feeling of another's life in his hands, but I regret to say it would be some poor girl from the slums that no one would miss. It would be quiet, unnoticed. This—' I pushed aside more of the flowers. The stain had spread all over the floor, '—this is screaming, "look at me!". There is no control here whatsoever. This is the very antithesis of all we know about him.'

'You think she was killed by a different man?' Mary asked, pushing her hair away from her forehead. I sat back on my heels and thought for a moment.

'No,' I said finally, shaking my head. 'It's too much of a coincidence that she should be so violated by two different men. Besides, think of him hurling Wiggins down the stairs.'

'Probably not the first time he's tried to get rid of a witness,' Mary pointed out.

'In broad daylight? In front of other potential witnesses? No, this and the attacks on Wiggins and Mr Shirley were impulsive acts. I think his control is slipping. I think his control is breaking down.'

Mary suddenly leaned forward and seized a pale pink rose from the flowers on the floor. She grasped it, squeezing it in her hands.

'All those years,' Mary whispered. 'He kept himself under such a tight rein. No one knew him or saw him for what he was. He made himself seem so ordinary, but underneath he was still there. Still evil, still mad, still wrong. It must have been such a strain, keeping up that pretence all the time. Even in his darkest, vilest moments, he could never let it entirely slip. And now...' She looked at me. The rose in her hand was torn to pieces. 'Jekyll is taking over Hyde.'

I nodded. It was an apt analogy. I had seen the play, though not read the book. I remembered that horrific moment of transformation.

'But why now?' Mary demanded, letting the crushed remains of the rose fall between her fingers.

'Something has changed,' I speculated, still kneeling on the floor amongst the flowers. 'Something is different, something new and uncontrollable has entered his life…oh.' I suddenly realized what I meant. 'Could it be us?' I whispered. 'We're the something new!'

Mary blanched, looking round the room.

'We caused this?'

'No,' I said firmly. 'He did this. He lost control. All we did was investigate, and we haven't even done much of that, not really.'

'We're the new player in the game, as Sherlock would say,' Mary said.

'But we're not that important!' I insisted again. I had never been that important.

'We're uncontrollable by his usual methods,' Mary said, striding round the room, her skirt disturbing the flowers and sending up wafts of fragrance. 'We have no one who is likely to believe any lies he tells about us. We have no secrets—well, I have none beyond fabulous but lost Indian treasure and some stories about the mutiny. I presume you have no dark secrets?'

'Not one,' I said ruefully.

'So here we are, two women—and he hates women—interfering in his life, and no way to control us. It must drive him insane.'

I shook my head. It didn't make sense. I couldn't see myself as anyone's implacable enemy.

'No, I don't think it's us,' I disagreed. 'There's something else here, something, someone we're not seeing. A different factor we know nothing about. If we're that dangerous, why not just kill us?'

Mary laughed, a harsh shout of laughter.

'Kill Sherlock Holmes' housekeeper and Dr Watson's wife? That would be a huge mistake!'

'Maybe he doesn't see us as his new opponent,' I said. 'Maybe he thinks his new enemy is Mr Holmes?'

Mary stopped pacing.

'Perhaps. Although I'm not sure if I'd be relieved or insulted if that were true.'

I bent my head for a moment, looking at the flowers.

'Well, we can ask him when we find him,' I murmured. Out of the corner of my eye I saw Mary glance at the book on the table. I knew she was imagining the Whitechapel Lady sitting here all alone, night after night, her life destroyed in so many ways by this man. And then, just when she had found some measure of peace, he had destroyed it again, utterly this time. And perhaps, just perhaps, it was because of us.

'He'll get worse,' Mary said quietly. 'He'll be like Jack the Ripper, and become more and more steeped in blood.'

'Or until we stop him.'

'No one stopped Jack.'

'He is not Jack,' I insisted. 'I know he isn't. Don't ask why.'

'But...'

'No, Mary,' I insisted. 'I can't tell you, not today.' Perhaps in the future I would, but it wasn't my story to tell her. A good housekeeper had to keep so many of her employer's secrets. I would tell Mary one day. I couldn't keep even that secret from her, but not on this day.

I slowly got up from my knees and walked over to the fireplace. The grate was cold now, but full of ashes. A great deal of paper had been burnt here. I leaned over to look. There was the tiniest scrap of white, just a corner of something left, right at the back.

When I turned, Mary was by the window. The harsh cold daylight cast deep shadows on her set white face. She stared at me, and I had never seen a look like that in *her* eyes before.

'It's not about finding him any more,' she said, in a low voice. 'It's not even about stopping him. I want him punished, Martha. I want him to burn.'

We didn't want to leave Whitechapel right away. To scurry away from the Whitechapel Lady's home would have seemed like a betrayal. Instead we wandered through the narrow alleyways and courts, listening to people talk. Most of them mentioned her, and her kindness and her generosity, and her sensitivity and her deep need for privacy. They talked of how they had gone to her for help, and she had never turned them away, nor preached to them. But amongst the tributes to her were other whispers. Ripped. Cut. '88. He's back. Him. Jack. The Ripper. Ripper.

'What did you take from the fireplace?' Mary asked, her voice low. I handed her the scrap.

'It fell down the back. Bits of paper often do when they are burnt. People always forget to look,' I said. She turned it over in her hand.

'A visiting card.'

'Yes, and yes, I read the name on it.'

There had been just a corner of a name, just the four letters: *lant.*

'Adam Ballant,' Mary guessed.

'Not necessarily,' I warned her, but I too had jumped to the same conclusion. Mary stopped suddenly on the street, grasping my arm, and getting in the way of an old woman in grey, who swore fluently at her. Mary ignored her.

'If you were hiding a pin, where would you put it?' she asked.

'I wouldn't hide a pin, I'm always losing the blasted things,' I told her.

'The best place to hide a pin,' Mary said softly, 'is on a pin-cushion, amongst all the other pins.'

She turned and walked on, lost in her own thoughts, barely aware if I followed or not. I did not need her to explain. The best place to hide a blackmailer would be amongst his victims—and we had both felt that Adam Ballant did not quite fit. Too secretive and yet too eager to talk. And too skilled at evading a pursuer. I could see Mary was up to something, and I would have laid a wager she was planning a visit to Adam Ballant.

Eventually we found ourselves on Whitechapel Road and hailed a cab. We sat in silence all the way back to Baker Street. I do not know how I looked, for Mary never glanced at me, but I recognized the set look of Mary's features. I had seen Mr Holmes look like that, when someone vulnerable and helpless had been hurt. I had seen John look like that, too. I knew that look. It was vengeance.

It's no surprise to anyone that Mr Holmes had a streak of darkness running through him. A man like that, who could think like that, with his strength and cunning, could so easily be tempted to take the law into his own hands, beyond detection into judgement and execution. But John had kept that side of Mr Holmes in check. And John, with his burning anger and his brief but sharp temper, could be checked by Mary.

But now here sat Mary, with the darkness etched onto her face. The same need to see revenge achieved, at any cost. Who would keep her safe? Who would stop the darkness claiming her?

I suppose that was supposed to be me. Yet when I thought of the flowers, I too wanted to see him burn.

When we arrived back at 221b, there was a large package waiting for Mr Holmes on the hall table. The address was printed, but I knew it came from Irene and contained the letters. I directed Billy to take it up right away.

Mary, exhausted, decided to go home. I set to cleaning the kitchen. I was in the middle of turning out a cupboard when Billy ran in and cried, 'I've just shown Sir George Burnwell up to Mr Holmes!'

'Really?' I wiped my hands on a dry cloth and rolled my sleeves back down. 'Billy, did Mr Holmes open that package he received this morning?'

'Yes, he did,' Billy assured me, 'but he only had time to glance through it.' I didn't seem to need to tell Billy what was in it. Between what Wiggins told him, what he had overheard from Irene and Mary and me, and his own intelligence, he seemed to have worked it out. He stood on a kitchen chair and opened the vent, and silently we sat down at the still-damp table.

Mr Holmes must have asked Sir George to sit down, and assured him of John's discretion. That was how these consultations always began. Of course John was there. Mr Holmes would barely see a client without him. I could imagine the scene clearly in my mind, Mr Holmes standing before the fireplace—where his face was in shadow and the light from the window shone directly onto his visitor's face—surprising his visitor with an example of his perspicacity. John sat in a chair behind the visitor, taking notes in his small brown leather book. Sir George would have sat on the sofa, and behind him, on the table, would be the parcel containing his ledger and his letters.

I could hear Mr Holmes talking in that tight, clipped manner he has when he dislikes his visitors. However, he has never allowed his personal dislike of a client to stop him taking a case, and I was apprehensive. What would Mr Holmes say if he discovered the criminal in this case lived under his own roof? I genuinely had no idea.

I listened as Sir George told Mr Holmes how he had returned home the previous Saturday evening, with a perfectly respectable companion he was not prepared to name. He had discovered three desperate ruffians in his study, had fought them off bravely, but they had managed to escape with some important papers, and burnt the rest.

'Mr Holmes,' Sir George said, in his suave voice, 'it is vital I retrieve the papers these men took!'

Men. Well, that was lucky. He had seen only Irene clearly, as she cheekily waved goodbye to him, and she had been dressed as a man.

'What exactly are these papers?' Mr Holmes asked.

'Private papers. The content is not important,' Sir George insisted.

'I say it is,' Mr Holmes insisted in his turn. 'If I do not know what these papers are, how can I tell to what use they have been put, or who is likely to have them? The truth, please, Sir George!'

It is difficult to lie to Mr Holmes' face when he demands the truth. His eyes bore through you, to the very heart of you. Sir George, I imagine, swallowed, his throat suddenly dry.

'A book,' Sir George said hoarsely. 'Merely a notation of some expenses. And family letters. Vital only to me, worthless to anyone else. Utterly innocent, I assure you.'

'I doubt that, Sir George,' John said, and I could hear the distaste in his voice. 'You have a certain reputation.'

I wonder how they knew? It occurred to me that perhaps some lady compromised by Sir George might have come to Mr Holmes for help before. Perhaps he already knew what he was dealing with.

'Shall we speak the truth, Sir George?' Mr Holmes said. 'The ledger is no doubt some sort of "book of love" and the letters are from ladies you have seduced. You mourn their loss because no doubt you hoped to use them for profit at some point in the future.'

'I am not a blackmailer!' Sir George snapped.

'Not yet,' John said. 'But when you are older, and have gambled your money away, and have lost your ability to charm coinage out of these ladies, you will become a blackmailer.'

'No! I…I need those letters…' Sir George insisted. I could hear the desperation in his voice. Why? He would acquire more letters, a new ledger, I had no doubt. Why did he need these so badly? If he only knew they were in that room, within his reach. If he only stretched his hand out to the table…

'Who was your companion?' Mr Holmes asked. 'I mean the night you were robbed, not any other night.'

'No one of any importance,' Sir George said sullenly. I could tell he was regretting his decision to come here.

'A woman?'

'Yes, a woman, damn you!'

'A society lady?'

'No!'

'Then who?' Holmes insisted implacably.

'A woman of the streets, not anyone of any importance,' Sir George said reluctantly.

'Did she know you had these letters?' John asked. Sir George was silent, and I heard him shift on the sofa. Then he spoke, in a quieter, almost ashamed tone.

'I was drunk. Very drunk. I may have boasted. It is a habit I have. Not a pretty one, I admit. I mentioned the letters, I think. Or…I'm not sure. She asked about them. She wanted to see how foolish these society women are. I don't remember much,' he admitted. 'Normally I handle my drink a lot better.'

I should imagine the same thought crossed Mr Holmes' and John's mind as crossed mine: he had been drugged. No wonder he had barely been able to stop us, had not even been able to recognize us as women. She had slipped something into his drink.

I felt a certain degree of satisfaction that Sir George had been tricked.

'She asked to see the letters?' Mr Holmes said sharply. 'You did not tell her about them first?'

'Yes…no, I don't know!' Sir George cried in anguish. 'No, she asked! I remember. I remember her name too,' he said viciously. 'Lillian Rose. That's her name. I found her in Whitechapel!'

Whitechapel. All roads led there. Half the criminals in London hid themselves in the mish-mash of Whitechapel. Was that the final stop, or only a staging post?

'She was a decoy,' Sir George realized. 'Find her, Mr Holmes. Get my letters back,' he pleaded.

'I will not,' Mr Holmes said coldly. 'No doubt Miss Rose and the burglars were sent to your house by one of these ladies you dishonoured to retrieve her letters. I will not help you find them, or hunt down your victims.'

'Then I'll find her,' Sir George said, standing up. 'I'll track down Lillian Rose…'

'You will not,' Mr Holmes told him, quickly, forcefully. 'You will go home and keep quiet. If I hear of any harm coming to Lillian Rose…'

'You daren't tell the police. Think of what I could tell them! I could ruin half the noble ladies of England!' Sir George shouted hysterically.

'There are the police—and then there is Dr Watson and I,' Mr Holmes said quietly. I heard the scrape of a chair as John stood up. I heard harsh breathing, as Sir George panted like a cornered dog. Then he darted out of the room, down the stairs, and out of the front door before Billy could reach it.

Upstairs, I heard John say, 'Holmes, have you seen what's in this package?'

I heard the rustle of paper as Mr Holmes glanced through the letters and ledger, then I heard his great shout of laughter.

'Well, that would have been the easiest fee we ever earned! Sir George begs us to find his papers, and here they are, not three feet behind him.'

'Who do you suppose sent them?'

'I have my suspicions,' Mr Holmes said, and I wondered if he meant Irene. 'But I'm not going to look this particular gift horse in the mouth.'

'The man is a cad,' John said. He must have been reading some of the letters. 'He really does deserve to be punished.'

'Oh, he will be,' Mr Holmes said. 'Put those papers carefully away, Watson. I've no doubt the name of Sir George Burnwell will pop up again.'

Lillian Rose. She sounded like a woman who could answer a few questions. But first we had to see Adam Ballant.

Mary arrived early the next morning, whilst I was still clearing away Mr Holmes' breakfast things. She had dressed as if for court, or battle. She was all in black, smart and slightly intimidating. Her hair was neatly pinned for once, a black hat with an upturned side brim replacing her usual straw boater. She was very pale, but resolute. She was determined to face Adam Ballant and have it out.

'Are you sure?' I asked.

'Certain,' she said grimly. As I was already, as always, all in black, we left to catch a hansom to Adam Ballant's house.

Mr Ballant lived in a very quiet, clean, expensive street in the west of London. Very few hawkers and muffin-sellers cried down this street, the servants kept discreetly indoors, anyone too scruffy would be moved on by the patrolling policeman— although this morning, the policeman was absent so we had the street to ourselves as we walked down it.

'I don't know what to say,' Mary admitted. 'What do we say to him?'

'We accuse him, I suppose,' I replied. 'I actually have no idea how Mr Holmes does this part. He always has his confrontations away from his rooms.'

'We have no proof,' Mary said, suddenly nervous, her hand tightening on my arm. 'Just a bit of card and a few suspicions. Maybe we should…'

'We can't wait,' I insisted. 'If we stop we will stagnate, and it is far too late for that now.'

'Of course,' Mary said. We had reached the steps of Mr Ballant's house, with its moss-green front door matching the moss-green curtains contrasting tastefully with the brilliant-white stone of the house. Mary put her shoulders back, stepped up to the door and rang the bell firmly.

The door was opened not by a footman or butler, as we expected, but by what seemed to be the scullery maid, sobbing violently. Mary's greeting died on her lips. The girl just stood there, crying her eyes out.

'What's wrong?' I asked gently.

'He's dead,' she cried out, gulping as she spoke. She seemed unable to contain herself now she'd started speaking. 'He's gone and hanged himself, he's dead, I saw it, he's dead!'

'Who?' Mary demanded.

'The master, right over the balcony, rope round his neck, like a common criminal, only he did it himself, he's dead and I saw it and I can't stop seeing it—and he's dead!' With that she broke down sobbing into her apron.

Mary and I stood there, utterly dumbfounded. Dead? Our prime suspect, a suicide? My gaze drifted upwards to the staircase that ran from the black-and-white tiled floor up to the first floor, sweeping around the hall. There was nothing there now, but I could see scratches on the banister, and smears of something on the highly polished floor, at least fifteen feet below.

A door to the right of the hall opened, and an elderly man with flyaway white hair came out. He saw the maid standing on the step babbling to us and hurried forward.

'Minnie, that will do! Go to the kitchen, now,' he ordered, not unkindly. 'I apologize,' he said to us. 'She should not have answered the door. I'm afraid we're all not ourselves this morning.' He seemed sad and worn and confused.

'Is it true?' Mary demanded. 'Adam Ballant hanged himself?'

'I regret Mr Ballant has died in unfortunate circumstances,' he said, remembering his duty and standing a little straighter. 'The police have been sent for. I regret the household cannot receive callers.'

'I feel faint,' I announced. 'May I sit down for a moment? Just here, in the hall?'

Mary, grasping my lie, hurriedly took my arm to support me. The butler hesitated, but I was only a woman, obviously not used to such shocking news, and ladies were prone to faint. From downstairs came a great cry—the servants were clearly getting worked up.

'It'll only be a moment,' Mary said sweetly. 'Then we'll be on our way. It's been such a great shock for her.'

'She knew Mr Ballant?' the butler queried.

'As a child,' I said weakly, hoping the butler had not been in the family back then. 'He was such a beautiful boy. Such promise, then to die so young and so tragically...' I allowed my voice to fade away.

'You don't want her fainting on the doorstep where the whole world can see her,' Mary pointed out.

The butler, prizing discretion above all—they all do—nodded, and guided me into the hall. There were some wooden chairs arranged there, against the wall, next to the door the butler had come out of, and Mary solicitously placed me in one. I could hear a woman screaming somewhere.

'It sounds like the servants are in uproar,' Mary said sympathetically. 'We will be fine by ourselves, if you wish to go and calm them. You wouldn't want the hubbub to alert the neighbours.'

The butler hesitated, glancing at the door beside us. Then, hearing raised voices, and something smash, he nodded quickly and left through the green baize door under the stair.

'That must where he hanged himself,' I said, looking up at the banister. Mary, in one swift movement, stood up and opened the door beside her.

'It's the billiard room,' she whispered to me. 'They've got him laid out on the table.' She stepped inside, whilst I just peered round the door.

Adam Ballant had been a magnificent young man in life. Now he looked diminished, laid out in the morning light on the table. His face was suffused with blood, and there was a livid purple bruise around his neck. He had not died easily. If he truly was our blackmailer, I was glad of that, and yet the sight of him made me feel sick.

'Keep watch,' Mary ordered. 'I'm going to examine his body.'

'Why? What are you looking for?'

'Just checking,' Mary replied, as she tilted Mr Ballant's head back to fully examine the bruise around his neck. I looked away, into the hall.

'How do you know what to look for?' I hissed.

'John's become quite the medical criminal expert,' Mary said, only half listening. She was peering closely at Mr Ballant's neck, moving the folds of skin aside. 'All kinds of people consult him now, not just Mr Holmes. I type up his reports, so I've learnt quite a lot too. Ah, that's interesting.'

'What is?'

'In a minute. Is anyone coming?'

The hall was empty, but I could hear voices. And of course the police were expected any moment—we didn't have long.

'He's quite cold,' Mary said, as clinical as John would have been. 'And stiff too. This must have happened quite a few hours ago.'

'The scullery maid found him,' I reminded her. 'They're normally up at six.'

'It's eight now,' Mary agreed. She had lifted up Mr Ballant's hands and was examining them closely.

'Mary, I think the butler's coming back!' I whispered urgently.

'All done,' Mary said calmly, replacing Mr Ballant's hand on his chest and sweeping out of the room, closing the door behind her. We sat just as the butler returned.

'My friend feels so much better now,' Mary said. 'Thank you so much for your kindness, we cannot impose any more, not on this day of all days.'

We stood and headed for the door, far faster than was polite. Hopefully he'd put our speed down to distaste at being at the scene of an unnatural death.

'Who shall I say called?' the butler asked as we hurried past him.

'It's of no matter now,' I said, weeping a little. 'Such promise—and all gone to dust. Farewell.'

And with that we headed down the steps as fast as possible and along the street.

As soon as we were far enough away, I asked Mary what she had found.

'Well, it's not a suicide,' Mary asserted.

'How on earth do you know that?'

'There were two bruises on his neck,' Mary said, gesturing to her own neck to demonstrate. 'One bruise around his neck, rising from the front to the back, knot under his left ear. A classic hanging bruise.'

I felt a bit sick, but Mary seemed calmly competent.

'However,' she continued, 'underneath that is another bruise, horizontally around his neck, and with no knot, just the two ends crossed at the back of the neck.' She clasped her hands round her throat to show me.

'The rope slipped?' I asked.

She carried on walking.

'No, I don't think so,' she said. 'I think someone wrapped the rope around his neck, enough to choke him into unconsciousness, maybe even to death, and then tied the rope around his neck and tossed him over the balcony to make it look as if he hanged himself.'

'He's too heavy!' I objected.

'Not really, it's all a matter of angles,' Mary said, lost in thought. 'Choke him from behind, at the top of the stairs, make sure he passes out draped over the banister, tie the rope around his neck, then using his own body as fulcrum, tip him over...'

'Mary!' I cried, eager to stop the picture she was building up in my mind. It was horrific.

'Sorry,' she said, seeing my white face. 'I couldn't help working it out. Mathematics was always my best subject as a governess,' she remarked inconsequentially, as I stood still, breathing deeply. 'I was terrible at French grammar though.'

I didn't smile.

'Are you sure?' I asked.

'That he was murdered? Yes,' she replied, as we walked on. 'I'm afraid there were scratches on his neck, and his fingernails were torn, as if he'd tried to pull the rope away from his throat. He fought for his life.'

'So, murdered,' I said. 'And therefore, not our blackmailer.'

'Probably not,' Mary corrected. She looked at my face. 'All right, almost certainly not. And therefore, the next logical step is that Ballant was killed by him.'

'He must have known him,' I said. 'If he let him in during the early hours of the morning.'

'Known him and trusted him. Probably like the Whitechapel Lady did…Martha?'

She was staring down the street ahead of us. A familiar figure, one I knew well, was approaching us. It was a little man with red hair and a permanently suspicious expression. He was counting the house numbers, with a constable by his side.

'Yes,' I said grimly. 'That is Inspector Lestrade.'

Unfortunately, at that moment he spotted us, and hurried towards us.

'Mrs Hudson? Mrs Watson? What are you doing here?'

I had to make a quick decision. What lie to tell? How much could I get away with? What would he believe? If he was heading towards the murder scene—and what else would he be doing here—the butler would be bound to tell him about the mysterious lady visitors. Inspector Lestrade was not clever, but he was perceptive and tenacious.

'I have a friend in service near here,' I said quickly. 'We came to visit her. She's not been well, poor soul. I took her some cake, to feed her up.'

'Bit early, isn't it?' he asked suspiciously. He was always suspicious.

'She's a very early riser. Alas, her illness means she does not sleep well at night, and is too tired for visitors in the afternoon. And you—are you here to visit the Ballant house?'

Beside me Mary gasped slightly—but how could I conceal our visit there, and our knowledge?

'How do you know?' he demanded.

'Martha felt faint as we walked down here,' Mary said, catching on quickly, thank goodness. 'We called at a house, any house really, for a rest, and unfortunately, it turned out to be Mr Ballant's house. Such a pity.'

'Quite a coincidence,' Lestrade said dryly. 'Own up, the pair of you. Mr Holmes sent you, didn't he?'

'Why on earth would he?' Mary demanded.

'He heard about this death—I don't know, he has his little methods—and sent you two here to get ahead of the game, didn't he?' Lestrade crowed, certain he'd caught us out.

'His housekeeper and his friend's wife?' Mary said scornfully. 'What on earth do you imagine he thinks we can do?'

'And what are you doing here?' I demanded myself. 'This is not your patch,' I said, slipping into the Irregulars' vernacular.

'Mr Holmes sent me here personally,' Lestrade said with pride.

'Sherlock sent you?' Mary asked, bemused.

'Not Mr Sherlock Homes. Mr Mycroft Holmes,' he said, visibly standing straighter. 'My reputation has spread far and wide, ladies.'

'I'll just bet it has,' Mary murmured. But Lestrade didn't hear her, and announcing he didn't have time to stand around in the street talking, he and the uniformed constable by his side walked past us and up the street to the Ballant home.

Well, Inspector Lestrade had a reputation all right. He was steady and persistent, but always tended to go for the obvious answer. His greatest cases had been solved by Sherlock, and Mycroft, as Sherlock's brother, would know this. So why send him out to this case? Lestrade would be bound to rule it suicide. And what was Mycroft's interest in Adam Ballant?

At the end of the street was a small garden with gravel paths and trees just bursting into bloom. It was rather pretty, even in the grey drizzle that had started, and we turned into the garden. We walked round and round the paths, arm in arm.

'Mycroft?' Mary said suddenly. 'John's mentioned him, Sherlock's brilliant older brother.'

'I've met him once,' I told her.

I had of course met Mycroft Holmes the previous year when he, quite unexpectedly, visited Mr Holmes at 221b to help a friend of his, a Greek interpreter. He seemed to me a very large man, slow and lazy in person, but with a quick and sharp mind behind grey eyes. He had glanced at me momentarily, and yet I had an impression that in that moment he had sized me up, classified me, docketed me, and put me aside to be remembered in case of future usefulness.

A few weeks later I had been asked by Mr Holmes to take a message to his brother at his club, as none of the boys seemed to be available at that time, and Mycroft Holmes had wanted the information instantly. I was instructed to go to the Diogenes Club, but on no account to talk or make any sound in those premises except in the Strangers' Room. The members prized silence and solitude. I doubted this would be a problem. As a woman, I would be lucky to get through the front door. I was only allowed in as I had a message from Mr Holmes marked 'Confidential. By Hand Only.'

Mycroft Holmes met me in the Strangers' Room. I entered as a young man left. He had obviously been in conference with Mycroft Holmes, and Mr Holmes still held the purple piece of paper he had given him. I gave Mr Holmes my message, for which he thanked me, and then he left. I followed him outside and watched him walk away towards Whitehall. He had again given me the impression of assessing me, not as a person, but as a possible tool. Sherlock Holmes liked to find out the details of a person out of curiosity, or an urge to help. Mycroft assessed them for what function they could fulfil for him.

As I stood on the steps of the Diogenes Club, I became aware the doorman was talking to me. He was a tall man, cadaverously thin and with a high-pitched Cockney accent.

'Good morning,' I said to the doorman. 'Do you enjoy your post?'

'I do not!' he said firmly. 'Standing 'round all day, not so much as a "thank you"; against club rules, apparently,' he said scornfully. 'And none too free with the tips either! Don't trust a man 'oo don't tip and don't talk, I say. F'r instance, you want to watch that one,' he said, nodding at Mycroft Holmes. ''E ain't safe.'

'What do you mean, not safe?' I asked. A gentleman I

recognized as quite a high-ranking minister had met Mycroft in the street and was talking urgently to him.

''E knows things,' he said, under his voice.

It must be difficult to work in a place where no one is allowed to say so much as good morning to you. He was obviously yearning to talk.

'I seen 'im, meeting all kinds of people down here, and getting 'em to tell him stuff. Know 'oo that is 'e's talking to right now?'

'Yes, I do,' I said. The man looked deeply distressed and Mycroft was soothing him.

'Well, that bloke's done things 'e ought not to,' he said. 'Things I can't tell a lady. 'E thought no one knew, but I heard that fat bloke tell 'im 'e knew everything.'

'Blackmail, do you mean?' I asked sharply. I saw Mycroft hand the purple piece of paper to the man, who sighed in relief.

'Gawd, no, not that sort o' thing, not 'ere!' the doorman said sharply. 'That fat bloke, Mr 'Olmes, just said 'e'd take care of things, and 'e'd be grateful if that minister could let 'im know a few things in return, that's all. Just a sort of exchange of information.'

'Exchange of information,' I said thoughtfully. 'All men of business do it. Why is he dangerous?'

''Cos it's not an exchange,' the doorman said. ''E has these men that work for 'im, all over the city, and they come and tell 'im stuff. Secret stuff. Stuff no one's supposed to 'ear or know. But 'e never tells anything in return. Oh no, not 'im. 'E watches and listens and collects all these secrets, but 'e never gives anything in return.'

'I see,' I said. It sounded as if Mycroft had his own collection of spies, not in a foreign country, but here, in England, spying on his own government and people and business.

'I 'ate this place,' the doorman said. 'This club. It's like people like you and me are just machines to 'em. Well, sod 'em. I've 'ad enough. It's my last day today. Can't stand the silence. Creeps me out, it does. 'Oo wants to be silent all the time?'

Someone who doesn't want to let a secret slip, I thought.

I told all this to Mary, adding that Mr Holmes—Mr Sherlock Holmes—was very proud of his brother, though of course, he tried not to show it. 'They all rely on him, according to Mr Holmes. He says Mycroft *is* the British government,' I said uncertainly. Although I had never met Mycroft when Mr Holmes told me of him, something about the way Sherlock spoke of his brother made me uncomfortable. 'He holds no official office, he has no title, no one below the upper echelons of government really knows he exists, and yet he is vital to them. He works behind the scenes, and is accountable to no one, except perhaps the Prime Minister I suppose—and even then…I'm not quite sure what exactly Mycroft does. He gathers information, I know that, he has a prodigious amount of facts in his head, and he is better than Mr Sherlock Holmes at drawing inferences from them. I suppose he must have a large circle of informers. He certainly influences policy. He sees patterns, and the way the pieces will fall in the game, whereas others will only see a corner of the puzzle.'

'You don't like him,' Mary observed.

'No,' I said softly. 'Do you remember when you were a child being taught about the Greek Fates?'

Mary nodded. 'Three old women who controlled the fate of all men—and women, too, I suppose. One spun the thread of life, one wove it and one cut the thread.'

'That used to give me nightmares,' I admitted. 'The idea of those women controlling the lives of everyone, choosing when they were born, and what they did, and when they died, and no one knew they were there, and no one could plead with them to change their fate. Mycroft Holmes reminds me of them, weaving and cutting the threads of someone else's life, and no one knows he is doing it.'

'So, a clever man, with presumably infinite resources,' Mary mused. 'And yet he sends not his clever detective brother, but

Inspector Lestrade—a man he knows to be unobservant—to investigate a case of murder dressed up to look like suicide.'

'He wants Lestrade to fail!' I said bitterly. 'He wants Adam Ballant's death to be ruled a suicide.'

'Why?' Mary asked.

'Mycroft collects secrets,' I said. 'He has an army of young men to do his bidding, and now one of his young men is dead. Goodness knows what secrets he had.'

'You don't know that Adam Ballant was one of Mycroft's spies,' Mary objected. 'That's just supposition.'

'A young man who does mysterious work for the government?' I pointed out. 'Mycroft sends Lestrade to investigate his death? A young man who, by the way, has the skills to evade the Irregulars?'

'Very well then, an educated guess,' Mary conceded. 'Even Sherlock isn't above those, given the right data. And we have lost our primary suspect. Do you suppose it's like this for Sherlock?' she asked, grinding her foot into the path. 'All dead ends and unexpected twists and unforeseen circumstances? Do you think he spends days chasing down leads, and is so sure he's right, only to run up against a wall, and find not only is he wrong, but he has nowhere to turn?'

'Probably,' I told her. 'But it won't be in John's stories. Mr Holmes wouldn't mind, but John does like to present him as all-powerful.'

'It was such a perfect solution!' Mary cried out, stamping her foot in frustration. 'It was such a clever scheme—the villain pretending to be a victim amongst victims! But it wasn't true. Everything seemed to lead this way.'

'It was a trick,' I said slowly. I was beginning to understand now. 'Like the trick with the safe. It's all tricks and games, all of it. Don't you see, Mary, someone is enjoying this. Someone is playing with us. All of this, it's one big game.'

I raised an umbrella and hailed a cab.

'Where are we going?' Mary demanded.

'The Diogenes Club.'

We were, of course, not allowed into the Diogenes. But I knew Mycroft would have to leave, sooner or later, and luckily, it was sooner.

'Mr Holmes?' I asked, stopping him on the street. It was one of the beautiful wide streets near Whitehall, with government buildings soaring above us on either side, carved angels of commerce and Empire gazing down at us. It was a place of power and influence, thronged by men—though it did not escape my notice that the angels were all women.

'Mrs Hudson?' Mycroft Holmes said, with only a moment's hesitation. He walked along the street as a man would walk along his garden path, secure and comfortable and knowing that all this belonged to him. 'And Mrs Watson, I presume,' he said, tipping his hat to her. 'A pleasure to meet you, finally.'

'And you,' Mary said, openly curious. 'John has mentioned you several times.'

'Ah yes, the estimable Dr Watson,' he said. 'And yet, ladies, you seem distressed. Is anything wrong with Mr Holmes? Or Dr Watson?' Ah well, in for a penny, in for a pound. I did not want to be subtle with this most subtle of men.

'Adam Ballant is dead,' I said. He did not flinch. Give him his due, that man knew how to control himself. Mr Holmes always gave something away, even just the iota of a movement, but not his older brother.

'I don't know that name,' he said.

'He came to see Mr Holmes,' Mary said. 'He said he was being blackmailed. He said he'd been sent to Mr Holmes.'

'By you,' I lied. Adam Ballant had not mentioned him at all. 'His employer.'

'I see,' Mycroft Holmes admitted. We stood there, this immensely secretive and powerful man, and two women, right there in the heart of government, and for a moment, we had him shaken. 'He should not have said that.'

'He was very worried,' Mary said. 'Perhaps he wasn't thinking straight.'

'Did Sherlock send you?' Mycroft asked, and I was suddenly aware that I should not overplay my hand. I did not want him to know that we were investigating. I did not want him to know that Mary and I were the detectives this time. I didn't want him to know anything about us.

'No, we bumped into Inspector Lestrade,' Mary said, as I pulled slightly on her sleeve. I wanted to end this now. I was afraid, all of a sudden. This was a mistake. We had to leave.

'Yes, I sent him,' Mycroft said, and his grey eyes were cold and assessing, and he was looking at us, really looking at us, and I knew he was trying to see who we were, what we were. 'So you see, I knew.'

'You said you didn't know him,' Mary pointed out, ignoring my growing uneasiness.

'He worked for me,' Mycroft admitted. 'But his work was secretive. It is a matter of habit to deny my...'

'Spies?' Mary finished.

'Agents,' he corrected.

'We don't need to know all this,' I said quickly. 'I just saw you in the street and thought you ought to know Mr Ballant was dead, as we had seen him at Mr Holmes', and he said he knew you.'

'And how did you know he was dead?' Mycroft asked, as smoothly as a blade through silk. 'I understand the body was only discovered this morning.'

'Coincidence,' I said quickly. 'We happened to be walking in that street this morning and...'

'Yes, I know,' said Mycroft Holmes. 'I have already had a preliminary report from Inspector Lestrade. Good morning, ladies.'

He left, walking away down the street.

'How odd,' Mary murmured, watching him go.

'He's more than odd,' I said. I was shaking. I felt like a rabbit trapped by a snake's gaze, and then the snake moved on.

'He might be Sherlock's brother, but I don't like him,' Mary said. 'He strikes me as a very strange man.'

Strange. Odd. A man who liked lies. A man with his own network of spies. A man with links to the police and the lawyers and the highest men in government. A man who liked power. An intelligent man who could see your secrets with a glance. In fact, a man who *collected* secrets.

Maybe there was a very good reason I didn't like Mycroft Holmes.

Surely it could not be true, and yet, he did fit all the criteria.

'Mary, what if it's him?' I said suddenly. 'What if Mycroft Holmes is the blackmailer?'

'It can't be,' Mary said firmly.

'Why not?' I demanded. 'We thought it was Adam Ballant just because he called at 221b. Why not someone closer? Why not Mycroft Holmes?'

'It can't be,' Mary repeated, but she was less certain this time.

'We need more evidence,' I insisted.

'We always need more evidence,' Mary said, as we walked away. 'I still refuse to believe it's Mycroft Holmes. I think you just don't like him. But we'll add him to the list.'

John often joked that if Sherlock Holmes had not been a detective, he would have been a truly great criminal. What if the other Holmes brother had taken that path, and used his skills not for good, but something truly evil?

I felt light-headed, dizzy almost, as we walked along the street. My mind felt full of names—Adam Ballant, Mycroft Holmes, John Ripon, Patrick West, unnamed men I hadn't even begun to think about yet. We seemed to hurtle from suspect to suspect, with no clear idea of where we were going or what we were going to do, and we were relying upon guesswork as much as cold, hard facts. I felt like this case was out of my control, a runaway train in danger of leaving the tracks. I doubted that Mr Holmes, with his cool precision and logical mind, ever felt like this.

And yet how did I know that? I walked along in silence, aware that beside me, Mary was also deep in thought. Who knew what Mr Holmes felt when he started a case and was met with a plethora of suspects and clues and events? Perhaps at the beginning it seemed impossible to make sense of it all for him too. Perhaps he could make sense of this one...But then I thought of Laura Shirley, alone and terrified.

I thought of the Whitechapel Lady, torn and broken in spirit and body. I thought of all the other victims out there, believing they were alone, living day by day in dread and persecution, thinking it would never end. No, I would not give up just yet. This was my case—mine and Mary's. We had sworn to help these people—these women—and by God, we would.

But we desperately needed a breakthrough.

CHAPTER 14

The House of Secrets

I saw a glimpse of the River Thames on the way back. It always made Mary smile a little. She said the river had brought her and John together, in a way. I never really knew what was happening in the case John called *The Sign of Four*, the case where he first met Mary Morstan. I had heard the original consultation after I had let Mary into the house, of course. I knew she had received a mysterious message inviting her to a meeting. It had come from the same person who had sent her six beautiful pearls, one a year. But that was all I knew. Most of that case happened away from 221b—which was very disappointing. I know that Mr Holmes had been very frustrated by his inability to find the boat the villain had taken to escape down the Thames, and he had paced in his rooms all night.

So when John arrived at 221b with Mary and called out to Mr Holmes, 'the box is empty!' I really had no idea what they were talking about. I was about to open the air vent to eavesdrop when Mary, all in white, appeared at the entrance to my kitchen.

'I thought you might like to know, as you were so kind to me when I arrived that first time,' she said softly, 'the treasure is lost.' She didn't look like she'd lost anything of great value. She was glowing.

'Treasure?' I asked, motioning her in.

'Don't you know?' she asked, as she sat down. 'No, of course, how could you? It must be very vexatious to live in this house with these men and see all these people come and go and hear odd little snippets here and there and sense something exciting is happening but never really knowing what is going on.'

It was such an accurate assessment of how I felt that I'm afraid I stared at her for longer than is polite, until the kettle on the hob whistled. She sat down at the table.

'I know what it's like to be on the outside looking in,' she told me. 'The Forresters were very kind, but I was still only a governess to them, neither one of the family nor one of the servants.'

'What were you saying about treasure?' I asked, as I poured the tea. 'I know of it, of course. Dr Watson mentioned it, but how did it come that you had this wealth waiting for you?'

So she told me the whole story of the Agra treasure. It was a wild, fascinating story of how a one-legged man called Jonathan Small and three Sikh soldiers had plotted during the Indian mutiny to kill a man for the jewels he carried, jewels he thought would keep him safe. Small and the others were caught, and imprisoned, with the jewels hidden still. Small had made a deal with Captain Morstan, Mary's father, and his friend, Major Sholto: his freedom in return for the jewels. Major Sholto had gone to find the jewels and, dazzled by their wealth, betrayed and deserted both Jonathan Small and Captain Morstan, returning to England a rich man. But he was never happy. He was sure that one day Small would return for his revenge. He was riddled with guilt over betraying Morstan.

The Captain had sent Mary to Britain years ago, but he had returned eventually. She planned to meet him—but he disappeared. Then the pearls started coming, once a year.

Mr Holmes and John had discovered her father had died of a heart attack brought on by an argument with Major Sholto. When Sholto had died, his twin sons had argued over the treasure. One said it belonged to Mary. The other, as greedy as his father, insisted on keeping it. The pearls they sent to Mary, one a year, were their compromise. But now one of the twins was dead, victim of Jonathan Small's revenge, and the treasure was gone.

'They say, by rights, the treasure is mine,' Mary added finally, as I poured her another cup of tea. 'But I don't think so. It's come to me via murder and blackmail and betrayal, and what kind of legacy is that? Besides, I don't want it. It's brought nothing but misery to anyone who owned it. Those stones are soaked in blood,' she said with a shudder.

'Where are they now?' I asked.

'Jonathan Small threw them into the Thames when he was being chased in a boat by John—I mean, Dr Watson and Mr Holmes,' she told me, blushing prettily over the lapse in using John's first name.

'You could have sold them,' I said to her. 'The money would have been useful.'

She shook her head. 'I want none of them,' she said vehemently. 'I would have liked a memento of my father, that is all. My mother died when I was born, but I can just remember my father. I remember a tall man with sandy hair and a moustache that used to scratch me when he kissed me. I remember him throwing me up in the air and catching me, and my ayah convinced he would drop me. And perhaps I wanted to remember India too,' she said, her voice dreamy, her gaze far away, beyond this London kitchen. 'I was so young when I left, only five, that what I can remember seems like a fairy tale. I cannot tell what is true, and what are stories my ayah told me. I can just remember heat so thick you could almost touch it, and dust that settled everywhere and caught in your clothes and the joy of a tall cool drink on an achingly hot day, and the colours. Oh, Mrs Hudson, the colours! I've never seen anything like it, not in this country. The buildings all dazzling white, and the clothes and the spices and the food and even children's toys all bright and shining and like jewels themselves, all shades of red and yellow and blue.'

She remembered where she was, and smiled at me. 'But it's only a vague memory,' she said. 'When I was five, my father sent me to Edinburgh.'

'I know Edinburgh,' I said. 'It's quite different from India.'

'Quite,' she said with a laugh. 'Thank you for letting me talk to you like this. I have no one to talk to, not really. Mrs Forrester is very kind, but...'

'But she is an employer,' I added. I remembered what Mary had said upstairs, in her first consultation. She had led a very reserved life, and had no friends. I didn't make friends easily myself. I was reserved too, as much by choice as anything else, but I felt if I reached out to her just now, Mary could be my friend. Could I do this?

'Can we be friends?' Mary said impulsively, reaching out a hand to me. I smiled and took it briefly.

'Of course,' I replied. 'It would be my pleasure.'

And then we became as close as Mr Holmes and John. She was my closest and perhaps only true friend. I doubt I would have gone as far as I had in this case without her encouragement, and her eagerness to solve this.

On the way back to 221b, I told Mary about Sir George Burnwell's visit. She found it irresistibly funny, and kept quietly chuckling to herself. She, too, agreed with me that Lillian Rose had been sent to distract and possibly rob Sir George that night. Unlike Mr Holmes, though, we didn't think she had been sent by one of the ladies in Sir George's ledger. We believed she had been sent by the very man we hunted.

Therefore, the best move was to find her. Find a prostitute, in Whitechapel.

Oh dear.

For this new line of investigation we needed one of Wiggins' boys again. He sent along Micky, who was very bright, very shrewd and very young. He had been charged by us to find Lillian Rose, and he had, and now he had come to lead us to her. Micky looked barely six, though he was probably older, but underfed. He had watchful eyes, and a large cap pulled down on his head. Wiggins sent him along with the recommendation that he wasn't much protection, but he was observant, and knew the people of Whitechapel well, which was exactly what we needed.

Wiggins had told Micky to do whatever we asked, and whistle if there was trouble. The Irregulars would be around somewhere, and would come running to the sound of their own distinct whistle.

Some instinct told me to take Irene along too.

We dressed as shabbily as possible, in stained, worn clothes. In Baker Street we looked like beggars. In Whitechapel we looked rich. Even the better-dressed women had thrice-turned dresses and torn hems. This time we followed the silent, stern Micky, not through the main streets of Whitechapel, but through the alleyways, the yards, the dark corners. We walked down streets that never appeared on any map, squeezed through tiny gaps into silent squares, hurried past dingy bars offering blind drunkenness for a penny. Whitechapel was bustling and busy in the daylight, people plying what trade they could, calling to each other, chattering and flirting and arguing, but there was a tension in the air that wasn't there before. The Ripper had been a story that was just beginning to fade the first time we visited. Now he was back, hiding behind every door.

Whitechapel always waited for darkness. At night, the desperate and the hungry and the criminal spilled out onto the streets—but now they felt like someone was stalking them again. They lived with death, even murder, day after day, but they were used to death in pub fights, arguments between couples, a robbery gone too far. But many of them believed that *he* had just killed again.

They were waiting to be murdered. They were waiting for Jack to come back. Perhaps he was already here, round the next corner, behind the door, in the back of the dark yards.

Once Micky stopped, and nodded towards a house on the corner. He was looking at the ground-floor room. I could see the windows were filthy and blackened, as if there had been a large fire inside. One was broken.

'That's where Mary Kelly was killed,' Micky told us. It was the first time he'd spoken since we entered Whitechapel. 'Ripper's last victim.'

'They still haven't caught him?' Irene asked. She had been out of the country for a while, after all. She had left before he struck. She didn't know. He was still there, still faceless, still haunting.

'No,' I whispered. We all stood there, stock still, staring at the tiny room. In my mind I could smell the blood, and the flames, I could feel her terror, the horror of the man who found her. By all accounts, this final scene had been devastating. Almost Biblical, someone had said, which I didn't understand, and then I read the Old Testament again. I shivered.

Beside me, Mary whispered, 'Martha, this man we're hunting, you don't think…'

'No, I don't,' I told her, more sharply than I had intended. 'The Ripper destroyed bodies. Our quarry destroys minds and spirits.'

'But the Whitechapel Lady was horrifically stabbed, eviscerated even.'

'Weren't like the Ripper,' Micky said laconically, leading us back down Dorset Street, away from Miller's Court. 'Us lads, some of us, not me, they saw Mary Kelly's body, and Billy and Wiggins saw Long Liz and Kate Eddowes too. Wiggins even saw Polly Nichols,' Micky told us, leading us through the maze of alleyways. People stared at us, hating us, but when they heard the names Micky mentioned, they turned away in silence. 'It was sickening, they said. Made your stomach turn, all their insides hanging out like that. But it was kind o' neat and tidy too, they said. Laid out proper. Neat cuts. All their stuff laid out at their feet. All done with a kind o' order.'

'Wait a minute—Billy saw this?' I asked suddenly, stopping in the street. He'd never said, never even hinted.

'Mr 'Olmes tried to stop 'im, but 'e insisted. That's what we were doing down 'ere then, working for Mr 'Olmes. Din't 'e tell you?'

'No, he did not,' I said quietly. This had been soon after John had married. Mr Holmes had been quiet and brooding. I knew at the time he might have been working on the Ripper case, but I assumed it was from his rooms, reading the newspapers, gathering information, thinking, perhaps going over the ground after the event. I never knew he had come here, seen the bodies, almost stepped in their blood. And to take Billy, too!

For a moment I was so angry I could barely see straight. How dare he involve the boys in this case, of all cases! But then I stopped. What else would Mr Holmes have done but investigate the Ripper? And as for Billy—you could never stop him when he was set on doing something. He had kept it secret, but then what were Mary and I doing?

Well, we were in Whitechapel, hunting down a horrific murderer, led by children, with no intention of telling Mr Holmes anything.

For me to be angry would be the pot calling the kettle black, to say the least.

I calmed down and nodded at Micky, who was staring at me worriedly.

''Ave I said the wrong thing?' he asked.

'No, Micky, I think you said exactly the right thing,' Irene said gently. 'So 221b is a house of secrets?'

'More than we realized,' Mary said dryly. 'Still, that's a problem for another time,' she added briskly. 'Let's get on, shall we? Micky, you said you saw the Whitechapel Lady's injuries?'

'Not me, some o' the older lads,' Micky told her. 'Before the police got there. Blood everywhere, they said, all torn up, but left just to lie. No neatness. Insides just tossed about all over the room. Like someone trying to be the Ripper, but not knowing how.'

'I see,' Mary said quietly. 'Anything else we should know?'

Micky looked around, then lowered his voice.

'The Whitechapel Lady—she 'ad her tongue cut out. And that was worse, 'cos we all know what that means.'

'Yes, we do,' Mary said, her jaw set. '"Don't talk". I do hope Lillian Rose hasn't heard about that.'

Micky led us on through cold gazes and filthy streets and chilly sunshine. About ten minutes later he took us round a corner into a street with two houses that glowered at each other across the sewage between them. They looked crooked and rickety, set to collapse at any moment. Micky led us into the one with the faintly green door. The house itself was crowded, every room let, every corner of the rooms sub-let. The stairs swayed as we climbed them, the banister crumbled to woodworm dust beneath our hands. There were no loud noises, just a constant rumble of moans and groans and complaints. The stench of boiling day-old cabbage just about shoved aside the foul odour of the drains.

Right at the top of the fourth and final set of stairs, Micky paused outside the door just to the right. Several of the panels had been kicked in long ago, but someone had nailed wood across them, and whitewashed the door.

'This is Lillian Rose's place,' Micky whispered. 'Take my advice, just walk in. If you knock, she'll think you're the rozzers and be out the back window and across the roofs in a flash.'

'We can't just walk in, she may be…you know…*busy*!' Mary said significantly. Lillian Rose was a working girl, after all.

'At eleven in the morning?' Micky said scornfully. 'She'll just be getting up.'

As it happened, when I opened the door, Lillian Rose was awake, out of bed, and very angry.

'Who the bleeding hell are you?' she demanded, hands on her hips. I was momentarily disconcerted. She was not what I had expected. I'd pictured someone blowsy and garish, colourful but ragged clothes slipping off grubby shoulders, hair dyed an unhealthy shade of blond. Or someone thin and gaunt, with hollow cheeks and over-bright eyes, already dying of some foul disease.

What I saw was a neat young woman with a rosebud mouth, a sweet complexion that owed nothing to make-up and neatly arranged black hair, wearing a very demure blue dress. With a shock I realized she could pass for a lady, if one in reduced circumstances, in any part of town. Only her green eyes were wrong, challenging and defiant, yet promising, in a way our eyes could never be.

The prostitute who doesn't look like a prostitute. Lillian Rose was clever.

The tiny room was too crowded for all of us, so Micky stayed outside, along with Irene, who'd taken an interest in the odd, bright little boy. I stood fully inside the room, in the centre of a faded rag rug, watching Miss Rose. Mary slid in beside me, staring round at the shabby but clean bed, the splintering wardrobe, the one small window and the single picture of a lake cut out of a paper and pinned to the wall, with unabashed and fascinating curiosity.

We'd interrupted Miss Rose in the middle of throwing her few possessions—another dress, green, lower-cut, some paste jewellery and a book, I could not see what it was—into a cardboard suitcase.

'You're running away?' Mary burst out.

'What's it to you?' Miss Rose demanded.

Her voice was rough, the accent sounded just like those of the people downstairs, yet it felt forced, as if it were a voice she had learnt. It was another hint that underneath the Whitechapel prostitute was someone else, a long way away from here, a lifetime ago. Lillian Rose had been better than this, and something told me she would lie, steal, perhaps even kill to be better than this again.

'Who the hell are you?'

'I'm Mary Watson,' Mary said impulsively. 'And this is Mrs Hudson. We've been investigating the death of the Whitechapel Lady, amongst other things.'

'Fancy yourselves detectives?' Miss Rose said scornfully. 'Isn't it nice, the games some people play? Bet you never get your hands dirty.'

'They're filthy now,' Mary snapped back. 'She died because of us.'

Miss Rose looked closer at Mary and must have seen the anger in her eyes.

'So you, being a detective, figured out I was your next port of call?' Miss Rose said softly. 'Leading him right to my door, aren't you?'

'You needn't be afraid of Sir George Burnwell,' I assured her.

She snorted derisively. 'Him? No, I'm not afraid of him.' Her accent had modified since she heard ours. She was obviously a woman who could adapt herself to any company. Her story must have been fascinating. I wish I could have heard it.

'Then the other man,' I said to her. 'The man you passed Sir George's secrets on to.'

She froze, utterly still. She did not even breathe. Only the scarf around her throat fluttered in the draught.

'No,' she whispered. The colour drained from her face, and she swayed where she stood.

'We know what you did,' Mary said, not ungently. 'We know you were there to steal letters from Sir George Burnwell.'

We didn't know, it was a guess, but a lucky one. Miss Rose stared at Mary, her eyes wide.

'Letters women had written to Sir George,' I said, almost making it up as I went along, feeling for the next step, judging my way by the shock on her face as we hit the mark over and over again. It felt cruel to distress her like this, but it also felt so intoxicating, so exhilarating. I could not stop now, no matter how mean it was. 'Were you given names? No, I believe not. You were expected to use your own judgement. You were to study these letters, and choose the most devastating, the most shaming, the most damaging. You were to pick the plums of the collection. You must be very clever.'

'Cleverer than them,' Miss Rose said, defiant again, but quieter, one hand resting on her hip, wanting to challenge me. 'How stupid of them, to put it all down in paper and ink like that. They wouldn't whisper those things they wrote, not them, but they wrote them easily enough. Then they're surprised when it gets used against them? Idiotic women.' Her voice belied her words. It was soft and sad now, a sob choked in her throat. Her accent was pure as mine. I wondered perhaps if there was a letter somewhere in her past.

'Why not just break in and steal the letters?' I wondered. 'Sir George was hardly the type to warn these ladies. Was it perhaps because some of the letters were not kept there?'

'The cream of the crop!' Miss Rose cried bitterly. 'He'd lodged them with Sir Peter York, his solicitor,' she explained. 'He called it his "insurance policy". I was to get those. It wouldn't be hard. He wanted to impress me. I have that effect.'

'I don't doubt it,' I said dryly, looking at the woman stood before me. She could be challenging, and unreachable, and yet somehow promising. It must be an irresistible combination.

'This man...' Mary said.

'No names,' Lillian Rose said quickly, her hand dropping from her hip. 'I won't tell any names.'

'Of course. He must have offered you a lot of money.'

'Thousands,' Miss Rose confirmed. 'Enough to get out of here. Enough to keep my mouth shut.'

'We just need a name,' Mary coaxed. 'Nothing else, just a...'

'Are you mad?' Miss Rose snapped, and her hand shot to the scarf at her throat. How odd, that a woman with barely enough to eat should wear a scarf like that. She pulled it and twisted it as she spoke. 'You saw what he did to the Whitechapel Lady. He cut her open and tore out her innards, and all she did was ask a few questions!'

'Questions?' I asked.

'Questions,' Miss Rose confirmed bitterly. 'Just lately, just to the women on the street. About if they'd ever been paid for letters. Or helped a blackmailer. Barely anything, really, and she ended up ripped!'

My stomach sank. I glanced at Mary, who looked as horrified as I felt. After we had left her, the Whitechapel Lady must have decided her sedentary life was no longer enough. She must have decided to track down this man herself—and she ended up in a pool of blood.

'We're sorry...' Mary stammered, but Miss Rose shouted her down.

'Do you think she was the first, eh?' she cried. 'A death like that doesn't just happen, he's had practice. There were others, women who talked, women who fought back. He's swimming in blood, and no one's ever done a damned thing to protect us!'

Mary suddenly gasped.

'There were reports in the papers,' Mary whispered, turning to me. 'When I was researching the society ladies, there'd be reports of chambermaids and prostitutes and governesses, some hanged, some poisoned, a lot with a cut throat or wrists. Most were considered suicides, one or two perhaps seen as murder. But, there were so many, so separate, all in different places, most of them not even seen as suspicious. How do you link the death of a duchess in London to the suicide of a nursery maid in Glasgow? I only saw them because I was reading so many newspapers. I never thought...I never realized it was connected.'

'Of course not,' Miss Rose continued, her voice shaking. 'Why would you? We're not the rich ones. We're not ones he likes to break. We're just the ones he uses and then discards. What use does he have for us? Even the ones that got away!' She ripped the scarf away from her neck.

A livid scar ran across her throat, raised and red.

'He didn't try very hard with me,' Miss Rose said. 'Just tried to cut my throat. Not for much, just for talking to a policeman I liked. He thought I was telling on him. As if I dared! But I survived and came here, and I was making a life, and then he found me again. Just one job, he said. Get the letters and I'll let you go. And I was leaving.' Her voice dropped to almost a whisper, and a tear ran down her face. 'He told me last night I'd done enough, and he gave me the money, and he walked away. I had escaped. But now you're here, and he'll know, and he'll track me down, and he won't be so careless this time.'

She looked up at me, her eyes full of tears, a hunted animal finally knowing it must lose.

'I don't want to die,' she told me.

'He won't know...' Mary started to say.

'He'll know!' Miss Rose spat. 'He knows everything!'

She tied the scarf back round her neck, then turned to the suitcase and snapped it shut. She reached out to the picture on the wall.

'Almost,' she whispered.

'Go now,' I said urgently. 'We're getting closer, he'll be concentrating on us, he won't have time for you.' She turned to look at me. 'Go to King's Cross and go to Scotland, right in the Highlands. I know a place, a private place.' I took down the picture of the lake and on the back, with a scrap of pencil from Micky, I wrote the address of someone my mother had known, long ago.

'It's not far enough,' Miss Rose said.

'Far enough for now,' Mary said. 'It'll give us time to stop him.'

'You?' Miss Rose said, disbelieving. 'You're going to stop him?'

'Of course,' I said, straightening my back and clutching my handbag. I was, as Mr Holmes would have said, the very embodiment of British Empire.

Miss Rose almost smiled. 'Maybe you will at that,' she said, looking me up and down. 'He'll never see you coming.'

And with that Lillian Rose slipped out of the room and down the stairs.

I felt my solid spine give way, and I sat down heavily on the bed. Mary leaned against the wall.

'A murderer too,' she said slowly. 'We knew that,' I pointed out.

'Not the scale of it. She's right, though, to leave a scene behind like the Lady's, you have to have done it a few times before.'

'He's not the Ripper, Mary,' I insisted.

'I didn't think he was, not now,' Mary replied. 'I mean, all those murders she said he did—no one ever linked them together. He just killed them, slipped away, and no one ever knew they were done by the same hand.'

'Whereas the Ripper was killing as if he were holding up a great big sign shouting, "Look at me! I'm a killer!",' I added. 'No, not the same man, but perhaps...'

'Ladies,' Irene interrupted, peering round the door. Truth to tell, I'd almost forgotten she was there. 'Micky has spotted someone he says has been following us.'

'Who? What does he look like?' Mary asked.

'Don't know who,' Micky said, appearing beside Irene. 'Not much to look at, really. Just ordinary. But too ordinary. Got a patch on 'is jacket arm, like 'e's tried to clean something off. 'E's been following us for a while. Weren't sure at first, but 'e's been stood outside this house, doing nothing, all the while you've been 'ere.'

'He didn't follow Miss Rose? The lady who left here?' I asked quickly.

'Nah,' Micky replied. ''E's still out there.'

'Right,' I said firmly. In the last day I had been frightened, had run for my life, heard terrible stories and felt so helpless I could scream. Time for that to end. 'I've had enough of this,' I said, standing up.

'Now what?' Micky asked apprehensively.

'That man's been following me for days,' I said to them. 'Now we are going to follow him.'

The Corners of Whitechapel

The sky had darkened, covered in thick black clouds, making the day as dark as night, though it was only noon. The air felt heavy and thick and sharp, presaging a thunderstorm, and all through Whitechapel people hurried indoors before the greasy rain fell. Micky pointed through a grimy window at the street below. There, lounging against a doorway, was a man, not tall, nor short, not dark, nor fair, wearing a jacket with an odd stain on the elbow, his face shadowed by a crumpled soft hat. He straightened up, anticipating moving soon. There was no doubt he was waiting for us.

'There's always another way out of these places,' Irene said, and I did not have time then to wonder how she knew that. 'Micky?'

'Down 'ere,' he said, and he led us through a door in the house that seemed to be nothing more than a crack in the wall. Once, it would have been a servant's hidden entrance, but now it led us down through the wall of the building, thick with rats and stench. Beyond the walls I could hear people's voices and moans. Micky did not take us all the way down, but stopped at another door. This led into a room, large and empty, though scattered with belongings. Micky did not hesitate but walked across the room and threw open the window.

It opened onto a flat roof. Irene led the way, then helped me out, hampered as I was by my skirts. Mary climbed after me, not needing help. We scurried across the roof and down an iron ladder into the street below. Down an alleyway, through another, and quickly nipping across the street, we found ourselves behind the Ordinary Man.

This was the point where Irene and Micky tried to persuade us to go home. Mary refused vehemently, in a hissing whisper so the Ordinary Man could not hear us. Micky turned to me, then said to Irene he'd seen that look on my face before and no way was he going to try to stop me.

'Fair enough,' Irene agreed. 'Look, he's going in.'

We peered round the corner. The Ordinary Man must have realized we were taking too long to come out, and had gone into the house to check on us. A moment later we heard him shout, and saw the curtain to Miss Rose's room twitch.

It began to rain. Just a few large drops at first, then thunder smashed across the sky, and the rain fell in earnest. It was falling as if there were no end to it, as if it planned to spend its forty days' and forty nights' allowance in that one afternoon, in great huge rods of rain that hurt when they hit you, and smashed on the pavements and dashed though any gaps in the houses. The rain was filthy, grey with the dirt of London, grimy with the soot of the smoke it fell through. It was a rain to send even the rats scurrying for cover, but it was perfect for us. It emptied the streets, so no one was left but us and the Ordinary Man, and it was so heavy it concealed us and forced him to keep his head down.

He took a long and winding journey. He seemed to wander aimlessly, though Mary guessed that he was taking a deliberately convoluted route to flush out followers—but both Irene and Micky were skilled at this game. Mary and I hung back, out of his sight most of the time, whilst Irene and Micky worked as a pair, alternating between following him and coming back to guide us. Micky was good at this, as were all the Baker Street Irregulars, but so was Irene, subtly changing her appearance and the way she walked, so he could never tell if it was the same woman who was behind him.

'Quite a skill she has,' Mary observed once, dryly. 'So useful for an opera singer from New Jersey.' She and I had exchanged significant glances.

An opera singer from New Jersey—yet I had never detected the trace of an American accent in her voice. Well, maybe she had lost it—but America was such a convenient place to begin again, to wipe out one's past and emerge shining and new. Where had she actually grown up? Where had she learnt to follow a man so she would never be caught? Where had she met locksmiths and thieves? What had she done in her past that she could be blackmailed about? When had she learnt the skills to wander the streets of London dressed as a boy, and to do it so successfully that she fooled even Mr Holmes?

I know he had tried to dig into her past. He had books of cuttings, labelled 'her work', 'possibly her work' and 'maybe her work'. He had found nothing solid though, only rumours and speculations. Nothing about her seemed real; just the fancy of a moment. All he knew of her that was tangible was the sovereign of hers that he kept on his watch chain that she had given him when he had witnessed her wedding, and a photograph he kept in a drawer. And there was one other note about her: he had once said she had a face to die for, yet he seemed unmoved by that. But he had remembered hearing her sing at a concert, once, long ago, and her voice, and only her voice that night, had moved him to tears. Mr Holmes could always be touched by music where beauty failed. And now here was the American songbird in front of me, using skills no music teacher had ever taught her.

We must have seen every corner of Whitechapel that dark afternoon. Mary and I walked on, keeping the Ordinary Man at the very edge of our vision, sometimes letting him slip away altogether, knowing that Micky and Irene had a closer eye on him, and would come back to point us in the right way. The clouds thickened until the streets were black as night, and the rain hammered down incessantly. The whole scene had an unworldly look, like one of the engravings of hell seen in some old book that had terrified me as a child.

Once Mary pulled me back into an alley, against the wall, and motioned me to be silent. I thought perhaps our quarry had spotted us and was heading back our way, but a moment later I saw why we had hidden. As I peered out of the alleyway entrance, Mr Holmes and John ran past us.

I drew back, but they had not seen us. They had some quest of their own to pursue.

'You have your revolver, Watson?' Mr Holmes called.

'Always do!' John called back.

'Good. He shall not escape us this time!' Mr Holmes answered, as they disappeared into the dark and the rain.

'What do you suppose that was all about?' Mary asked, once she was sure they were gone.

'I have no idea,' I said, watching the street they had run down. I had not listened at the vent so frequently, and didn't know what Mr Holmes was currently working on. 'I don't suppose we'll ever know.'

We couldn't ask them, not without admitting we'd seen them. How odd that we should all be in Whitechapel on this day, hunting down villains, entirely separate from one another.

'Oh, John will tell us one day,' Mary said lightly. 'And then I'll tell him what we were doing here.'

The clocks were striking four in the afternoon, and the skies had clouded over. In the narrow streets of Whitechapel this made the day seem as if it was almost twilight. Micky scurried back to us and said, "'E's home. Miss Irene says we've found 'is lair. We've been hanging around outside for ages and 'e hasn't come out yet.'

We followed the boy up Commercial Road, and then down one of the streets, until we were almost in Stepney. Before us was a huge grey-brick warehouse. The name on the side had long since faded away, and the walls were blackened with dirt and the traces of a long-ago fire. The few windows were boarded, and the huge great doors were securely bolted. Only one small side door remained unsealed. I looked around. We were surrounded by other great warehouses, and the streets were empty and abandoned. Irene stood by the one small door that she had just finished unlocking. It was open now, and an odd white light spilled into the street. We stood there, only a few feet away from the Ordinary Man.

'Maybe we should...' Mary started to say, but I would not let her finish. I was angry, so very angry. I thought of Laura Shirley and the Whitechapel Lady and all those others I had never met or known. I thought of the lives taken and the lives smashed and the damage done and the blood spilled and the hearts broken. I thought of all this man had taken, assuming his right to do so. My anger flared and soared and burnt, and, without stopping to be careful or wary, I walked straight through the doorway into the warehouse.

I was surprised. I am not sure what I expected to find, but it was not this.

Most of the warehouse had been screened off with heavy curtains, leaving a large room about twenty feet square. This room was very brightly lit with gas lamps. Highly polished mirrors directed the light to various areas. The curtains them-selves were either velvet, or had highly improbable country scenes painted on them. Various items stood about the room—larger plaster Greek urns, mismatched sofas and chairs, fake statues. Along one wall stood a rail, and from this hung several items of clothing—all rather gaudy and diaphanous. In the centre of the room, on a violently coloured Turkish carpet, stood a woman, perfectly still, posing as if for a portrait. She wore a Greek helmet, sandals—and nothing else.

'Close the bleeding door, love,' she called out. 'I'm freezing my tits off 'ere.'

Mary gasped, half laughing. Irene did laugh, then turned the wide-eyed Micky round and sent him outside. I looked behind me to where I expected the painter to be. Instead I saw a large wooden box, about two feet square, balanced on a tripod. A large glass lens was inset on the side facing the girl. A cloth hung over the back of it, with a man underneath the cloth.

So, a camera. And being operated by the Ordinary Man. He even wore the same jacket with the same white stain on it. The one I had spotted over and over again, the only mark by which I'd recognized him. He came out slowly and glared at me—though more with annoyance than anger, to my surprise.

'You again,' he said wearily. 'You just keep popping up, dontcha? What the 'ell do you want?'

I had nothing to say. I just stared at him, with the uneasy feeling creeping over me that I had made a horrible mistake—again.

Mary had walked over to a table at the back of the room. There were boxes of photos on it, and she shamelessly began poring over them.

'Pictures,' Mary said. 'Dirty pictures. Very dirty pictures!' she said, a little shocked, but not all that horrified. She turned one round and round in her hand. Irene, suddenly curious, went over to join her. I did not move.

'Pornography,' I muttered. 'Not blackmail.'

'Look, who exactly are you?' the Ordinary Man demanded,

quite reasonably given the circumstances. In passing, I noted that I had been asked that question rather a lot recently. Maybe I should give thought to acquiring business cards.

He must not have seen me properly before. Perhaps I was in shadow, as always. But as he came out from behind the camera, he turned one of the mirrors towards me, so the light was full on my face. It was very bright, but I did not flinch. He, however, did. He must have recognized me, as a woman he'd followed. He did not speak. Neither did I. We merely stood there, the shadows flickering between us, watching each other for a reaction we could understand.

The naked woman sighed, relaxed her pose, and rubbed her back. Spotting an opportunity, Mary hurried over to her with a dressing gown and started chatting to her, leaving the photographs to Irene. Mary had an art of putting anyone at their ease, and within moments she and the young woman, named Ruby, were talking brightly about photography. Mary's questions sounded artless, but she was gradually drawing out of Ruby who the man photographed, how he photographed, could he take a photograph in secret?

'According to the name on these pictures,' Irene called out to me, 'this man is called Robert Sheldon.'

'Leave those alone!' he ordered, but he didn't take his gaze from mine.

I had expected defiance. I had expected anger. I had even expected, perhaps, horror at discovery. I had not expected his fear. The blood drained from his face, his eyes opened as wide as could be, his hand trembled. What could he possibly fear from me? He had brazenly followed me all over London, but he had never looked at me this way.

That was when I got the first inkling. Perhaps I had not taken the wrong path. Perhaps I had merely taken a necessary detour.

'The Whitechapel Lady,' I said quietly. Over in the corner Irene still turned over the photographs. At the other side of the room Mary and Ruby chattered happily, and fruitfully. Yet at that moment there was no one else in the world but him and me.

'I didn't kill her,' he said. His pale eyes bored into mine and I believed him.

'You were outside her home,' I insisted. 'You followed her. You followed her all over Whitechapel and when I visited her, you followed me. Then she dies in a pool of blood.' I had no idea I could be so inexorable. He looked as if the curse had come upon him.

'I watched you, that's all. Just watched!' he said, in a low, intense voice.

'Why?'

'I thought you were a do-gooder. I thought you'd try to get me stopped. I wanted to see who you talked to about me.'

'Why would I talk about you?'

''Cos people like you do talk, doncha,' he said bitterly. 'You decent people. Talk about morality and doing good and cleaning up the streets and all you're doing is doing people like me and Ruby out of a day's wages. Whitechapel's full of women like you, you know, wanting to stop us. I've met your kind before, and had to move on 'cos of it. I'm not 'aving your lot interfering again.'

And I knew that was a lie. Never mind, for now.

'And was the Whitechapel Lady a do-gooder?'

'Yeah.' He sneered. 'Dangerous profession.'

'Do you know who killed her?'

'No,' course not!' he insisted, turning pale. 'I just wanted to see what she did. Wanted to check she wasn't going to interfere with my work.'

'Liar,' I pronounced. I moved forward, the light behind me now, so my face was in shadow. 'Someone told you to follow her. Someone told you to watch her. Someone told you to report on her. And when that someone heard I had visited her, had asked questions, someone told you to kill her. And how long, exactly, was I going to last before I too was found in a pool of blood?'

'I didn't kill her!' he stammered, shaking. 'I saw her, I saw all that blood. I went up there—he asked me to go up there...'

'Why?' I demanded. He became suddenly silent. 'It was a warning, wasn't it? This is what will happen if you talk to anyone. But I am here now, and he is not. Tell me,' I insisted. He glanced around, like a trapped animal. 'Tell me,' I said again, but then, like a trapped animal does sometimes, he lashed out, the heavy mirror beside him suddenly pushed down onto me. I had a second, barely a second, to step out of the way, before it smashed onto the ground next to me. The shattered glass flew up and scratched my hands and face.

A moment before I had felt like Nemesis herself. Now I felt like a little old lady once again.

Irene ran forward and caught him by the wrist. He squirmed, but her grip was like iron.

'Are you hurt?' she asked me.

'No,' I said, my voice suddenly weak. Mary ran over and studied my cuts and scratches.

'You're fine,' Mary confirmed. 'Just superficial cuts. Lucky for you.' She turned on Mr Sheldon. 'If you had hurt her...'

'So what!' he cried. 'Do you think I'm afraid of you? Whatever you could do to me, he could do much worse. I'm under his protection, do you understand!' he screamed, his voice rising, trying to convince me as much as himself. 'If you try anything, you'd be dead before you left Whitechapel!'

'Maybe,' Irene said, letting him go. 'But we have protection too,' she whispered, enjoying what she told him. 'If you hurt any of us, we know a man who can and will hunt you to the ends of the earth, and tear your heart out.'

We were at an impasse. He was too afraid to speak, our protectors were silent, invisible and deadly, and no one knew what to do next.

'Leave 'im alone, can't yer?' Ruby said, not angrily. 'Look, 'e ain't a bad man, not a good one neither, but 'e's been all right to me and I like this job.'

'Do you?' I asked, surprised.

'It's indoors,' Ruby said, going to stand next to Robert Sheldon, laying one hand on his arm. He didn't turn to look at her, but he did cover her hand with his for a moment. 'In the warm, no one touches me or paws me—so I'd say this was pretty good, and 'e found me, and 'e gave me this, so stop scaring 'im, will yer?'

'Sorry,' Mary said, spontaneously. 'It's just…'

''E follows people,' Ruby said. Sheldon seemed to be getting his breath back, and was standing a little taller. He was watching Ruby with astonished eyes. I don't think he had known she cared. ''E's good at it, and no one notices 'im. But I swear that's all 'e does.'

'I don't recognize anyone in the photographs,' Irene said. 'But I doubt he'd keep the juicy ones here.'

'Is that what you did?' I asked. 'Take secret photographs? Hidden behind a curtain?' But my accusations sounded weak even to me.

'I'm not sure it works like that,' Mary said. 'This equipment is hardly discreet.'

I turned back to Robert Sheldon. I had an idea. There was a way to eliminate at least one suspect.

'Have you seen him then? This man?' I asked. He shook his head. He would not answer, but Ruby did. She didn't seem to be afraid. Perhaps she didn't know she was supposed to be.

'I did,' she said. 'Just once. 'E came to see Robert. Yeah, I know I shouldn't 'ave been looking,' she said in response to Robert Sheldon's horrified look, 'but I couldn't resist a bit of a peek. 'E never saw me. Besides, I didn't really see 'im. It was all dark in 'ere, and 'e was leaving. I just saw sort of a shadow on the door, that's all. Just an outline. Not enough to tell you what 'e looked like.'

'Was he a large man?' I asked.

'No, just normal sized. Bit skinny really,' she said, shrugging.

Robert Sheldon stared at her in silence, and then moved away. 'I didn't hurt anyone,' he insisted. I could not gauge the truth of that. 'Probably not,' I told him. 'You're a coward.' I had intended to provoke a reaction, and I got one. He drew himself up to his full height and marched down on us.

'You insult me, you invade my work, you damage valuable equipment and you make foul accusations!' he cried. Suddenly he was not the cringing little man any more, but someone with a bit of power. Even his accent had changed, from Whitechapel to somewhere more salubrious. I wondered who he'd run to once we were gone. 'If you come near me again, I shall call the police. If you wish to question me again, contact my solicitor,' and he shoved his solicitor's card, drawn from his waistcoat pocket, at me as he ushered me through the door, 'who I'm sure will be happy to charge you with libel! I'm not scared of you,' he said, one last blow as we tried to leave with our dignity. 'How could I be scared of a bunch of women?'

Clues and Traps and Patterns

Outside, mercy of mercies, Micky had found a cab large enough to take us all home. It was an ancient, rickety old thing that must have been fashionable a hundred years ago. It still bore traces of gilt paint here and there, and the upholstery, though worn and torn, held hints of the rich green colour it had once been. I was so tired. I had been kept going by the excitement of the day but now, as the clocks struck five and the murky daylight became night, I was exhausted. Judging by her yawns, so was Mary. Micky held the door open as Mary and I clambered in. We offered him a lift, but he said he'd rather walk. Carriages made him sick, he said. Irene paused and shook hands solemnly with the boy.

'A pleasure working with you, Micky,' she said. 'I hope to meet you again sometime.'

'And you, Miss Irene,' Micky said, obviously impressed by Irene's street skills.

Irene climbed in, and I leaned out of the window. 'Micky, here's the five shillings we owe you; it was a good day's work,' I said, handing him the money. 'Come to the kitchen at 221b tomorrow, and I'll have hot gingerbread for you.'

His thin face lit up, and for a moment, he looked just like the little boy he was. Then he controlled himself and said, 'Enough for the others too, missus? We share what we got!' They looked after each other, the Irregulars.

'I shall make plenty for everyone,' I promised him, 'and you may take it back to them, but I want to see you in the kitchen, to thank you personally.' Not just to thank him, but to make sure he suffered no ill-effects from the day's adventures. Someone in this game was vicious enough to harm a child, I was sure. Micky grinned, tipped his hat to me, and left.

I settled down into the back of the carriage, Mary lolling sleepily beside me. That woman could sleep after living though a battle. Irene sat opposite me, her back to the driver, watching to see if anyone followed us. She must have been satisfied, because she leaned out of the window and told the driver where to go. She sat back down, and we continued in silence, Irene watching, Mary dozing, me thinking, turning the card Mr Sheldon had given me over and over in my hand.

'Well, at least it's not Mycroft,' I said. 'He's a large man, exceptionally large. Neither the man the Whitechapel Lady knew nor the man Ruby saw was large.'

'They may have been representatives of the blackmailer,' Irene pointed out.

'I don't think so,' I said, pinching the bridge of my nose wearily. I would have liked to have just lain down and gone to sleep. 'The blackmailer gets personally involved with his victims, otherwise how does he see their pain? The Whitechapel Lady said he enjoyed seeing her agony close up. I think he stays close to them, to watch what happens and to do that he has to blend in, he has to look unnoticeable. Mycroft Holmes stands out. He is very large, and very visible.'

'Besides, he's too lazy,' Mary said. 'I really don't think he's guilty.'

'Not of this crime, no,' I agreed. I didn't trust the man. I never would. But this wasn't his crime. He was capable of the events, but not, I think, capable of the lack of control this black-mailer was beginning to show.

'Dead end,' Irene said, after a while. She wasn't talking about the road.

'When Mr Holmes hits a dead end,' I said to her, 'he goes back to the beginning and re-examines the evidence.'

'How many dead ends does Sherlock Holmes hit?' Irene said wryly.

'Not many,' I admitted.

To be perfectly honest with ourselves, we didn't have all that much solid evidence. This case was all emotion and suppo-sition, instinct and guesswork. There was no solid basis to it. It constantly shifted and changed, always just one step ahead of us, the entire story just a wisp of smoke that would disappear as soon as we tried to grasp it. The task seemed so huge. I sagged in my seat.

'I feel so tired,' I admitted. 'Yet I doubt I could sleep.' Beside me, Mary yawned widely, her eyes still closed, and I smiled. Obviously she was not having the same problem.

'Mr Holmes stays awake for hours and days on end when he has a case,' I told Irene, keeping my voice low so I did not disturb Mary. 'I used to wonder how he did it. Now I think he has no choice. He cannot sleep.'

Irene smiled, a little sadly, and stared out of the window at Oxford Street. The roads were brightly lit now, the gas lamps were alight, and the shops still open—some would be open until midnight. The streets were busy and crowded, and we moved slowly, but I was in no hurry.

'What's that?' Irene asked, nodding at the bit of cardboard in my hand.

'Oh, Mr Sheldon said if we were to contact him again, we'd have to do it through his solicitor. Something about libel.'

'I didn't hear him say that...Horrible little man,' Irene muttered.

I turned the card over. John Kirkby, solicitor at law. Not a well-regarded one, by any means, judging by the grubbiness of the cheap card. Not like...not like the Whitechapel Lady's solicitor, Sir Richard Halifax.

And then, all of a sudden, there was one solitary spark in the darkness. I felt my breath catch. Oh my. Oh my indeed.

'I can't talk to Laura Shirley,' I said, half to myself. 'I doubt she'd talk to me now.'

'What's that?' Irene asked. I looked up.

'I want to talk to a victim, but the only one I know is Laura Shirley, and I believe she's doing her best to put the blackmail behind her and help her husband recover. I don't think she'd appreciate me calling on her, not now,' I told her, suddenly sitting forward in my seat. 'I don't know any of the other victims, or rather they don't know me, I don't think they'd want me turning up on the doorstep saying I know you've been blackmailed, can you...'

'You know me,' Irene said calmly, interrupting me.

Of course. I'd come to think of Irene as an associate, but she was a victim too. That was the entire reason she was here. I leaned forward.

'I may have an idea,' I told her. 'I need to work this through in my head, get it clear. Will you be so kind as to answer a few questions?'

'Of course,' Irene said, amused.

'The blackmailer: did he know about your liaison with the King of Bohemia?'

'He did, which is why I had to suspect Sherlock in the first place.'

'Who else knew of that liaison?'

'No one.'

'No, people did,' I insisted. 'Name everyone, Irene. Everyone who had the slightest inkling. The King's servants?'

'Always blindfolded, and faultlessly loyal, or they wouldn't be the King's servants. And they are all in Bohemia,' Irene said, looking puzzled.

'We can rule the King out as a suspect, can't we?' I asked.

'We can,' Irene said dryly. 'He may not be completely honourable, but he's not clever enough to do all this.'

'Me, John, Mr Holmes...' I went through the list.

'Obviously not blackmailers.'

'Your husband?'

'No, he never had a clue until I told him. And he wouldn't care if he did. The whole affair belongs firmly in the past.'

'There was a photograph of you and the King together. You took it with you, didn't you?'

'No, I left it here,' Irene told me. 'In a very safe place.'

'Where, Irene?' I insisted, leaning further forward so I almost touched her. 'Where did you leave that awfully incriminating photograph? Where did you leave all your incriminating papers, Irene?'

'In a sealed box with my solicitor, of course,' she told me, puzzled. And there I had my answer. She must have seen my face light up. 'My solicitor!' she breathed. 'But the box was sealed...'

'Anyone can open and reseal a box,' I told her. 'Especially a solicitor who has access to all kinds of ways of sealing boxes. Who is your solicitor?'

'Kettlewell,' Irene said breathlessly. 'Sir Jacob Kettlewell. I trusted him...'

'Everyone does,' I told her. 'I have left all kinds of papers with my solicitor. So have John and Mr Holmes. We never dreamed they'd be anything but utterly secure and safe.'

'Kettlewell,' Mary said vaguely. 'Very pretty little village in Yorkshire. John and I went there once.' She stirred out of her doze and saw Irene and I staring at her, our eyes wide. 'Did I miss something?'

'Kirkby,' I said to her.

'That's in Yorkshire too,' Mary said, sitting bolt upright. 'What's going on?'

'I glimpsed the name of Sir George Burnwell's solicitor in his study,' Irene said, as excited as I was. 'Peter York!'

'The man that threatened the Whitechapel Lady was called John Ripon. That's in Yorkshire too. Why are we talking about solicitors?' Mary asked. So we told her.

A woman has no safe places to hide. Everything she has belongs to her husband. He may read her private papers and letters if he so wishes. So women—especially ones with secrets— lodge all their papers and letters and private boxes with their solicitor, who is under oath not to reveal their secrets. The women imagine their papers safe. After all, a solicitor is a representative of the law. Who would imagine that a solicitor would break open the seal, read the secrets, blackmail and kill and destroy? And if you did suspect, how could you tell? Imagine all the secrets he kept back, ready to use, just to keep you silent.

'It's the same man,' Mary said, in the end. 'All those solici- tors with names from Yorkshire, they are the same man.'

'Why choose Yorkshire villages?' Irene asked. 'And wouldn't he be rather busy with all those clients?'

'Aliases are difficult to remember,' Mary said. Irene nodded. So, she knew that too? 'Far easier to remember who you are if you know it must be a village in Yorkshire.'

'Maybe he comes from there,' I said, staring out of the carriage window, willing it to push through the crowds and go faster. I was having to suppress an urge to cry, 'the game is afoot!' No wonder Mr Holmes charged about the entire city when he was solving a case. I felt like I could run from Buckingham Palace to Baker Street in pursuit.

'When was the last time you saw your solicitor?' Mary asked Irene.

'I saw him when I hired him,' Irene said. 'A little old man. Since then, all my transactions have been by post.'

'Well, there you are then. That's how most people deal with their solicitor. One or two initial meetings, and the rest by post. It's simple. A few disguises, or a few willing actors to play a solic- itor for the initial meetings…'

'He did seem suspiciously solicitor-like,' Irene agreed. 'He did remind me of a solicitor in a play.'

'Precisely!' Mary exclaimed. 'And after that, whichever office you directed your mail to would be nothing more than a clerk redirecting your mail somewhere else. Or even just a letterbox he visits twice weekly.'

'That would be safer,' Irene said. 'But wait—Lillian Rose was sent to Sir George Burnwell by the blackmailer to retrieve papers from his solicitor. Why do that if the solicitor is the blackmailer?'

'To test Lillian Rose?' I said. I could think of half a dozen reasons now. 'To prove he owns her? To test Sir George? To see how loyal Sir George is, or what he would do for a pretty face? To get them together for some reason? To make sure Sir George isn't holding anything back? Or just to play with them; moving pieces around in his elaborate game to see what happens for fun.'

'I can see that,' Irene said. 'With a mind like this, like the one we're dealing with, all that is possible. You know, it works! That all actually works!'

'We found him! Well, almost found him, we've found him out, it's just a question of research,' Mary said excitedly. 'But we're within reach now! Martha, Irene, the game is very much afoot!' she laughed, and then her face suddenly froze. I knew why. She had the same thought I'd had just a few moments before.

'Martha,' she said, quieter now. 'We met the Whitechapel Lady's solicitor outside her home, when she was murdered. You talked to him, I didn't. What did he…'

'Halifax,' I told her. 'He said his name was Halifax.'

'In Yorkshire,' Mary murmured. 'Oh, Martha, we spoke to him. I shouted at him!'

'Yes, I spoke to him,' I said, my body cold, both with anger and fear. 'I stood in the street, and spoke to her murderer, the blood barely dry on his hands, and I never knew. I never even guessed.'

'Maybe it was one of his actors,' Irene said.

I shook my head. 'For what reason?' I asked. 'He didn't need to speak to anyone there. The only person he knew there was the Whitechapel Lady, and she knew him as himself, although under a different name. Besides, I think he was gloating. I think he'd come back to revisit the scene of his crime, to see how clever he'd been. To exult in what he'd done. Mr Holmes says criminals often do that. No, that was our man, I am sure.'

'Did you tell him your name?' Mary asked. I told her no.

'He knew,' Irene said. 'He would have found out. I'm very much afraid this killer, this solicitor, has known who you are for quite a while now.'

'Why hasn't he done anything?' Mary asked.

Irene turned to her. 'He's a hunter. He's stalking you. He's stalking his prey, until you are in the right position.'

Until he had us firmly in his sights.

All those solicitors—Kettlewell, Kirkby, York. I'd lay good odds that Ripon was a solicitor, too—maybe not the Whitechapel Lady's, but of someone she knew. Why would she mention that? Solicitors are so unimportant! All of them supposed to be quiet, good, loyal men, all to be trusted with the power and the secrets they held in their hands. I could imagine them—*him*—sitting in his office long after dark, the shutters closed, the dusty room lit by a single candle, taking down the black deed boxes inscribed with noble names, breaking the seals he knew how to replace, and reading each and every one of those secret papers they thought they had kept so safe. How he must have loved that. Standing in those grand houses, standing as they sat, and gave him orders, and condescended to him, and made him wait, how he must have stood there and thought. 'I know. I know every one of your dirty, grubby, vile little secrets. I know exactly what you did. I know exactly how you covered it up. I could ruin you.' It must have been such a small step from thinking that to one day, pushed too far, humiliated just that little bit more, actually saying, 'I know'. And then would have come their fear, the begging and the promises, and he must have realized that of it all, he liked the fear the best.

But after a while, just fear alone became dull. He didn't have enough secrets. So first he found more, and then he made them up, and then came the blackmail, and control, and terror and joy in someone else's destruction, and then their death and then—and then how long before he found blood on his hands, and realized he liked that too?

And now he was a madman. Small steps from the curious solicitor to the murderous madman. All because of those secrets. How he must love his secrets.

We all sat back in our seats, just like before, yet changed. Now we knew. That knowledge made us all different. Mary leaned her head back and stared into the streets passing by with a satisfied little smile on her face. Irene sat in her corner, staring out the window, clenching and unclenching her fist, her face tight with anger, once muttering 'Stupid, stupid!' to herself. And I—I sat a little more upright. My hands rested in my lap, lightly clasped. I looked out of the window, searching and watching and knowing, now, that he was out there. And I would find him.

'We're on Serpentine Avenue,' I said, noticing the street name.

Irene stirred and looked around her. She called to the driver to stop. 'It's late,' she said, noticing the dark and empty street. 'I'll make sure he takes you home.' She got out and called up to the driver to take us to 221b, giving him enough money to complete the journey. Then she leaned in at the window.

'That child Micky...' she started to stay.

'Will be safe,' I assured her. 'Wiggins takes care of his boys.'

'On the streets,' Irene finished blankly.

'I think perhaps those children are safer on the streets than in the workhouse, or in service to someone who will abuse them,' I said to her.

She nodded. 'We all find our ways to survive,' Irene said thoughtfully. 'Wait a moment.'

She ran into the house, and came out ten minutes later.

'These are all the papers I have in connection with my solicitor,' Irene told me. 'Bills, letters, and so on. Hopefully you can find something helpful in them.'

'Don't you want to look through them?'

She shook her head.

'This is your work,' she insisted. 'You and Mary have been the ones doing the investigation. I've just been along for the ride. Besides, I'm too close to this. My view is distorted. You, on the other hand, see very clearly. You have a gift for seeing the entire puzzle.'

I took the papers and folded them up tight in my hand.

'What will you do now?' Irene asked. Behind her, the horses stamped a little, impatient to be gone. I glanced at Mary, peacefully sleeping in the corner.

'I shan't do anything until tomorrow,' I told Irene. 'I'm an old woman, I need my rest.'

Irene snorted. 'Old woman, not a chance! You pretend you're fully middle-aged, creeping into old age, but I've been watching you. You're not all that much older than I am.'

With that she stepped back and let the cab continue on its way.

I sat back and, for a moment, allowed myself to remember. Twenty years ago, almost to the day, my boy had died. My seven-year-old mischievous, delightful, intensely alive little boy. And when he died, instantly I became old. My hair became threaded with grey, and I pulled it back into a tight knot, taming my curls. I put away my pretty dresses and wore only black. I walked slowly and never smiled and when I sat down, I winced as if my bones ached, though they did not. My boy died, and I became a seventy-year-old matron immediately. I'd stopped being Martha and became Mrs Hudson, the respectable housekeeper and land-lady. I knew when people looked at me they saw a little old lady, grey and worn, all in black.

In truth I was only forty-eight.

The cab rattled through the streets. I clasped Irene's papers in my hand, and tried to work out what to do next. I knew now what Mr Holmes had meant about the faith that was placed in him and now in me, and I also knew what he meant about the terrible fear that you will somehow betray that faith.

When we arrived at 221b, Billy ran out to meet us and opened the door.

'Mr Holmes and Dr Watson aren't home yet,' he told us, as Mary yawned herself awake.

'No, I don't suppose they are,' I replied, remembering the men running past in Whitechapel. It looked as if their chase would go on for a while. 'Mary, why don't you take the cab and go home?'

'I'm not tired,' Mary asserted, just like a schoolgirl who wants to stay up late with the grown-ups.

'Liar,' I told her, calling up the address to the driver.

'I shan't sleep until John gets home anyway,' she told me, slightly truculently.

'Then best you "don't sleep" in your own home,' I told her, closing the door of the cab. It left, and I turned to Billy, who looked unaccountably angry.

'What's wrong?'

'First Mr Holmes and Dr Watson off chasing down a villain,' Billy replied, 'and then the three of you running around goodness knows where. And don't tell me you weren't doing anything because Wiggins told me you took Micky! You had me worried, you know! Yeah, me, worried!'

I smiled, touched by this young boy's concern.

'I'm sorry,' I apologized. 'I should have told you. But I need you now. Would you like to help me solve this?' I asked him. He grinned, good humour restored.

Inside, in the kitchen, I spread Irene's papers out on the table. I gathered together all the notes I had written on Laura Shirley and the Whitechapel Lady. I sent Billy upstairs to retrieve Sir George Burnwell's papers. Hopefully amongst this mass of documents I would find the vital clues I needed.

How to proceed? I closed my eyes, took a breath and let my mind wander. *The Lady, the victims, the blackmail, the murders, the pornographer, the Yorkshire towns, the secrets, the solicitors.* It all kept ringing in my head. I heard voices—Laura Shirley, begging for help, the Whitechapel Lady revealing her face, the murmurings of people on the street, Irene saying, 'My view is distorted. You see the whole puzzle'.

My eyes snapped open. Puzzle. Games. Clues and traps and patterns.

I looked at the clock. It was eight at night.

'Billy, I need a map of London,' I told him.

'I've got lots of maps of London, all kinds. Mr Holmes says I should learn every street in London.'

'Do you have a large map of London including its suburbs, with all streets named?'

'I do. I'll get it.'

I may not have known how my deductions would end, but I knew where to start them.

Putting Together the Pieces

A few weeks ago, Mary had been sitting at my kitchen table, turning over the pages of one of Billy's books. It was an old history book one of his tutors had left behind. Billy had expressed an interest in the Wars of the Roses—sparked, I am sure, by lurid tales of the battlefield John had told him.

'I could teach Billy,' Mary said suddenly. John was out with Sherlock, on one of their four-hour-long walks around London. Mr Holmes hadn't had any new cases for a few weeks, and he was restless. Billy was out with Wiggins somewhere, and I was trying a new bread recipe.

'Why?' I asked, mixing the flour and baking powder and only half paying attention to Mary. 'I thought you were happy to stop being a governess.'

'I was happy to stop being a governess because I didn't like the position,' Mary said, restlessly playing with a teaspoon. 'It can be very lonely, and not at all satisfying. But I did quite enjoy the teaching. It was a challenge, trying to find a way to impart complicated information to a child's mind. I like a challenge.'

'Well, you could teach Billy, if you wanted to,' I said, leaning over the table to read the recipe. 'He has tutors, and Mr Holmes and Dr Watson, of course, but he is always willing to learn more.'

'He doesn't really need me, you mean,' Mary said disconsolately. 'I could teach Wiggins, perhaps, and the Irregulars.'

'I'm not sure they'd be quite so eager,' I told her over my shoulder as I went into the pantry. Would I need more eggs? These recipes always needed a little adjusting. 'They might see it as interfering in their lives.'

'I'd like to know more about their lives, as a matter of fact,' Mary said, putting the teaspoon down with a clatter.

'Their lives are dangerous,' I said, meaning to warn her off.

'A little danger would be very enjoyable,' Mary said wistfully. 'Just enough to make life interesting.'

I wasn't listening. I was paying attention to the bread. I didn't hear the yearning in her voice.

Mary was, however, far from my thoughts right now. I had sent her home, she was safe, with John when he came back, and I had work to do right here in my kitchen. Billy brought the large map to me, and we spread it out on the kitchen table, weighing down the corners with the tea, coffee, sugar and spice caddies. The map covered all of London and its suburbs, for several miles, with most streets named, albeit in tiny writing. I took my pen, and the red ink I used for checking the butcher's bills—he could never be relied on to add up amounts correctly.

'Right,' I said. 'Let's begin.'

'What are you doing?' Billy asked. I had given him a summary of the evening as we had laid the map out, and had told him about the names, and the clues, and the solicitor himself, with his network of spies and informers and victims.

'I've already found one pattern,' I told him. 'The solicitors' names all come from Yorkshire. And where there is one pattern, there is often another.'

I looked through the papers Irene had given me, and found a bill with her solicitor's address on it. Billy found this on the map, marking it in red ink. I read out the address on the card from Mr Sheldon, and again he found it and marked it.

Together we looked through Sir George Burnwell's papers. He was terribly disorganized. If Lillian Rose could have found anything quickly in this mess, she deserved an award. Eventually a crumpled piece of paper covered in wine stains proved to be a solicitor's bill, complete with address. We again marked it on the map.

Three red dots. They seemed to form no discernible pattern. They were scattered all over the city, in middle-class areas. I needed more data.

'Yorkshire names,' I murmured to myself.

'Why do that?' Billy asked. 'Why use the names of villages in Yorkshire? Surely he realized someone would notice it, sooner or later?'

'Well, no one did notice until now,' I said to him. 'Maybe it's like Irene said, it's just easier to remember the aliases better if they're all linked. He probably grew up in Yorkshire. Perhaps he has no idea he's doing it. Or perhaps...'

Another thought crept its way into my mind. Games...

'Perhaps he's doing it deliberately,' I said slowly, thinking as I talked. 'He is hoping that one day, someone will look at all these names and see they are connected. He wants someone to realize that it's all a puzzle. He's playing with us. It's a game to him—one great game.'

'He wants to entice you?' Billy said, uncertain. 'I mean, you, specially?'

'With anyone clever and dedicated to start to track him down,' I explained. 'I doubt he was expecting it to be Mary and me, he was probably hoping for...oh. Oh, Billy, it wasn't meant to be us at all!' I suddenly understood.

It had puzzled me for a while. Mary and I should have been victims by now. If he could kill the Whitechapel Lady, he could easily hurt us too. We had been getting so close, he must have noticed us. He should have turned on us. He had had us followed. He had even talked to me. He was capable of great violence, yet we had not been so much as threatened. We had not even had a letter, and he had written so many letters. Why?

This man had been playing games for years. He had worked so hard, been so clever, found the weakness, found the almost invisible cracks in these women's lives and bit by bit played his game until he had all the pieces in the right place and then destroyed these women. But he was too good at it. The game had become too easy. His victims were too guileless, not subtle or devious enough to fight back. He had become bored.

He wanted a bigger game. He wanted a more dangerous, more complicated game. He wanted to play with an adversary worthy of giving him a fight. He wanted the ultimate adversary. He had laid out an invitation. I laughed, all of a sudden. He hadn't threatened us because he thought we were just pawns of someone else. He thought he was battling someone else. He thought his great opponent was Sherlock Holmes.

I smiled to myself, and it was not a kind smile. It was this man, in the disguise of a solicitor, who had sent Laura Shirley, and perhaps Adam Ballant, to 221b. This man had laid down an invitation for Mr Holmes to play, and I had picked it up.

I'd been underestimating my own skills for years. I'd been a clever landlady and a skilled cook, but I'd never appreciated what else I could do. I never knew I could think like this, put the clues together, jump from idea to proof to theory to certainty. I'd barely known what I was capable of. If I could solve these problems, what else could I do? I'd be damned if I let this evil sod underestimate me too. I'd play the game he'd set for Mr Holmes, and I would play it well. I, at least, had the element of surprise.

I looked at the map. Giving myself stirring speeches was all very well, but I still had to perform the task itself.

'Mary's better at this sort of thing than I am,' I muttered.

'What sort of thing?' Billy asked. I had been lost in my own thoughts and I hadn't actually realized he was sitting at the table watching me, his chin resting on his folded arms, looking up at me.

'This,' I said, waving at the map. 'The practical elements. The clues. The science.'

'Then what do you do?' Billy asked.

'People,' I said to him. 'I think I'm good with people. And patterns. I see patterns. Perhaps. I hope so.'

'I think so,' Billy said, standing up and stretching. 'Do you want to leave this until morning?'

'Yes...no,' I told him. I was restless and wouldn't be able to sleep or read or bake anyway. I wouldn't be able to concentrate on anything else. 'Let us at least make a start. Occupy ourselves until Mr Holmes returns. Is there such a thing as a register of solicitors?'

'Yes, Mr Holmes has one,' Billy replied. I asked him to get it, and a gazetteer of Yorkshire.

Ten minutes later we crouched over the table, matching names from the gazetteer to names from the register. Some of these names would be innocent, of course—many solicitors were called Leeds or Halifax without being cold-hearted murderers. But some of them would be him. They must be. If he was playing a game, he would insist on sticking to the rules.

Bit by bit, the scattered red crosses on the map grew. There seemed to be no rhyme or reason to them. His offices were scattered all over London, with no particular pattern to them. Poor areas, rich, middle-class—he was everywhere. It worried me, how many names could be him.

As we were marking the twentieth cross, I heard a commotion from upstairs. Someone was banging on the door, and shouting.

'That's John,' I cried out. Billy ran up the stairs and opened the front door, with me just behind him.

'Sorry, couldn't get my key,' John gasped. 'Give me a hand.'

He was supporting a pale and collapsing Mr Holmes. We helped them over the threshold. Blood dripped from Mr Holmes' arm, his jacket draped over it, the shirt torn where John had treated the wound. I gave a cry when I saw the injury, I must admit.

'Don't fuss, Mrs Hudson!' Mr Holmes snapped.

'Ignore him,' John said. 'He always gets in a foul mood when he's been stabbed.'

'Stabbed?' I gasped, as was expected of me. I wasn't actually that worried, just mildly concerned. This was not the first time Mr Holmes had come home in such a state. In fact, I believe it was the fifth. 'By whom?' Was it the quarry we had seen him chasing earlier? Had he become tired of Mr Holmes chasing him?

'A common thief,' John said, hauling Mr Holmes towards the stairs. 'It's nothing really, just a graze.' He must have seen my dubious look, for he whispered to me, as Mr Holmes shrugged him off and insisted on climbing the stairs himself, 'It looks worse than it is. This is more exhaustion than blood loss. You know how he works himself.'

'Too hard,' I replied grimly, following Mr Holmes up the stairs. Honestly, he was dripping blood all over the carpets. Never mind, I had long ago come up with a chemical formula of my own to remove blood. 'I'll send him some warm water and hot tea.'

'Not hot tea, I beg of you!' Mr Holmes cried, opening the door himself, despite John pushing past me and reaching for it. 'I'd as soon drink tepid pond water!'

'You'll drink it, and do as your doctor tells you!' John insisted. To me he said, 'That would be helpful, thank you. With plenty of sugar.'

I nodded in acknowledgement, and looked over John's shoulder into the rooms. Mr Holmes leaned against the back of the sofa, staring, in the very dim firelight, at some bookshelves—or rather, at the gaps left by the books Billy and I had borrowed. He turned and looked at me, puzzled. I remained imperturbable, my hands folded in front of me, the very picture of a respectable, not too intelligent, very commonplace housekeeper.

'Good night, Mr Holmes,' I said to him, as he opened his mouth to speak, and then I gently closed the door.

I did smile as I went down to the kitchen. I didn't know how long it would last, but for a moment there, I had confused the great Sherlock Holmes!

I sent Billy up with the water, tea and sandwiches, then I quickly mopped up the worst of the blood. What was left would dry to the same red-brown as the stair carpet and be unnoticeable by morning. Once that was done, I sat down at the table and looked at the map. I heard Billy come in and sit down at the table. He was still wide awake, but, I confess, I was starting to feel a little sleepy. Perhaps it could wait until morning.

'Mrs Hudson?' John called, coming down the main stairs. I hurried out of the kitchen before he could come in and see what I was doing.

'Is he all right?' I asked, standing in the hall.

'Mr Holmes is fine,' John replied. 'He's asleep. I gave him a sedative; he won't wake for hours. Is Mary here?'

He looked so worn. Looking after Sherlock Holmes was an exhausting job.

'No, Mary went home hours ago,' I told him.

'I have to go to Scotland Yard,' John told me. 'I have to find Inspector Gregson. The man who stabbed Holmes is still out there, but if we wait until morning, we may lose him.'

'I understand. I'll send Billy to let Mary know,' I reassured him.

'It's so late. I'll be out all night,' John told me.

'Billy's still awake,' I reassured him. 'And Mary would like to know.'

He nodded and left, briskly walking down the street. I sent Billy out a moment later, with a handful of cash for the cab. Then I went back down to the kitchen, and stared at the work I had done.

The candles had burnt down—it was almost half past nine at night. The remaining light was dim, and flickered across the room. It was so dark in there now, so quiet, after such a busy day. I had twenty crosses marked on the map. Let us say, at a conservative estimate, that just over half of those were legitimate solicitors. That left approximately nine names. Nine men taking secrets and promising to keep them safe, these nine men actually one foul fiend, a liar, a cheat, a blackmailer, a murderer. How many stories had he heard? How many women had sat before him, some weeping, some defiant, some ashamed, and confided in him, only for him to turn and bite? Only for him to bring about the very ruin they came to him to avert. All for the thrill of a game, for him.

How many had he killed? Some of those secrets he had taken from maidservants and prostitutes and other women not quite as important as his quarry. He hadn't played at being their solicitor, he had been their tormentor. They had seen his true colours when he threatened and used and abused them. Even the ones that had started out as allies had become his victims. He couldn't rely on them to keep silent. They must have died— we knew some had. I remembered when we were researching, way back in the beginning, I had spotted some incidents that now, given what I knew, would fit. The occasional report in newspapers of the death of an unimportant girl—often blamed on a male follower, someone of her own class. But the reports had become that bit more disturbing, the murders that bit more heinous, the wounds that bit more horrific, until it culminated in the ripping apart of the Whitechapel Lady. He would not stop there. As in the blackmail, as in his games, he had refined and perfected his technique of murder, and he would not stop. Like Jack the Ripper, his crimes would become more and more gruesome and horrific.

Of course, Jack had stopped. But I had my own theories about that, and they were not along the lines of sudden remorse or satiation.

I sighed. It was late and I was tired and my thoughts were

becoming gloomy. It was time to stop. Mary could look at this in the morning with fresh eyes. I had no doubt she would see something I had missed. I blew out the candles. As soon as Billy returned, I would go to bed.

As I had that thought, Billy hurtled through the front door and down the stairs into the kitchen. He was out of breath.

'Not there...' he panted. 'She got a note...' He held a scrap of paper out to me. It was a folded note, and the writing on it was startlingly like Mr Holmes'. It read 'Come at once. Watson hurt'.

'There was a carriage,' Billy said. 'The housemaid said it took her away.'

'Sit down,' I ordered, suddenly wide awake. 'Dr Watson is fine; Mr Holmes did not send this note.' I studied the note intently. The handwriting was unfamiliar, the paper not mine. It was a moment before I realised what had happened. 'It was a trap, he's taken her.'

'Taken Mrs Watson?' Billy cried. 'Why? What do they want?'

For a moment I nearly said 'me', and then I thought—no. I looked up, to the rooms above me, where all was silent now. Kidnapping Mary was far more likely to draw out Dr Watson, and hence Mr Holmes. This man was tired of waiting for Mr Holmes to put together the clues and had decided instead to lure him. He would be expecting John and Mr Holmes. He might even be watching them. As for me—I was just the housekeeper. I was unimportant. I was just another pawn.

'Mr Holmes gets that look,' Billy said softly, staring at me. 'That sort of frozen look you've got now. Only when he's really angry. Dr Watson says it frightens him. Mr Holmes will stop at nothing when he looks like that.'

'Yes,' I said, placing the letter on the table. 'I am very angry.'

'Should I find Dr Watson?' Billy asked, standing up.

'No,' I said firmly. 'I won't place them in danger, too. Besides, he is out at Scotland Yard and likely to be out all night.'

Billy sat down again. He did not argue.

I was afraid, and upset, and confused, and tired, but most of all I was angry. A white-hot anger that burnt bright enough to scorch. I was angry that those I loved were being used by this man, I was angry at being overlooked, I was angry that Mary had fallen for such an obvious trick, I was angry at myself for giving up on my life but most of all I was angry at *him* for every man and woman ruined, every life ended, every happiness destroyed, every drop of blood spilled, every woman who felt lost and alone and afraid.

I looked down at the map, and the papers. The clue was here somewhere, and I would find Mary. I would change the rules and cheat and lie and win.

'I will play the game.'

CHAPTER

18

Following the Clues

'What first?' Billy asked. I looked down at the map. All I really had was a mass of red crosses scattered randomly across London, and a game I knew only half the rules to. And the fear, of course. The fear that Mary was trapped, and helpless and afraid, and that I, in my stupid pride, was condemning her to death. That I could not do this alone, that I had no way of doing this, that I did not know what to do next, and it would be Mary who suffered.

'He charged them for everything,' Billy said, seemingly from nowhere. 'Not just work, but papers, pens, meals, cabs, everything.' I turned to look. He was reading a bill that he had picked up from Irene's papers.

'Solicitors do,' I told him, taking the bill. 'Especially this one. He'd charge you for the air you breathed if he thought...' My voice trailed away as I read the bill. Amongst sundry other items—carefully catalogued—was one particular charge.

Cab to Briony Lodge, Irene's house. 9 ¾ miles.

I picked up another bill. There it was, below the expenditure on seals.

Cab to Claridge's. 11 ½ miles.

Oh, for goodness' sake. I caught my breath so sharply I swayed a little and had to clutch the side of the table.

'He left us clues!' I said to Billy, who looked alarmed by my sudden breathlessness. 'He had to lay a trail, so he left us clues!'

'He did?'

'The cab rides—he has given us the length of the journey from his home to these locations,' I explained, holding out the bill. 'Find me all the bills you can. I know we only have Irene's and Sir George's but hopefully that will be enough.'

'What if the cab rides weren't from his home?' Billy asked, as he riffled through Sir George's papers. 'What if they came from his office?'

I hunted through the kitchen drawer where Billy kept his school equipment for his lessons.

'No,' I said emphatically. 'For a start, those offices either don't exist, or are nothing more than letter-drops. I doubt he goes anywhere near them. For another,' I continued, as I found the ruler and the compass with a pencil that I was searching for, 'he wants us to find him. Well, he wants someone to be clever enough to find him, I should say.'

I took the sheaf of bills from Billy's hand, and he went round the table, replacing the burnt-out candles with bright new ones.

'Billy, read out the first distance again.'

'Briony Lodge, 9 ¾ miles.'

I measured out 9 ¾ miles against the guide at the edge of the map. Then I stretched the compasses out to the correct distance. I put the point of the compass roughly where Briony Lodge was, and drew a circle.

It was crude, but it was a start. The circle encompassed a wide area of West London, and some of the centre too. There, within that circle, somewhere near the edge, we would find our solicitor.

'But it could be anywhere inside that circle,' Billy pointed out. 'London's streets all twist round each other. Five miles could be two roads over.'

'Read the bill,' I countered. 'At the top, there's a pre-printed message.'

'"All meals charged for are undertaken on client's business",' Billy read. 'A justification for the charges?'

'Read on.'

'"All charges for sundries such as pen, ink, paper etc. are undertaken at standard rate commensurate with hours worked on client's business. All distances are measured 'as the crow flies'." So five miles really would be...?'

'Five miles from his destination,' I confirmed.

'That doesn't seem right. Isn't it a bit obvious?' Billy asked dubiously.

'Billy, this is a trap,' I said gently. 'From the moment Laura Shirley came here, to the death of the Whitechapel Lady, even the kidnapping of Mary, this has all been a trap. And what use is a trap if you do not lay a trail for your quarry?'

'I see,' Billy said, peering at the bill. 'Difficult, but not impossible.'

'Quite.'

'But...would Mr Holmes have done it like this?' he objected. He picked up one of Sir George Burnwell's bills. It was printed with the same instructions at the top. 'Look, these are obviously printed at the same place. They even have the same irregularity at the corners. Mr Holmes...'

'Not if Mary's life were in danger. He would have followed the trail, as I am doing,' I asserted firmly, though not entirely sure I was right. Mary would have tracked down the irregularity in the printing too, but there was no time, none at all! I glanced up at the clock.

By ten o'clock, I had my solution. I knew what he was doing. I would find out where he was. I knew how to find him. And

Mary, whilst she might be afraid, would never be helpless. She was clever and devious. We would win. We *had* to win.

'Next measurement.'

The bills were full of cab rides. Sir George had met his solicitor all over London—at his home, theatres, hotels, coffee shops. Irene had requested his representative pick up papers from all sorts of people, again all over London. We had a good number of distances to work from.

It was odd though. The thought struck me halfway through. Why now? Why, after all these years, try to entrap Mr Holmes? Who had suggested it? Was there, perhaps, someone standing further in the shadows, guiding him, pointing him in the right direction, suggesting clues to entice and lead?

I shook the thought away as soon as I had it. I had no time for speculation, not now. But I would return to that thought in the years to come.

The clock was striking half past twelve as I drew the last circle. Billy had fallen asleep, his head pillowed on his hands. The rooms upstairs were silent. It felt as if I were the only one awake, not just in this house, but in the whole world.

I looked at my map of London, covered in crosses and circles. The circles all intersected at one place, on the edge of Richmond.

A completely blank field.

I sat there, staring at the spot on the map. Had my calculations been wrong? Was my clever idea not so clever after all? What was I failing to see that was there before me?

I held my head in my hands, grasping my hair, trying to force myself to think. I needed one more deduction, one more leap from clues to knowledge, but it would not come. According to the map, according to my theory, Mary had been taken to an empty field. Was that possible, even probable?

That was when a candle flickered in the draught and I caught sight of the date of the map. It was two years old. And as I noticed that, I remembered something I had seen in today's newspaper. I reached over to where I had placed it on the chair beside me. Halfway through the paper was the advertisement. Newly built homes in Richmond, suitable for professional men and their families. Some already built and available for viewing, the rest to be built by the end of the year.

Not an empty field then. A field of half-built houses.

I left a note for Billy to say that if I wasn't back by seven in the morning, he was to let Dr Watson know what had happened, and to be sure to say it was all my fault. I had thought of asking for help: perhaps this would all be beyond me. But Mr Holmes was drugged, and who knew when Dr Watson would return? There was no time to wait. I reached for my hat—and stopped. No hat. No sign of respectability this time. I merely fastened my coat. As I reached the front door, it occurred to me that the solicitor could have someone watching the house, so as to be forewarned when Mr Holmes finally came after him. I went through the back door, to the exit from the yard Mr Holmes thought I did not know about. I slipped through the faulty fencing into next door's yard, and then through the hole in their wall that they had never had fixed. I squeezed through the narrow gap, almost too tight for me, down the side of the houses, into the next street. I walked along there until I could cross to the Marylebone Road, where I was sure to get a cab.

That escape route should have been convoluted enough to throw off any pursuer. It certainly left me breathless and grubby, and the cab driver almost didn't stop for me. You can get almost anything in London, at any hour, and there is always a cab waiting to take you where you need to go. I told the driver the address, and though he objected to the distance, I promised him a large tip. I settled down as the cab rattled through the night to Mary—and to the solicitor.

Perhaps you think I should have woken Mr Holmes or fetched John, or brought Billy. Perhaps I should have called on Irene. Perhaps I should have gone to Scotland Yard and laid it all before Inspector Lestrade or Inspector Gregson. Perhaps I should have waited, and sent someone else, anyone else.

Or perhaps you understand why I did not do any of those things, why I had to do this alone. And if you do, perhaps you understand more than I did, for I did not really understand at all. I only knew that I must play this final act alone, centre stage.

One way or another, by the time the sun rose, this would all be over.

CHAPTER 19

Stepping out of the Shadows

It was a long drive to Richmond, long and silent and dark. I finally had time to reflect. Mary: she must have known what was happening when she got into that carriage; she must have done this deliberately. She had walked right into danger. She could get hurt. She could die! How could she go?

How could she not. She was Mary, after all. I remembered that first sight of her, so steadfast, so sure of herself. I remembered her excitement at hearing of Mr Holmes' cases. I remembered her longing for something, anything to happen. And with all that came other memories. Her comforting hand over mine. Her laughter at her terrible scones. Her request to be my friend. The instinctive way she turned to me and became my partner in this game. She let herself be taken into the trap because she knew I'd come after her. She was sure I'd follow the last clues and track her down. She had absolute faith in me. She had more faith than

I had. She was my friend. She was my only, most precious friend. I couldn't lose her. I would not lose her. I would *not*. I called up to the driver to go faster.

I had anticipated using the lengthy cab ride from Baker Street to Richmond to plan my attack—what I should say, or do, how I could rescue Mary, how to tie together the loose ends that still dangled before me. And yet, all through the night ride, my mind remained blank. My hands knotted together where they rested on my lap, and I stared unseeing out of the window as crowded streets gave way to gentler peaceful roads, giving way to the blank darkness of countryside, and still my mind would not think.

I seemed to be separated from the world outside the cab. The noise of the wheels on the road, the feel of the cracked leather seat, the faint, hot smell of the tiny cramped space and the soft sound of my own breathing was all I was aware of. I could feel only the pinch of my clothes on my flesh, the scratch of a badly placed stitch on my gloves, the knot where the stocking had turned in my shoe. Nothing else in the world existed.

The journey seemed to last for hours. The roads were empty, the horse fast, but the night seemed to stretch on and on in front of me and I found I could not imagine a dawn.

I did not have any plan at all when the driver pulled up in Richmond, and called down to me that we had arrived.

I climbed out and held up my fare.

'Please wait,' I said.

'Here?' he asked. 'In the middle of nowhere, in the middle of the night?'

'Well, you can go back to the centre of London by yourself, or wait here for a short while and return with a paying fare,' I said, more sharply than I intended. Of course, the paying fare might not be me. There was a chance instead that the solicitor would come running out, and flee in this cab, but it was a chance I had to take.

The cab driver nodded his assent and I looked around. It wasn't quite the middle of nowhere, but close enough. The street itself was only half-built and gas had not yet been laid on for the lighting. Foundations had been dug on both sides of the street, and the houses were in various states of completion. Some had walls and roofs and doors, but some were just great piles of bricks looming out of the darkness, shapeless and formless. The beginnings of the houses looked like ancient monolithic ruins in the dim light. This place felt heavy and old and evil, less a place of modern innovation, more a place of ancient sacrifice. The air was cold and still. No one was here. Nothing stirred. The building had frightened the wildlife away. The entire street felt like it was waiting, unfinished, needing something else to complete it, and I remembered old stories of blood sacrifices in ancient homes.

But then I ordered myself not to be such a silly old woman.

I gave a shake, and berated myself for a lack of logic and cool thinking. I looked around. Most of the street was dark, but there was a little light coming from one of the very few completed houses. I could see a low, two-storey villa, surrounded by a high hedge, and a path to one side, presumably leading to the back garden. This must at one time have been the show house for this development, and had stood here, complete, as the others were built around it. From there a pale milky light bled through into the night. It appeared to be the only inhabited building on the street. This, then, was my destination.

I headed towards the path at the side. I felt calm now. Not peaceful, but with this odd stillness instead. It reminded me of what Hector had once said about how a soldier becomes just before a battle. It is almost relief that the waiting is over, and the worst has now come, and now all he has to do is face it head on, and get it over and done with.

I was right; the path led to the wooden panelled fence of the back garden. The gate was not locked. I slipped through onto the lawn. I remained in the shadows as I took in what I could see.

Before me were large French windows, leading to a room that seemed to be some kind of study. One window was open onto the garden. There was a desk up against the wall, a table, book-lined shelves against three walls, all lit by two oil lamps, one on the desk, one on the table by the window. A green leather chair was up against the desk, and, incongruously, a rough kitchen chair right in the middle of the green carpet. And on that chair, bound to it by rough ropes, was Mary.

She was half facing me, but slumped, and her eyes were closed. Her wrists were bound to the straight arms of the chair, another rope passed around her middle. and her feet were also tied to the chair's legs. There was blood on her dress, a bruise on her cheek and a cut on her forehead. Her dress was torn and her hair hung loose and bedraggled.

Mary had fought. Once she knew what was happening, she'd fought like a tigress. She had left her mark before he bound her.

There was a man standing there: of middling height, slightly plump, dark hair oiled down, rounded shoulders. His dove-grey coat was torn, and I could see the back of his hand bound with a bandage. This was the hand that held the gun, pointed at Mary.

There was another gun on the desk, close by his hand, ready loaded, I imagined. These were not revolvers, but single-shot guns, very old-fashioned. I wondered why he used these? Perhaps this was all he had. He did not strike me as a man who liked to use guns. His preferred weapons were words, and if he could not use words, then knives. I moved closer, across the lawn.

'Who's there?' he called, and turned.

I froze still.

It was him: the man I had talked to outside the Whitechapel Lady's home. Her solicitor—her murderer. His face was pinched and plump, and he still had pince-nez firmly clamped to his short, slightly bulbous nose. His eyes were small, but his face was very much what you would expect to find behind the desk of a legal firm. His hair—which I guessed was dyed that unnaturally dark colour—was parted in the middle and plastered down to his head. He was all very much as he was before, when I talked to him in the street and Mary was rude to him, the very pattern of a solicitor. He stopped for a moment, talking off his spectacles, laying them down, then pinching his nose. They must hurt him. He was obviously very tired. He turned, suddenly.

'Holmes, I know that's you!'

He did not look like a man to be afraid of. He looked like a man to be overlooked, to have his skills used, but never to be befriended. He was a man to be ever so slightly mocked. Someone to be found always in the background, someone to be underestimated, someone to be ignored.

Well, him and me both. I stepped into the light.

'Who the hell are you?' he asked.

'I am Mr Sherlock Holmes' housekeeper. I am Mrs Hudson.'

I stepped into the room, through the window, making sure to keep him between Mary and me. I wanted to make sure he could point the gun at only one of us. With Mary unconscious, he chose me. He kept the gun aimed in my direction, turning as I entered the room and peering at me, obviously bitterly disappointed.

'Mrs Hudson?' he repeated, confused.

Once his back was to Mary, her eyes opened, she saw me, and winked—obviously the unconsciousness had been feigned. She sat upright and began to pull at her bonds. I wasn't sure how successful she could be, but the longer I kept his attention, the more chance she had to get free.

'We've met, I think,' he said, squinting at me. Perhaps he really needed those pince-nez he had worn before. Perhaps he just wasn't seeing anything clearly any more. His eyes were crazed, like a trapped rabid dog.

'Outside the Whitechapel Lady's home,' I told him.

'Oh.' He waved his hand. I was of supreme unimportance. He'd forgotten me as soon as he saw me. I had not played any part in his calculations, either as Mr Holmes' housekeeper or the woman he met in Whitechapel.

'I have introduced myself,' I said to him, very evenly. 'It is only polite you do the same.' He laughed, but there was no amusement in it. There was, however, a trace of mania. I had not expected him to be sane, but I had expected him to be under control. After all, this was a man who thrived on control. And yet…there was something about him. His control was slipping.

'Kirkby, York, Skipton, Overblow, take your pick,' he told me. If I had seen that look in his eyes when I had talked to him in Whitechapel, I would have known him to be more than a mere solicitor. And yet then he had been so utterly calm.

'Those are aliases,' I said. Behind him, I could see the rope around Mary's wrist was loosening. She twisted and pulled at it, and the rope stretched. She had tiny hands, she wouldn't need to pull it much further to slip out of it. 'Your real name, if you please.'

'I'm not sure I remember,' he said slowly. 'It's been so long since I used it. When will he come? I've been waiting.'

He saw my gaze slip past him, and he turned round to face Mary, but she was fast and she quickly slumped in her chair. He stared at her, suspicious.

'What's happened?' I asked him. 'What's changed, you've changed?'

He turned back to me, unsure, wavering.

'I don't…nothing!' he insisted. 'All is as I planned it.'

'Not quite,' I said dryly.

'It will be,' he declared. 'This is just an extra step. He is still expected. I was promised.'

'I see,' I said calmly. So the plan was still to go after Mr Holmes, was it? This re-arranged plan of his, was that what was shaking him to the core? He was always mad, I'd wager, but he had his limits. Yet something, someone, had pushed him beyond those limits. Had someone given him a monomania fixated on Holmes, and pushed him over the edge at the same time? Or was it always destined to end like this for him?

'Then we have time to talk,' I said to him. 'Tell me, the Yorkshire names—a deliberate clue? As with the cab ride bills?'

He smiled, and I have never seen such a cruel smile.

'Such clever clues. So subtle! He was right. I laid such a clever trail.'

'Who was right?' I asked.

'Him,' he insisted. 'Just him.' Either he did not know the name, or even in his madness, he would not reveal it.

Mary had slipped one hand out of the rope now, and she was pulling at the bond round her other wrist. If he turned, he would see her hands were almost free. Given his current state of mind, there was a good chance he'd shoot her there and then. I had to keep his attention on me.

'A trail I followed,' I reminded him gently. Always be gentle with a madman, I had heard the phrase somewhere. I kept my voice soft and low.

'You're just a woman. You haven't the mind to work it out,' he said dismissively. Behind him, Mary shot him a glance of sheer hatred. I felt a flash of anger myself, but I controlled it. He had a loaded gun pointed right at me, his finger on the trigger, and a mind rapidly losing its grip on reality. Any of us could die in a second.

'You're right, of course,' I said soothingly. Mary yanked at her bonds, obviously angry. 'Mr Holmes worked out the clues. He's coming soon.'

'I know. I was told...what was that?' he shouted suddenly. Outside a fox had screamed, those terrible screams that sound like someone being murdered, in an extremity of pain. For a moment the gun swung towards the window. I stepped forward, but he swung it back to me. It was barely inches from me, and I felt a frisson of fear.

'Just a fox,' I reassured him. 'You should be used to it by now.'

He nodded. I realized he thought he would stay, that tomorrow morning, his life would go on as always. He had not planned for, or even expected, failure.

'I suppose you're tired of waiting,' I went on, breathless now, afraid, but somehow intoxicated by how close to the edge I was. I could not have stopped now for all the tea in China. And besides, Mary had her other hand almost free. But she still had to work loose the ropes round her waist and feet. 'That's why you kidnapped Mary Watson, isn't it? You thought it would pull Dr Watson, and therefore Mr Holmes, towards you.'

'I still have Mary Watson,' he said quietly. 'And I have you. He'll come.'

No. No one would come. Even if Billy woke now, and even if Mr Holmes and John could come immediately, it was still such a long way from Baker Street to here. And there was no time to wait. This man in front of me, this man with a gun in his hand, had lost all control. I could see his hand shake and his eyes dart towards the garden and the way he jumped at every sigh. The man I had met outside the Whitechapel Lady's home had been a restrained man, ordered, playing his part perfectly, but that had all gone. It had slipped away.

He babbled and talked and whispered, half to himself, half to me, but sometimes, I felt to another person in that room, someone else behind Mary and me, someone he was convinced was listening. His secrets, kept for years inside his mind, spilled out of him. The scandals and the truths and the names! All his silent years in the background had ended. He laid the pieces of his game in front of me, and I listened, and I watched his gun, and I knew no one else would come.

It would end here and now, between the three of us in this room. The housekeeper, the wife and the solicitor. No great hero. No staunch companion, just us three.

Very well then. Let us end it.

The Final Act

He gibbered on and on, secrets spilling like wine from a broken bottle. He could barely keep up with his own words. He looked exhausted, drained to the dregs, but he would not stop. It was as if, after being silent for all those years, he had to tell everything on this final night. All those secrets, all there, in his head, bursting to be told—and tonight, he finally revealed them all.

He walked up and down, up and down in front of me, desk to window and back again, watching me, all the time. If ever he started to turn towards Mary, I called him back to me. And then, every time he looked at me, he pointed the gun at me. He walked to the window and stared out of it, telling me some foul tale, the gun hanging loose in his hand, and then, in a moment, his arm would come up and the barrel would point at me again, and I knew I could be dead in seconds. As long as he didn't look at Mary. As long as he kept talking to me. Mary was very tightly tied. It seemed to take an age for her to completely free herself, for him to talk on and on, but in truth, it couldn't have been more than ten minutes. Occasionally he'd mention a name, just the beginning of one, but the same name, over and over again. I didn't catch it, but he mentioned promises and endings and glory, all from this name he kept whispering under his breath.

But after a while I couldn't bear to listen to any more. The love stories and betrayals and secret children and letters, so many letters, were driving me out of my mind. I had to stop him. If he was going to keep talking, I was going to get a few answers for myself.

'How long have you been planning this?' I asked, interrupting him.

'Not long,' he said, surprised. 'I hadn't even heard of Sherlock Holmes until a couple of years ago. But once I knew he existed—it was so marvellous. It has been wonderful. Such joy, matching wits with him, Holmes, the greatest mind of the age!'

'Who? Who told you about Sherlock Holmes?' I asked, but he just stared at me, puzzled. Somewhere in his mind was a blank spot, and every time I asked who had led him to this, it pushed him a little further over the edge. When that happened, his grip on the gun tightened, and he pointed it more firmly in my direction. Whatever was in that part of his mind, he did not like me digging into it. It made him want me dead. I wonder if others had asked? I wonder if perhaps the Whitechapel Lady had asked the very same question and it had pushed him over the edge? But I had no intention of playing the heroine for truth's sake. It was time to take a different tack.

'Where is he?' he moaned, like a woman waiting for a recalcitrant lover.

'He is in a cab now,' I assured him. 'He is just leaving Baker Street. Can we talk, until he comes?'

Perhaps if I kept him talking, Mary would free herself, escape and manage to get help. Besides, I desperately wanted to find out who was really behind this. He nodded in agreement.

'You must have been so bored,' I said gently. 'A clever man like you, playing all those complex mind games with such easy victims. It must have been such a thrill when you first realized you could control these women. It was all so easy, and you never failed. And no one even knew who you were? It must be deeply unsatisfactory, to be so clever and so devious and have no one know. No one knows exactly what you can do.'

'You don't know either,' he said darkly, turning round towards Mary suddenly.

'I know everything!' I shouted, distracting him so he wouldn't register that her hands and waist were loose. He turned back to me, puzzled and angry and wary. In that moment, I realized I really did know everything. I had all the pieces in my head, and I had thrown them all up in the air, and they had fallen neatly into place, to create the perfect picture.

'I should imagine you started as a country solicitor,' I said quickly. 'And one day, someone, a rich someone, a lady, gave you a secret, and instead of keeping it safe, you blackmailed her. You did it so cleverly and so subtly, you weren't caught, and so you did it again and again.'

'I know you're only killing time until Holmes comes,' he said to me, and I saw the madness flooding his eyes as he spoke. And yet he watched me and did not turn to Mary. The gun was raised, and pointed at my head, and for a moment, he thought about killing me. But then he lowered it again.

'Not till he gets here. That's what's supposed to happen,' he said. 'That's how I planned it. I sent Laura Shirley to him. I even sent him Adam Ballant. How could Holmes ignore the death of his own brother's man?' I could not let him know I was afraid— but I could not let him know I was his adversary either. Mary pulled at the ropes around her feet. He had tied her so tight.

'You made so much money you were able to move to London. You need never work again if you didn't want to. You didn't need to blackmail any more, but you liked the power. You stole secrets, not for money, but power. You snapped your fingers and they danced to your tune. Oh, Mr Holmes will be so impressed!'

'He promised me he'd come. He swore he'd be here,' he kept repeating.

'He will, he's so close, he's almost here. Let me finish, please? When they didn't have secrets, you made them up,' I extemporized. 'Such clever lies, so easily told, so easy to believe. Who'd suspect you? Quiet, unassuming, professional. You whispered in ears, spread tales, told the lies, forced others to spread the poison for you and still no one believed it could be you.'

'I was promised a final battle. It must come.' He was barely listening. This wasn't good. A battle? Is that how he thought of this, one soldier against another? He kept glancing towards the garden and the door. He was waiting, for Mr Holmes or someone else. What would he do when he realized no one else was coming? He'd gone to the edge and he was too close to draw back now. I had to keep his attention a little while longer, try to force him to retain some semblance of control, or he would snap and start shooting. But for how long could I do that? And what then?

Mary stood. She was free. I waited for her to run, but instead, she reached for the poker beside the fireplace. Oh, for heaven's sake, Mary.

'Robert Sheldon is afraid of you.' I had to keep him watching me. I had to make him talk to me and only me. Mary was moving achingly slowly, trying not to make a noise, to ease the poker into her hand without banging it against the fireplace.

'Who?'

'The Ordinary Man. The one you use to follow people. He's frightened of you.'

'So he should be!' He was actually proud of that. Proud he'd made weak, soft Robert Sheldon afraid of him. 'I sent him after you. I forced him to follow you, even if it meant following you in the dark and the rain, for hours and hours. I even made him afraid of you. He believed every word I said about you!'

Mary had the poker in her grip. She crept towards him. If he turned, he'd shoot. Just a single sound, just a feeling and he'd turn and kill her.

'And then the women started dying,' I said softly. The mania slipped a little from his eyes then. Somehow, the thought of their deaths had calmed him.

'I'm not supposed to say,' he said quietly. 'Not to you. I have to tell him. That's what I was told. I was too good to waste my talents. He told me that over and over again, rammed it into my head until I could barely breathe.'

The madness had always been there, latent inside him, but controlled, so very firmly controlled. But I was correct: someone else had been there, and made his control slip away with promises of the great final battle against the great thinker, Sherlock Holmes. Who could slip inside a madman's brain like that and play it so well?

'Well, practise on me,' I said to him. The more he talked, the more chance there was he would let slip who was behind this. 'You want to get it right when he gets here, don't you? Tell me, so you know what to say when it matters.'

'I must get it perfect,' he said, nodding. 'It's very important. And you don't matter...I only saw the first one,' he continued, trying to explain. 'The very first woman I led to death. One hot summer day by the sea, on those high cliffs at Beachy Head, surrounded by friends, I told her what I was going to tell her husband. Oh, it was horrible, what I was going to tell him. It would have destroyed them both, and a few others too. Do you know, she didn't cry? Not even beg. She just stood up, walked to the edge of the cliff, and jumped to her death. Oh, it was wonderful! I'd done that, do you understand? I'd taken her life, I had utter control. Do you know how intoxicating that is?' His eyes sparkled. I'd heard the phrase 'drunk with power' but now I was seeing it.

That was when Mary struck. She raised the poker and slammed it down on his arm. He cried out, but he didn't drop the gun. Instead he fired—the shot was wide, but it was enough. She cried once, and fell, hard against the bookcase. They were duelling pistols, they only had one shot each, but one could be enough. I leapt forward for the other gun, but he was so fast, much faster than me! He spun and charged into me, slamming me into the wall, leaving me breathless on the floor. He raised the other gun.

'No!' I cried, holding out my hand. I could barely breathe. I could see Mary had hit her head badly. Blood poured down her cheek, and there was blood on her dress too. She seemed to be unconscious, but breathing. I had to keep us both alive.

'Tell me!' I insisted. 'You owe me. Tell me.'

'Tell you?' he said, hesitating.

'How else can I tell the world, once you've killed Mr Holmes?'

For a moment, he wavered. Sanity and madness warred within—but madness won.

'You murdered girls,' I accused him.

'Yes,' he insisted. 'Only kitchen maids who were going to tell their mistresses. Prostitutes who held back their secrets.'

'You liked it,' I told him, trying to sit up. My stomach hurt so much, and I could barely catch my breath.

'Aren't you clever?' he said, surprised. 'No, not you. Did Mr Holmes tell you all this?'

I wasn't sure. True, what I had come up with was half deduction, but also half guesswork. It just so happened my guesses were right. Was this how Mr Holmes worked? Deductions and clever guesses?

Mary's eyes were fluttering.

'Yes,' I murmured. 'He's so close now. He is in the lane outside. He will be here soon. Please, tell me it all. I have to know.'

'That look in their eyes as you slide in the knife, Mrs Hudson,' he said to me. 'Their own blood dripping to the floor as they watch. Looking at you, knowing they will die, but not yet, not until you decide they will—that's power, too, Mrs Hudson. Although I admit it's not quite as good as destroying their minds. I have always loved watching someone slip into that moment of destruction. Which path will they choose? Anger, sorrow?'

He stepped towards me, his pale eyes burning, the gun wavering in his hand. He had to tell someone.

'Why you?' he asked suddenly. 'Why am I telling you this?'

'People always tell me things,' I said, pulling myself up, hanging on to the table. I held his gaze calmly.

'Sometimes they begged, sometimes they pleaded. Sometimes they became autocratic and ordered me to stop. That always made me laugh! And sometimes they offered me things. I have been offered fabulous jewels, and women's bodies, men's bodies, and huge amounts of money.'

'I can't imagine that would appeal to you.' Behind him, Mary's eyes opened. She slowly wiped the blood away from her face, and glanced down at her dress. She was awake, but was she aware? Could she help? Because truth to tell, I had run out of moves to play now. I had reached the end of my game, and I had no idea how to win this. The only ending I could see was with the two of us dead.

'You should know,' he said to me. 'Now it's about to end for you too. There's no real loyalty in the world, Mrs Hudson. No love. No one would die for anyone else. Romantic novelists' claptrap.'

He'd never loved, never touched, never had a moment's affection. He had been damaged and never saved.

'Blood's different,' he told me. 'It never lies. It's real, when it's warm and sticky on my hand. The secrets were important, the secrets were life, but the blood—I didn't want it at first. He insisted.'

'Who?'

'Him,' he said, as if it were obvious. Did this figure even exist? Had the solicitor imagined a force driving him onwards to commit even worse acts? I was no longer sure who he meant by 'he'. Mr Holmes, his guide, or someone else entirely?

'Once the blood was there, my heart beat like a lover's, and I wanted more. Secrets and blood, the two sweetest, truest things in all the world.' He was lost now. No one was coming. Mary was pulling herself up on the bookcase, hand over hand, but how could she help? He was so fast, so strong.

'I see.'

'Life is full of secrets,' he said softly. 'I've always known the biggest one. There is no love.' This was it. He had gone as far as he could go. The end was here. He looked up at the garden and knew it was empty.

I had moved, just slightly, whilst he talked, to keep his back to Mary, and now I realized I had made a mistake. He was between me and the garden. There was no escape route now.

'Is he here? Is he listening? Please tell me he's here,' he said, looking at me. He seemed so tired, and I swear there was a tear in his eye. 'It needs to be over now.'

'Soon,' I promised. 'It'll all be over soon, for both of us.'

'Soon,' he mocked. 'See, I was right! They didn't even come for you. Not even his own wife. He was right. Time to end this.' He raised the gun so I could see directly down the barrel. Mary couldn't see, blinded by her own blood. Play dead, Mary. Maybe you can escape if he believes he's already killed you.

'Do you know why I blackmailed women? Why I killed them?'

'No,' I said, lying. I had realized that ages ago. Just for the same petty reason all the Law and the Church and the men in charge were against us. The same stupid lie.

Please, Mary, don't try again, he'll kill us both. I wished this so hard, as Mary began to move, but I didn't dare speak, or even look at her.

'You're so weak!' he announced. 'So feeble. You can't even think straight. You never knew, none of you ever knew. As for fighting—you couldn't! You all just whimpered and cried and begged. You, all you women, you made it all so easy!' he exulted.

It all came back to me. The patronizing smiles. The men who told me 'not to worry my pretty little head'. The doors that were closed to me, the rules that barred me, the small, pointless role I was forced to play in my own life. I thought of all the women who were afraid and alone, all the women he had destroyed, all the women he had been allowed to destroy, and I thought to myself: I can fight. I can fight the same way he does. He destroys with words—well, I can do that too.

'All those women weren't enough of a challenge,' I said to him.

'No, not quite. I needed a game worth the playing.'

'But Mr Holmes didn't play!'

'Oh, he will. I have been assured he will. I thought tonight was the final move, but it was only the beginning of the end. The check before checkmate. Remove the queen, leave only the king.'

'Holmes?' I said, disbelievingly. 'He's not the one here now, is he?'

'What do you mean? You said he was coming!' he cried. His grip was tightening on that gun. It may not have been a weapon he used often, but he seemed to like the feel of it in his hand more and more.

'I lied,' I told him, with as much contempt as I could muster. 'Mr Holmes didn't follow the clues. He knows nothing about you. I followed the clues. I came tonight, and I came alone. Sherlock Holmes is not coming.'

'You're just the housekeeper. You're nothing. You are background detail!'

'Yes, I was in the background, and standing there, I have watched. I have listened. I have learnt. Mr Holmes, your great adversary, found the puzzle too boring, so he passed it on to me, his housekeeper.' I stood up straight, my anger blazing, daring him to kill me. I poured all the scorn I was capable of into my voice. 'Is that what you've been trying to do? Get Sherlock Holmes' attention? Like a boy sitting at the back of the class, raising his hand and begging, "oh please, sir!" whilst the teacher ignores him? You just weren't clever enough, I'm afraid. Even I'm bored by you now.'

'Stop it!' he screamed.

'So this is your final battle, is it?' I demanded. 'Go on, shoot me, forget her, kill me, but I swear I'll make you suffer before I die, you miserable little worm of a man. Not with the great Mr Holmes, not even with Dr Watson, but with an ordinary little housekeeper. A woman. What an ending for your game.'

The hammer of the gun clicked as he drew it back, but I would not flinch. I would not close my eyes. I stared into his eyes. He didn't understand. He was shaken. He was…afraid! I'd had my moment of triumph, even as I was certain I was about to die.

In the background Mary had stood up, picked up the chair she had been bound to, and with a great cry, swung it round at his head. This time it connected, knocking him sideways, knocking the gun out of his hand, and he staggered against the desk. The gun fired as it hit the floor, but the bullet struck the window and it shattered. Mary fell backwards, against the bookcase again, this time grabbing onto a shelf—but something clicked and the bookcase began to move. She had, unawares, revealed a secret door.

'Well, look what I found!' Mary breathed, as she straightened up again.

I stepped towards her, reaching out for her, and saw what she saw. Behind the bookcase was a secret room, at least five feet by five feet. The walls were covered with shelves, and the shelves were full to bursting with files and boxes and pictures.

His secrets. His precious secrets.

Seeing it revealed like that pushed him too far. He half crawled, half lurched into the room, gathering the papers to him. I ignored him, rushing to Mary's side.

'Are you all right?' I demanded. 'He shot at you!'

'No, it's fine; it just missed me, I just hit my head on the bookcase. But look, Martha!'

I walked up to the open door of the hidden room, and looked around at its overflowing records.

I live in a house of secrets. Dozens of secrets, told day after day. All those people who climbed the seventeen steps up to Mr Holmes, and said to him, 'Help me, rescue me, save me—but no one must know'. And Mr Holmes and John took those secrets and liberated them and destroyed them, and let the light shine into the darkest corners, and saved their clients. All secrets were uncovered in 221b Baker Street, eventually.

But here, in this house, were secrets too. Secrets recorded, stolen, hidden, kept to fester and rot and burn in the dark.

Another house of secrets, but this house was where despair and death and darkness spread.

He stood there, staring into this room full of lives already destroyed, and he smiled. His eyes shone like a lover's, he glowed with desire for those secrets.

'He'll be so impressed,' the solicitor murmured. 'He'll be so proud. Look at the power I have!'

I was no longer certain of whom he spoke. Holmes, or his own mysterious mentor? Instead, I moved away, back to the desk, and motioned Mary towards the French window. Time to end this ridiculous farce. No more talking.

'No, no more,' I said to him. 'This ends, here and now.' I picked up the oil lamp from the desk. It was heavy, and the oil splashed about in it. The lamp was almost full. He turned and saw me, and knew what I intended to do. He jumped up, snarling, meaning to rush me and strike me down once more, but instead I threw the lamp towards the room of secrets. It shattered, the oil spreading over his shirt, then pooling into the room full of dry, dusty old papers. Amongst the oil, the wick lay, the flame sputtering.

I had only meant to burn the papers, I swear. I thought he'd get out. He was supposed to run!

The draught from the window blew in and caught the flame. For a moment I thought it would go out, then it flickered, grew stronger and brighter, and then leapt up, hungry for the fuel all around it.

'Oh God,' I breathed. He was covered in oil, he should have moved away, but instead he cried, and reached out for his precious papers. His secrets, all those letters and papers, his only reason to live, his pride and joy, about to burn. He could not help himself. Without them he did not exist. He walked into the flames.

'Martha!' Mary called. I dashed to the window, but I could hear him cry out. The flames spread up and over and around that room, burning the papers and files and pictures, and in the centre he stood, seemingly untouched, gathering scraps of paper to his chest, scraps of scorched paper.

'Run!' I cried to him, but he would not. He was nothing without his secrets. He was just an empty man, losing the only game he could ever play. He reached for a scrap as it floated past him—and the oil on his shirt finally caught flame.

I remembered the Whitechapel Lady, and Adam Ballant. I remembered blood. I remembered loss, and pain. I remembered what he had done, and I remembered that he had enjoyed it. Calmly, I stepped out of the window, into the garden, into the night.

His house of secrets had claimed one last victim.

CHAPTER

21

The Suspicion of Lestrade

The cab was still waiting for us as I slipped out of the garden door and into the street, Mary beside me. All that had taken only an hour. The driver was staring at the flames beginning to show above the fences. The entire house was going to burn.

'Baker Street, please,' I said calmly to him, as he watched the fire. He turned to look at me.

'Was that you? Did you do that?' he demanded, gesturing towards the burning house. Mary clambered inside the cab.

'Of course not, I'm just an old woman,' I told him. 'Baker Street. Two-two-one-b Baker Street,' I repeated, but he did not move.

'We're making a daring escape!' Mary called from inside the cab.

'Daring escape—oh, I see, Baker Street!' he realized. 'You work for Mr Holmes?'

'If you like,' I said wearily, climbing into the cab.

Mr Holmes was well known amongst the cabbies of Baker Street. He was forever ordering them to follow some other cab, or leading them on some improbable journey to the unlikeliest of places. It seemed easier to use that reputation.

We set off slowly, through the half-built homes of Richmond. It would be dawn soon, but for now, the sky was still an intensely dark shade of navy blue. I stared out of the window into London, passing by—safer now, but who would know? From somewhere I could hear clanging bells. The fire engines were already on their way. And then the story would be spread through the tele-graph wires, told over the telephone, printed in the papers—but no one would ever know what really happened.

I sat back, looking at Mary. Her face was still covered in dried blood. I took out my handkerchief and tried to clean it off. She smiled shakily at me, and I smiled back. After all that, we were alive.

'He deserved it,' Mary said firmly to me. 'He deserved to die like that.'

I wanted to feel guilt. I wanted to feel remorse. I wanted to feel even just a trace of sorrow for the man that had just died, and the part I had played in his death, but there was nothing there. There was no triumph either, no gloating. Not even satisfaction. Just a feeling that now the job was done, and I could stop. There was just—a blankness. Had I forgotten how to feel?

'Perhaps he should have had a fair trial,' I ventured.

'Do you honestly think he could have had a "fair trial"?' Mary cried indignantly. 'What with all those secrets he had? He would have had the prosecuting barrister and the judge and half the jury and the police and, for all we know, the Home Secretary in his pocket. Who would have dared testify against him, and ruin themselves in court? In the end, he would have just walked away.'

'And yet, to die like that...'

'Listen,' Mary told me, sitting up and taking the hand-kerchief off me. 'I knew it was a trap, as soon as I got into the carriage. I thought, this is stupid, Sherlock would never send for me like this. But I went into that man's home anyway, because I wanted to know. I wanted to ask him questions.'

'I can understand that,' I agreed, watching her. Dawn was rising, not a dull grey as usual, but as an opalescent sheen that lit up Mary's face.

'So I asked him, and he wanted to tell. No one had ever known what he had done, and he wanted to boast. Don't we all want someone to know how clever are we are, otherwise what's the point of being clever? So he told me.'

She shivered, and looked away, into the half-dark of the morning.

'He'd done horrific things,' she said softly. 'Those he'd driven to suicide, those murdered by others because of what he said, those he murdered himself. He told me things I will never tell you, because no one should speak words like that ever again. He gave those women slow, painful, agonizing deaths, and he gave others perpetual pain, and he enjoyed every last second of it. You heard some of it yourself! I heard far more.'

She turned back to me, her face fierce and strong in the first of the light.

'He had an easy death compared to them. He deserved much worse.'

She was right. Yet still I felt empty now, a drained and echoing shell. Outside, people had started to stir, to go about their daily business, calling to each other and walking about, and I felt oddly disconnected from them, as if either they or I weren't real. I did not know how to get back to my normal life after what I had done. It had all gone now, the excitement, the challenge, the stimulus, the danger, and it felt like nothing was left behind.

For the first time I understood why Mr Holmes used his 7 per cent solution of cocaine.

I thought back. The solicitor had said there was someone who had guided him, pointed him towards Mr Holmes, nurturing his darkest urges. Was this person real, or just another aspect to his personality, his own personal Jekyll?

'We can't tell anyone,' Mary said suddenly.

'About tonight, or all of it?' I asked. 'I wasn't planning on telling anyone what we did tonight. I don't think it reflects well on us.'

'All of it,' Mary said seriously. 'All those secrets. We know so much; if we went to the police, we'd have to tell everything we knew. All about the Whitechapel Lady and Adam Ballant and Irene, and then everything would come out in the inquest and end up in the papers and everything we worked for would just fall around our ears.'

'That's not all,' I added. 'Did you hear him say there was someone else in the background? Someone with an interest in Mr Holmes?'

'Do you think he was real?' Mary asked.

'I don't know,' I mused. He had mentioned a name in his ramblings, just the merest murmur under his breath that he hadn't wanted me to hear. But my hearing was excellent. 'Perhaps not. But if so that could be anybody, and if he knows what we did…'

'He could take revenge on us.'

'Use us to take revenge on Mr Holmes,' I interjected. What was the name? Moore? Morris? 'If this person believed Mr Holmes carried out tonight's work, then killing us would be a suitable response. No, you're right. No one must know.'

I stared out of the window again. No one would know what we had done—both the good and the bad. We had been working as much in the dark as the solicitor had.

I'd never even found out his real name. I don't suppose it mattered.

'I'm so tired,' Mary said sleepily, resting her head on my shoulder.

'I'll ask the cab to drop you off at home,' I said to her.

'No, we'll go to Baker Street,' Mary insisted, yawning. 'The stories always end at the house at Baker Street.'

I smiled to myself. It didn't matter what I felt right now. I was being ridiculous. Mary was safe, Irene and Wiggins and Mrs Shirley and numerous unknown women were safe. That would have to do for now. In fact, that would do very well.

'Stop, stop,' I cried suddenly. We had turned into Baker Street, finally, having been caught up in the dawn traffic. There, across the street, waiting for us, were the Irregulars. The boys were scattered, some in doorways, some lounging against a wall, some sitting on the kerb. Wiggins stood alone in the centre of the street, the morning light showing his face clearly. He was angry.

I jumped out of the cab.

Wiggins strode towards me.

'What the 'ell have you done?' he growled.

I stood back in surprise. He had never spoken to me like that before.

'Are you all right, missus?' the cab driver called.

'Perfectly, thank you. This is a friend of mine,' I said, never taking my eyes off Wiggins, hoping it was true.

'You were seen,' Wiggins told me, his voice low and angry. 'Think you can get out of Baker Street without one of us seeing yer? You got a cab hours ago, going south—to Richmond, wasn't it?'

'Yes…'

'Where there's a fire!' Wiggins shouted. 'And a man dead, a man with a lot of people interested in what 'e did and how 'e died!'

The cab driver studiously looked away, making it clear he heard none of this.

'How do you know?' I said. I was badly shaken.

''Cos I got a boy at Scotland Yard,' Wiggins said, quieter, but still furious. ''E cleans boots. 'E cleans Lestrade's boots, and he 'eard that Lestrade was personally taking over a case that 'ad just come in, a respectable solicitor burnt to death, and some very prominent people were taking an interest. 'E'll be in Richmond by now.'

'Oh,' I said feebly. Lestrade knew. On the one hand, he could find it all an accident. He probably would. But what if he brought in Sherlock Holmes? What would he discover? And what prominent people did Wiggins mean? Had someone else begun to suspect?

'Was it you?' Wiggins demanded between clenched teeth.

Could I lie to him, this boy? Should I? I looked round at all the boys gathered on the street. They had all been in my kitchen, had eaten my cake and drunk my tea. Micky saw me, and tipped his cap. They respected me, and liked me and maybe even looked up at me. Could I tell them what I had done?

'Yes,' I said softly.

Wiggins stepped back, drawing his breath in sharply. He turned away, so I wouldn't see his face, then came back to me.

'Was it 'im?'

'It was him,' I told him. 'And now he's dead. The man that hurt you, and killed the Whitechapel Lady, and hurt so many other people and did awful things...' My voice trailed to a halt as Wiggins stepped closer. He was as tall as me. When had that happened?

'You stupid woman,' he hissed. 'How dare you do that alone!'

'I wasn't alone...'

'You were alone, both of you! Anything could have happened!'

'Anything did,' I said shakily.

'It's not funny!' He was worried, really worried about me, and I realized the anger came not from disappointment or disillusionment, but anxiety, like a mother shouting at her child when he runs away.

'I had to do it alone,' I told him quietly.

'Why? Wot do you think we're 'ere for? It's for you! It's for all of you in that 'ouse!' He gestured towards 221b.

'I had to prove it,' I insisted.

'Prove wot?'

'That I'm not a silly old woman who's only fit for baking cakes!' I shouted.

Wiggins' face cleared up. He understood that. He had to prove himself over and over again. He'd never survive on the streets if he didn't. He had to prove he was more than a boy every day.

'Well, you're not that,' he said, and mercy of mercies, he grinned. 'Though you do make decent cakes.'

I nodded my thanks. Between us two, that was as good as a hug.

'Promise me you won't do it again, though?' he asked.

'I can't,' I told him. 'Look, can you promise me you'll never cheat, or lie, or steal? Never, not even to protect your boys? Because I can never promise I'll never get into trouble again, not to save someone who needs my help.'

Wiggins looked round at his boys. He'd do anything to protect them. And now, looking at me, he recognized a kindred spirit of sorts.

'How's the arm?' I asked. His other hand went hurriedly up to his injured arm.

'It's all right,' he said grudgingly. 'Sorry I bled on your floor.'

'Probably not the last time,' I told him.

He smiled sardonically.

The sun was up now and the street was beginning to get busy. The cab driver yawned pointedly, loud enough to cover the yards between us. I ignored him. 'Micky's invited for gingerbread this afternoon,' I said to Wiggins. 'Will you join him?'

He hesitated, then nodded. He peered into the cab at Mary.

'You'd better get her inside,' he said to me. 'She don't look none too clever.'

'I will, thank you,' I said. And thank you for wanting to protect me, thank you for looking after me, thank you for bringing me Billy, thank you for bringing yourself, thank you for coming to my kitchen to eat gingerbread. I could never say those words, he'd hate them, but we both knew I was thinking them. I walked round to Mary's side of the cab.

'And look out for Lestrade,' Wiggins called. 'He wants to solve this one.' Then, in a moment, the Irregulars melted into side streets and alleyways and had all disappeared.

'Thank you,' I said to the driver as I helped Mary out of the cab. I paid the driver well, and gave him a huge tip. Mary was very tired, which was hardly surprising given the night we'd had. 'If the police should ask, by the way…'

'I ain't seen a thing,' the driver said, tapping the side of his nose. 'Mr Holmes and the police don't always get on, do they? Well, I'd rather be on Mr Holmes' side.'

'Right…um, thank you,' I said, as he drove away.

Mary and I stumbled through the door of 221b, utterly exhausted, drained, bloodstained and scorched. That was when we saw Mr Holmes, standing at the bottom of the stair, fully dressed, his wound apparently healing nicely, staring at us as we came in.

'You'll wake Watson,' he said.

'No we won't, he sleeps heavily,' I said to him.

'What have you been doing?' he demanded, apparently in amazement.

'Can't you guess?' Mary asked sleepily, leaning on me.

'I don't guess,' he said coldly. He looked us up and down, saw the state of our clothes, the expressions on our faces, the tiredness in our eyes, and a new look crossed his face, one I had never seen before. I am not sure if it was confusion, or worry.

'Mary?' he asked, looking at her intently.

I've only ever heard Sherlock Holmes use Mary's first name twice. One I shall tell you of when I have the nerve. The only other occasion was now.

I turned to look at Mary. She was not just leaning against me, she was slumped against me. She was weak, barely able to stand, her face white, her breathing shallow. As I clasped her, I realized that there was a bloodstain all along her side—and it was fresh, and dripping. In our exhilaration at solving the case, neither of us had recognized how badly hurt she was.

'I think the bullet may have struck closer than I thought,' Mary murmured. 'In fact, I'm not sure he did miss me.' Then the last of her strength gave way, and she collapsed.

Mr Holmes leapt forward and caught her before she hit the floor.

'Watson!' he bellowed, sweeping Mary up into his arms,

seemingly unconscious of his own injury. 'You and your medical kit are needed in the kitchen immediately!'

I moved to follow as he carried Mary to the kitchen door, but at that moment the doorbell rang. What a moment for callers! I stepped away from the door, I was going to ignore it, but Mr Holmes stopped me.

'It's Lestrade; I saw him coming down the street,' he said, shifting Mary's weight in his arms. She moaned, but did not seem conscious. 'You have to answer it, but don't let him in, and don't tell him anything.'

'What shall I say?' I demanded to know, half-frantic.

'Lie, Mrs Hudson,' he told me, manoeuvring Mary down the kitchen stairs. 'It's easy, I lie all the time.'

And with that he was gone. John came hurtling down the main stairs, carrying his bag, his shirt half hanging out of his trousers where he had dressed hastily. He stopped when he saw blood drops around the front door. I pointed mutely at the kitchen. I did not have the courage to tell him it was Mary who was hurt. I took a shawl that had been across the newel post and flung it around me, hiding, I hoped, the bloodstains and the scorch marks. Then I took a deep breath, patted my hair down, straightened my skirts, and in a stately manner, opened the front door.

Inspector Lestrade stood there, two police officers flanking him. He sniffed when he saw me, his pinched face crumpled with tiredness, and yet his eyes were bright and eager.

Oh dear. He was on the trail. He'd heard the news, humming over the wires to Scotland Yard. A mysterious fire, the body of a man no one really knew and the remains of thousands of files. I wondered if perhaps there were a few names left in the ashes, just enough to pique the interest of some very important people indeed.

Now Inspector Lestrade was here to ask Mr Holmes to solve the case. This case of the burning man. It would be manslaughter, and we had caused the death. It could even be murder at worst: we had not tried to help, we had not called for assistance, we had merely driven away. We could end up in jail. We could be hanged!

And all those secrets we fought to keep would be revealed.

If Inspector Lestrade came in, he'd follow the blood on the wooden hall floor to the kitchen, and find Mary there, a table full of letters and a map pointing towards the dead man's home.

All those thoughts crossed my mind in seconds, and, I hope, did not show in my well-trained face. I merely stood straight and tall, and hoped he couldn't see what state my clothes were in under the shawl. I wondered if he could smell the smoke on me.

Mr Lestrade asked if Mr Holmes was in. I, in my very best housekeeper manner, replied that he was not; he was busy right now.

'At this hour of the morning?' Inspector Lestrade asked.

'Mr Holmes works all hours,' I told him. 'As, obviously, do you.'

'Maybe he's already on the case,' the inspector mused, and turned to leave.

That was when John called out, 'What the hell happened?' very loudly, from the kitchen. He must have just seen the state of Mary. I ignored the shout, and settled my face into its usual imperturbability.

Inspector Lestrade turned round to me again, and this time his sharp eyes were suspicious.

'That was Dr Watson,' he said.

'Yes, Mr Holmes is not here, but Dr Watson is,' I said slowly, as if explaining to a small child. 'And the doctor has a patient, so if you will excuse me...' I tried to close the door, but the inspector held it open.

'Mr Holmes has left without Dr Watson?' Inspector Lestrade asked disbelievingly.

'They're not joined at the hip!' I snapped. Out of the corner of my eye I saw blood spots on the floor right in front of Inspector Lestrade—Mary's blood, fresh and red. I slid my foot across to cover them. 'Especially since Dr Watson got married. And I will not let you intrude on the doctor when he has a patient.'

Inspector Lestrade peered past me and up the stairs. I glanced over my shoulder. Just out of his eye line was a trail of blood along the hall leading to the kitchen. My God, how much blood had she lost?

If he came in, he'd see it, and insist on finding out what was going on.

I looked back at the inspector, trying hard to maintain my respectable coolness, as all housekeepers showed all the police. He watched me sharply. Mr Holmes had often referred to him as a terrier. The inspector was not clever, but he was tenacious. Once he found the smallest thread, he grasped it and worried it until he got to the end. If he came in and saw the blood, he would find the truth.

'There was rather a worrying incident last night,' the inspector said to me. 'There was a fire, a man died and his home was destroyed, along with many confidential papers. It is believed to be an accident, but it's just possible it may be murder. There are some small inconsistencies, the kind of thing Mr Holmes can usually find a great deal of importance in. If I could consult him...'

'Inspector Lestrade,' I said firmly, 'I am sorry a man has died, but as I said before, Mr Holmes is out, will be all day and I don't know when he'll be back. Now if you don't mind...'

I tried again to close the door, but Inspector Lestrade stuck his foot in the gap.

'If I could just leave a note in his rooms...' he started to say.

'Inspector Lestrade!' I insisted, exasperated. 'I am taking the opportunity of Mr Holmes' absence to give his rooms a thorough clean. The carpets are up, the floor is being polished and if you think I'm going to let you tramp all over my clean floors and get in my way to leave a note Mr Holmes probably won't read you're very mistaken!' I said firmly, but loudly, every inch the aggrieved, harassed landlady. One of the policemen took a step away, the other sniggered.

'Mrs Hudson,' Inspector Lestrade tried to say, soothingly.

'If you want Mr Holmes that badly,' I continued, 'I suggest you try and find him. You are a detective after all! He's been spending a lot of time at the docks lately. You can start there, and leave me to get on with my work. Good day!'

And with that, I successfully slammed the door in his face.

I heard him go down the steps and into the streets, petulantly upbraiding the policeman who had laughed. I turned round and leaned against the door, shaking. I had never been rude to a policeman before.

'*Brava*, Mrs Hudson,' Mr Holmes said softly. I looked up to see him standing in the hallway, at the top of the kitchen stairs.

'Mary?' I asked.

'Merely a graze, exacerbated by exhaustion and excitement,' he assured me, walking towards me in the bright morning light. 'Watson is a very skilled physician. She will be all right.'

I took a deep breath and closed my eyes. We might, perhaps, have got away with it all. Except...

'Billy also said that he packed away all your papers and put them somewhere safe. He refused to tell me what papers, despite the fact I pay him!' he said, gently frustrated.

'Yes, but I feed him.'

Mr Holmes walked into the light and faced me.

'Can you tell me what all this is about? Mrs Watson refuses to say a word.'

I think perhaps I wanted to say, just to tell him what I had done, that he was no longer the only detective in 221b Baker Street, but I could not.

'No,' I said softly, shaking my head. 'I cannot tell you.' He took a deep breath, and looked at me.

'I could find out,' he said.

'Don't,' I pleaded.

He looked at me for a moment, then said, 'Very well, Mrs Hudson. For your sake, I shall leave this mystery alone.'

He offered me his arm. 'The docks?' he asked.

'I understand you can catch some very nasty diseases down there,' I said venomously. He chuckled.

'Come to the kitchen,' he said. 'I made tea. I understand it to be good for shock.'

He made tea? Sherlock Holmes had made tea for me, Mrs Hudson, his housekeeper?

'Did you warm the pot first?'

Epilogue

Mary and I held firm. John asked over and over again what had happened. Mary refused to tell him, and when he got angry, she snapped at him.

'Tell me about the Giant Rat of Sumatra then!' she countered. 'You're not allowed to, are you?'

He blushed then. He appealed to Mr Holmes for help, but the detective merely leaned against the dresser, drinking his tea.

'Sorry, Watson, I made a promise,' Mr Holmes said, glancing at me. 'As, I suspect, these ladies have.'

'She was shot, Holmes!' John shouted. His hair was all over the place, his trousers hastily pulled on over his crumpled nightshirt.

'Which makes Mrs Hudson the only person in this room never to have been shot,' Mr Holmes said coolly. 'At least, I presume...?'

'Not even once,' I told him. 'John, please understand, we have indeed made promises...'

'Mrs Hudson, I intend to tell Inspector Lestrade it was quite clearly an accident. Whatever it is he's asking me. Watson, I believe this is the time to get your wife home so she can rest.'

John looked round to Mary, who sat at the table, stronger now, but still pale.

'Mary,' he said beseechingly.

'I will tell you,' she promised. 'But other people's secrets depend on it, so not for a long while yet. Please trust me, sweetheart.' She smiled at him bewitchingly, with true love, and he gave in. Grumpily, John agreed to take her home. As I helped her into her coat, she told me she would write to every woman we knew who had been a victim of this man, including Lillian and Irene. The letter would not say anything beyond the words 'you are free'.

Mr Holmes locked himself in his rooms all afternoon, with piles of old papers and his reference books. I left him alone, and cleaned blood out of the carpets—not for the first or, may I add, the last time. At sunset, I carried tea up to Mr Holmes' rooms— but I stopped before I went in. He was playing the violin—a sweet Scotch tune that I had loved as a child and that I myself had hummed to Mr Holmes. He knew it was my favourite but he rarely played it, saying it was too simple a piece to please him. And yet tonight, the notes floated through the air towards me, and filled my heart. Cold as Mr Holmes could be, his music was always full of emotion. I sat on the stair and listened, and wept, I know not why.

Once the music had finished, I let myself into his rooms, and placed the tea tray on the table. Mr Holmes sat by the window, in the large, battered leather chair he favoured. His jacket lay on the floor, the waistcoat beside it. At his feet lay various newspapers. I could see they contained a report of the attack on Mr Shirley, various reports of some suicides, including Adam Ballant, and the murder of the Whitechapel Lady.

'I think I see a pattern I did not see before,' Sherlock Holmes said softly. 'A story I was not aware of. People I turned away.'

The flaming red light of the sunset outlined his profile, sharp and unforgiving, a man for whom mountains would move because they felt they must.

'They needed help,' I said gently, neither needing nor wanting an explanation. He had found some of the truth. 'They came to you and...'

'And I said no,' he added, not turning to look at me. 'I did not find their problems of sufficient complexity. Or I would not allow them to keep their secrets. Or I could not see the despair behind their seemingly trivial requests. I was wrong,' he admitted. 'I am, occasionally. Far more than Watson allows for, or you realize.'

'You were wrong,' I agreed. 'But you will be right next time.' I had been placing the tea things on the table, and now I took the empty tray. Always unfailingly courteous, he rose to open the door for me.

'But this time, you were right.'

'They needed help. They were lost,' I said to him.

'And you found them. As you do with lost souls.' I looked up into shadowed eyes I could not read.

'Good night, Mrs Hudson. Eggs in the morning, I think,' he told me.

He walked away to stand before the window, tall and sharp and dark against the glorious turbulent sky.

'Mrs Hudson,' he called, as I was almost through the door. I stopped. 'Will you ever tell me the story of what has happened in the past few days?'

'Perhaps,' I said. He did not turn. 'One day, when we are both very old. But not today.'

'Why not?' he asked, turning to me finally.

I thought for a moment, then said to him, 'Because this was not a Sherlock Holmes story. This was a Mrs Hudson and Mary Watson adventure.'

ACKNOWLEDGEMENTS

It turns out writing a book is not quite the solitary occupation I always imagined it would be. I had a lot of help, and thanks are due.

First, my agent, Jane, for taking this book on, and helping me shape and expand and improve this story, and generally looking after me.

My editor, Natasha, who has put an enormous amount of work into this book.

Everyone at Pan Macmillan, who have been so enthusiastic about this book, it quite takes my breath away.

To the Shh…girls, just for being lots of fun when I needed to relax, and because all those discussions about books were very useful, and especially Shyama—it's so good to have another writer to talk to. Only writers understand writers!

Arthur Conan Doyle himself. Without his wonderful stories, I wouldn't have written this book.

And finally all the librarians and English teachers and booksellers who fostered a love of books in me, encouraged me, and always found the exact book I needed, even when I didn't know I needed it.

RESEARCH MATERIALS

This novel involved a lot of research, and any mistakes are my own, not those of any of the authors below.

There are a number of excellent books on Victorian life. I relied on Judith Flanders' books *The Invention of Murder, The Victorian City* and *The Victorian House* to find out exactly what life was like for a woman in Victorian London. I also found Ruth Goodman's *How To Be a Victorian* and Lucy Worsley's *If Walls Could Talk* very useful when researching what it took to look after a Victorian home. Henry Mayhew's *London Labour and the London Poor* had a lot of fascinating information about life on Victorian London's streets and John Christopher's *The London of Sherlock Holmes* helped me navigate the streets of Holmes' London (and I'd like to thank the Waterstones shop assistant who, when I asked vaguely for a book about what London was like in Victorian times, pointed me immediately to this title).

Lee Jackson's website www.victorianlondon.org was utterly invaluable for finding maps and newspaper articles and all kinds of information.

The timeline for the Sherlock Holmes stories is often in dispute. I used the one at www.sherlockpeoria.net/sherlocktime-line.html. It's very well researched, and fitted my ideas of the timeline.

The Sherlock Holmes exhibition at the Museum of London was fascinating, and gave me a chance to see lots of the typical Holmes items in real life (and a glimpse at an actual manuscript for *A Study in Scarlet*!).

The online newspaper archive at my local library was very

useful. It gave me access to newspapers of the time, including the wonderful advertisements.

And finally—I am indebted to the wonderful stories of Arthur Conan Doyle himself, without whom there'd be no Sherlock Holmes, no Dr Watson, and no Mrs Hudson and Mary Watson to tell stories about.

Library of Congress Cataloging-in-Publication Data

Names: Birkby, Michelle, author.
Title: All roads lead to Whitechapel / Michelle Birkby.
Other titles: House at Baker Street
Description: First US edition. | New York : Felony & Mayhem Press, 2019. |
    Series: Baker street inquiries; 1 | A Felony & Mayhem mystery | Summary:
    "The women in Sherlock Holmes's circle-Mrs. Hudson and Mary Watson-step
    in when Holmes himself declines to help a terrified young bride"--
    Provided by publisher.
Identifiers: LCCN 2019038754 | ISBN 9781631942242 (hardback) | ISBN
    9781631942204 (trade paperback) | ISBN 9781631942211 (ebook)
Subjects: LCSH: Hudson, Mrs. (Martha)--Fiction. | Holmes, Sherlock--Fiction
    | GSAFD: Mystery fiction.
Classification: LCC PR6102.I75 H68 2019 | DDC 823/.92--dc23
LC record available at https://lccn.loc.gov/2019038754